"TALK," SAID THE GOON

"I deplore your choice of friends," Mr. Mountjoy said to Howard. "Does your father know the company you keep?"

The Goon looked bored. "Have to stay here all night," he said to Howard. He propped himself on the fist that was holding down Mr. Mountjoy's hands and yawned.

Mr. Mountjoy gave a strangled squeak and struggled a little. "Let go! You're squashing my hands, and I'll have you know I'm a keen pianist."

The Goon unpropped himself. "Can always do it again," he told Howard reassuringly.

"Diana Wynne Jones writes some of the quirkiest, most original fantasies around."

—*Isaac Asimov's Science Fiction Magazine*

Diana Wynne Jones
ARCHER'S GOON

BERKLEY BOOKS, NEW YORK

This Berkley book contains the complete
text of the original hardcover edition.

ARCHER'S GOON

A Berkley Book / published by arrangement with
William Morrow & Company, Inc.

PRINTING HISTORY
Greenwillow Books edition published 1984
Berkley edition / June 1987

ISBN: 0-425-09888-5

A BERKLEY BOOK ® TM 757,375
Berkley Books are published by The Berkley Publishing Group,
200 Madison Avenue, New York, NY 10016.
The name "BERKLEY" and the stylized "B" with design
are trademarks belonging to Berkley Publishing Corporation.

PRINTED IN THE UNITED STATES OF AMERICA

To Fiona

AUTHOR'S NOTE

This book will prove the following ten facts:

1. A Goon is a being who melts into the foreground and sticks there.

2. Pigs have wings, making them hard to catch.

3. All power corrupts, but we need electricity.

4. When an irresistible force meets an immovable object, the result is a family fight.

5. Music does not always soothe the troubled breast.

6. An Englishman's home is his castle.

7. The female of the species is more deadly than the male.

8. One black eye deserves another.

9. Space is the final frontier, and so is the sewage farm.

10. It pays to increase your word power.

ARCHER'S GOON

CHAPTER ONE

The trouble started the day Howard came home from school to find the Goon sitting in the kitchen. It was Fifi who called him the Goon. Fifi was a student who lived in their house and got them tea when their parents were out. When Howard pushed Awful into the kitchen and slammed the door after them both, the first person he saw was Fifi, sitting on the edge of a chair, fidgeting nervously with her striped scarf and her striped leg warmers.

"Thank goodness you've come at last!" Fifi said. "We seem to have somebody's Goon. Look."

Howard looked the way Fifi's chin jerked and saw the Goon sitting in a chair by the dresser. He was filling most of the rest of the kitchen with long legs and huge boots. It was a knack the Goon had. The Goon's head was very small, and his feet were enormous. Howard's eyes traveled up a yard or so of tight

1

faded jeans, jerked to a stop for a second at the knife with which the Goon was cleaning the dirty nails of his vast hands, and then traveled on over an old leather jacket to the little, round fair head in the distance. The little face looked half-daft.

Howard was in a bad mood anyway. That was Awful's fault. Awful had made him meet her coming out of school because, as she said, he was her big brother and supposed to look after her. When Howard got there, there was Awful racing out of the gates, chased by twenty angry little girls. Awful was shouting, "My big brother's here to hit you! Hit them, Howard!" Howard did not know what Awful had done to the other little girls, but knowing Awful, he suspected it was something bad. He objected to being used as Awful's secret weapon, but he did not feel he could let her down. He swung his bag menacingly, hoping that would frighten the little girls off. But there were so many of them and they were so angry that it had ended by being quite a fight. And the little girls called names. It was being called names that had put Howard in a bad mood. And now he came home to find it full of Goon.

He banged his bag down on the kitchen table. The Goon did not look up. "Who is *he* supposed to be?" Howard asked Fifi.

Fifi jittered nervously. "He just walked in and sat there," she said. "He says he's from Archer, whoever that is."

Howard was big for his age. On the other hand, so was the Goon big for whatever age he was. And the Goon had that knife. Howard thumped his bag on the table again. "Well, he can just go away," he said. It did not come out as fierce as he had hoped.

Here Awful put her word in. "You go away, Goon," she said. "Howard's bag's covered with the blood of little girls."

This seemed to interest the Goon. He stopped cleaning his nails and gave the bag a wondering look. He spoke, in a strong, daft voice. "Don't see any blood."

"And we don't know anyone called Archer!" Howard snapped.

2

The Goon grinned, a daft, placid grin. "Your dad does," he said, and went back to cleaning his nails.

"He smells," said Awful. "Make him go. I want my tea."

The Goon did smell rather, a faint smell of gasoline and rotten eggs, which came in whiffs whenever he moved. Howard and Fifi exchanged helpless looks.

"I want my *tea!*" Awful yelled, in the way that had earned her her name. Her real name was Anthea, but she had been Awful from the moment she was born and first opened her mouth.

The piercingness of Awful's yell seemed to get to the Goon. A slight quiver ran through the length of him, though it stopped before it got to his face. "Shut up," he said.

"Shan't," said Awful. The Goon's little face and daft round eyes turned to look at Awful. He seemed amazed. Awful looked back. She drew a deep, careful breath, opened her mouth, and screamed. Dad always said that scream had cleared clinics and emptied buses since Awful was a month old. Now she was eight it was truly horrible.

The Goon cocked his small head and listened to it, almost appreciatively, for a second. Then he grinned. "Aw, shut up," he said, and threw his knife at Awful.

At least that was what seemed to happen. Something certainly zipped past Awful's screaming face. Awful ducked and stopped screaming at once. Something certainly flew on past Awful and landed *thuk* in Howard's bag on the table. After it had, the Goon went placidly back to cleaning his nails with what was obviously the selfsame knife.

Howard, Fifi, and Awful stared from the knife in the Goon's hands to the raw new rip in Howard's bag. Awful longed to scream again but did not quite dare. "How—how did he do that?" said Fifi. "He never moved!"

The Goon spoke again. "Know I mean business now," he said. He sounded rather smug.

"What business?" said Howard.

3

"Stay here till I get satisfaction," said the Goon. "Told her before you came in." And he went on sitting, with his legs spread over most of the kitchen. It was plain he meant what he said.

Since there seemed no way of budging the Goon, Fifi and Howard began trying to get tea around the edges of him. This turned out to be impossible. The Goon took up too much space. They kept having to climb over his legs. The Goon made no attempt to stop them. On the other hand, he made no attempt to get his legs out of their way either.

"Serve you right if I spill hot tea over you!" Howard said angrily.

The Goon grinned. "Better not."

"Or," said Howard, "if I trip, you could get a peanut butter sandwich in the face."

The Goon thought about this. Fifi interrupted hurriedly. "Would you like some tea, Goon? Tea in a cup, I mean, and a sandwich to hold in your hand?"

"Don't mind if I do," said the Goon. And he added, after thinking deeply again, "Not stupid, you know. Knew what you meant."

This was so clearly untrue that Fifi and Awful, scared though they were, spent the next ten minutes hanging onto each other trying not to laugh. Howard crossly pushed a mug of tea and a sandwich at the Goon. The Goon put his knife away and took them without a word. *Slurp*, he went at the tea, and he ate the sandwich without once closing his mouth. Howard had to look away.

"But why have you come?" he burst out angrily. "Are you sure you've come to the right house?"

The Goon nodded. He gulped down the last of the sandwich and then got his knife out again to scrape bits of bread from between his teeth. "Your dad called Quentin Sykes?" he said around the sharp edge of it. "Writes books and things?"

Howard nodded. His heart sank. Dad must have written

4

something rude about this Archer person. It had happened before. "What's Dad done?"

The Goon jerked his little head at Fifi. "Told her. Sykes got behind with his payment. Archer wants his two thousand. Here to collect it."

The smiles were wiped off Fifi's and Awful's faces. "Two thousand!" Fifi exclaimed. "You never told me that!"

"Who *is* Archer?" said Howard.

The Goon shrugged his huge shoulders. "Archer farms this part of town. Your dad pays, Archer doesn't make trouble." He grinned, almost sweetly, and sucked the last bit of bread off the point of his knife. "Got trouble now. Got me."

"Phone the police," said Awful.

The Goon's smile broadened. He took his knife by its point and wagged it at Awful. "Better not," he said. "Really bett'n't had." They exchanged looks again. It seemed to all of them, even Awful, that the Goon's advice was good. The Goon nodded when he saw them look and held his mug out for more tea. "Quite peaceful really," he remarked placidly. "Like this house. Civilized."

"Oh, do you?" Howard said as Fifi filled the Goon's mug. "Just as well you like it because Dad won't be in for ages yet. It's his day for teaching at the Polytechnic."

"Easily wait," the Goon said.

"Does Mum know about Archer?" Awful asked.

"No idea," said the Goon.

This had been worrying Howard, too. He was sure Mum did not know and would be very upset when she found out. She worried all the time about how short of money they were. He realized that he simply had to get the Goon out of the house before Mum came home. "Tell you what," he said. "Why don't you and I go along to the Poly? We can find Dad there and ask him."

The Goon's little head nodded. The grin he raised from

5

drinking tea was big and sly. "You go," he said. "Me and the little girl stay here. Teach her some manners."

"I'm not staying with *him*!" Awful said.

"Eat your tea," said Fifi. "We'd better all go, Howard."

"That suit you?" Howard asked the Goon.

The Goon considered, idly scraping the point of his knife around his mug of tea. The noise made them all shiver. Chips and gouges of china fell out of the mug onto his faded jeans. That knife, Howard thought, must be made of something most unusual, something which could cut china and come back to you when it was thrown. "All go then," the Goon said at last. "All keep where I can see you." He put the scraped, carved mug on the floor and waited for Awful to finish eating. When she had, he stood up.

They found themselves backing away from him. He was even larger than they had thought. His little head grazed the ceiling. His long arms dangled. Fifi and Awful looked tiny beside him. Howard, who was used to finding himself as big as most people these days, suddenly felt small and skinny and feeble beside the Goon. He saw it was no good trying to run away when they got outside. They would have to trick the Goon somehow. He was obviously very stupid.

Fifi bravely rewrapped her scarf around her neck and crammed a striped hat on her head. She took hold of Awful's hand. "Don't worry," she said in a small, squeaky voice. "I'm here."

The Goon grinned down at her and calmly took hold of Awful's other hand. Awful dragged to get it free. When that made no impression at all, she said, "I'll bite you!"

"Bite you back," remarked the Goon. "Give you tetanus."

"I think he means it," Fifi said in a faint squeak. "Don't annoy him, Awful."

"Can't annoy me," said the Goon. "No one has yet." He must have gone on thinking about this while Howard was leading the way down the side passage into Upper Park Street. It was getting dark by then. The Goon's head seemed to get lost

6

upward in the dusk. When Howard looked up, he could hardly see anything beyond the Goon's wide leather shoulders. "Funny," the Goon's voice came down. "Never been really angry. Wonder what would happen if I was."

"I shudder to think!" Fifi said, more faintly than ever. "Howard, would you like to hold my other hand?"

Howard was going to refuse indignantly. But it dawned on him in time that Fifi was scared stiff. So was he. When he took her hand in what was supposed to be a comforting grip, his hand was as cold and shaking as Fifi's. Joined in a line, they turned right and walked the short distance to the Poly. It could have been a shorter distance still, but Fifi took one look at the empty spaces of the park, and another, shuddering, at the gathering dark in Zed Alley and took the longer way around by the road and in through the main gate of the Poly.

By the time they got there bright strip lights were on in most of the windows of the Poly, and the forecourt, where the diggers were at work excavating for the new building, was well lit, too. There were a lot of people about, students hurrying home and men working on the site. It should have felt safe. But the Goon still had hold of Awful's hand, and none of them felt safe. Fifi cast longing looks at several people she knew, but she did not dare call out for help. Howard twitched at her hand, trying to tell her that they could give the Goon the slip inside the building. They could go up in the elevator, down the stairs, through the fire doors, up in the other elevators, and shake him off in the crowds. Then they could phone the police.

They went up the steps into the litter of paper cups in the foyer. Howard turned toward the elevators.

"Don't be too clever," the Goon said. "Know where you live."

Howard turned around and looked up at him. The distant small face held the usual grin, but just for an instant, before Howard looked clearly, it did not look quite as daft as he had thought. In fact, he could have sworn the Goon looked almost clever. But when Howard looked properly, he realized that it

7

was just a sort of slyness. That was bad enough. Howard changed direction and led them all up the stairs instead, to the room where Dad usually did his teaching.

Dad was there. They heard his voice from behind the door, raised in a yell. "Good heavens, woman! I don't want to know what the Structuralists think! I want to know what *you* think!"

Dad sounded busy. Howard raised one hand to knock at the door, but the Goon reached a long arm around him and tore the door open. Inside, there was a row of people sitting in metal chairs and holding note pads. They all turned irritably to look at the door. Quentin Sykes, propped on the back of another metal chair, turned around as irritably as the rest. He was smallish and fattish and barely came up to the Goon's armpit. But, as Howard knew, you could rely on Dad not to panic. Quentin went on looking at them irritably and raked his hands through the rather fluffy remains of his hair, while he took in the Goon, Howard's and Fifi's scared faces, and Awful's angry glower.

He turned back to his students. "Well, that about wraps it up for today," he said smoothly. "We'll save the Structuralist view for next week. Come in, all of you, and shut the door—you're making a draft. I think we'll ask Miss Potter to introduce next week's discussion, since she obviously knows so much about Structuralism." At this the thinnest woman with the largest note pad sat upright and stared in outrage. "The rest of you," Quentin Sykes said, before she could speak, "had better read these books in order to keep up with Miss Potter." And he rapidly recited a list of books. While the students, including Miss Potter, scribbled them down, Quentin took another look at the Goon. "See you all next week," he said.

The students took a look at the Goon, too, and all decided to leave quickly. Everyone hurried out of the room, except for Miss Potter, who was still looking outraged. "Mr. Sykes," she said. "I really must complain—"

"Next week, Miss Potter. Put it all in your paper," Quentin said. "Show me how wrong I am."

8

Miss Potter, looking more outraged than ever, squared her shoulders and marched out of the room. Howard hoped that Dad would be able to get rid of the Goon this easily, too.

"Now what *is* this?" Quentin said, looking at the Goon.

"Meet the Goon, Dad," said Howard.

The Goon grinned, almost angelically. "Overdue payment," he said. "Came to collect two thousand."

"He just walked in, Mr. Sykes!" Fifi said angrily. "And he—"

Quentin stopped Fifi by holding one hand up. It was a knack he seemed to have with students. "Nonsense," he said. "My payment isn't overdue."

It was the Goon's turn to hold one hand up, grinning still. Since he was still holding Awful's hand, Awful came up, too, dangling and yelling. He said something, but nothing could be heard but Awful. He had to shout it. "Should have had it two weeks ago! Archer's annoyed—" This was as far as the Goon got before Awful somehow managed to climb up her own arm and fasten her teeth in the Goon's knuckles. The Goon must have felt it. He turned to her reproachfully. "Drop you!" he shouted above the noise Awful was still making.

"No, you won't. You'll put her down," said Quentin. Long practice had given him a way of enlarging his voice so that it came through Awful's. "Or you will if you want to hear yourself speak."

This seemed to strike the Goon as a good idea. He lowered Awful to the floor, where she stood putting her tongue in and out and making disgusted faces. "He tastes horrible," she said. "Can I go on yelling?"

"No," said Quentin, and he said to the Goon, "I don't know what you're talking about. I've never heard of this Archer. The man I deal with is Mountjoy."

"Don't know Mountjoy," said the Goon. "Must go to Archer in the end. Archer didn't get it."

"But I tell you I sent it," Quentin insisted. "I sent it last week. I know it was late, but Mountjoy never bothers, as long

9

as it's the full two thousand words." He turned to Fifi. "*You* know I sent it, don't you? It was that long envelope I gave you last week to drop in at the Town Hall."

It seemed to Howard that Fifi gave the faintest gasp at this, but she said promptly, "Oh, was that what it was? Yes, you did."

"Well then?" Quentin said to the Goon.

The Goon folded his long arms and loomed a little. "Archer didn't get it," he repeated.

"Then go ask Mountjoy about it," said Quentin.

"You ask him," said the Goon. His round eyes slid sideways to the telephone on the desk.

"All right," said Quentin. "I will." He went to the telephone and dialed. Howard, watching and listening and by now quite mystified, knew that his father really did dial the Town Hall. He heard the switchboard girl answer, "City Council. Which office, please?" And Quentin said, "Mr. Mountjoy. Extension six-oh-nine." After a pause he could hear a man's voice, a rich, rumbling voice, answering. Quentin, looking unlovingly at the Goon, said, "Quentin Sykes here, Mountjoy. It's about my two thousand words. Someone seems to have sent me a hired assassin—"

"Not killed anyone yet!" the Goon protested.

"You shut up," said Quentin. "He says the words are overdue. Now I know I sent them to you, just as usual, nearly a week ago—"

The rich voice rumbled on the telephone. And rumbled more. Quentin's face clouded and then began to look exasperated. He cut through the rumbling to say, "And who is Archer?" The voice rumbled some more. "Thank you," said Quentin. He put the phone down and turned to the Goon, sighing.

The Goon's grin grew wide again. "Didn't get them, did he?"

"No," Quentin admitted. "They do seem to have gone astray. But he'll give me another week to—" He stopped because

10

the Goon's little head was shaking slowly from side to side. "Now look here!"

"Archer won't wait," said the Goon. "Want to go without electricity? Or gas? Archer farms power."

"I know," Quentin said angrily. "Mountjoy just told me."

"Do the words again," said the Goon.

"Oh, all right," Quentin said. "Come on, all of you. Let's get back home and get it over with."

They marched silently back with the Goon looming over them. Howard was aching to ask his father what on earth was going on, but he did not get a chance. As soon as they reached the house, the Goon took up his former place, filling half the kitchen, and Quentin hurried to his study. The sound of typing came from there, in little rattling bursts, with long pauses in between. Awful went to the front room, where she turned on the television and sat brooding on bad things to do to the Goon. At least, Howard thought thankfully, Mum had not come in yet. He hoped very much that Dad could finish his typing and get rid of the Goon before she did.

In the kitchen Fifi was climbing back and forth across the Goon's legs again. "Help me get supper started at least, Howard, there's a love," she said. "Your mum's going to be so *depressed* when she comes in and finds all this going on!"

Catriona Sykes came in five minutes after that. She came in with her eyes shut, tottering, meaning it had been a bad day. Her job was organizing music in schools, and she got headaches from it. She put a stack of music, the evening paper, a tape deck, a bundle of recorders, and a set of cymbals down on the table and fell into a chair by feel, with her hands to her head. Howard watched the relief fading off her face as she listened to the sounds in the house and began to realize something was wrong. He saw her locate Awful by the sound of the television, and Quentin by the clattering of the typewriter, then Fifi by the hurried pouring of hot water into the coffee mug Fifi had ready. Howard saw Catriona follow the haste with which Fifi handed the mug to him and locate Howard by

11

his footsteps hurriedly stepping over the Goon's legs to give her the coffee. A frown grew on her face. As she took the mug, her head tilted to catch the scraping from the Goon's knife as he sat cleaning his nails. She took a deep drink of the coffee, pushed her hair back, and opened her eyes to look at the Goon.

"Who are you?" she said.

He grinned his daft grin at her. "Goon," he said.

"I mean," said Catriona, "what is your name?"

Howard's mother had a very strong personality. But so had the Goon in his way. The room seemed thick with them. Howard and Fifi both held their breaths. "Goon will do," said the Goon, and went on grinning.

Catriona gave him a long, level look. Then, to Howard's surprise, she smiled quite pleasantly. "You look strong," she said. "There's a set of drums in my car. Help Howard get them in before they get damp or stolen."

And to Howard's further surprise, the Goon got to his feet and loomed through the room. "Where to?" he asked Howard.

The Goon was so strong that all Howard needed to do was show him the car and unlock the back. The Goon carried the drum set, bumping and booming, and set it down with a further boom in the hall. Then he went back to his chair in the kitchen. There Howard could see his mother had been asking Fifi what was going on. Fifi was looking upset. Catriona was taking it all much more calmly than Howard would have expected. She was just looking gloomily mystified.

"I don't mind as long as he's quiet," she said to Howard. "I've been listening to school orchestras all day—have you done your violin practice?—and my head's splitting." And before Howard needed to lie about the violin, she looked at the Goon and said, "Who is Archer?"

The Goon looked back. He had a short think. "Farms power," he said. "Gas and electricity. Money, too. Won't worry you. You come under Torquil."

"You mean he's a town councillor?" Catriona asked.

That amused the Goon highly. He threw back his little head

12

and laughed and clapped his long thigh with his vast hand. "That's good!" he said. "Look like the Council, do I?"

"No, I can't say that you do," said Catriona. She seemed utterly unable to find the Goon alarming. "He seems harmless enough," she said to Howard as she got up to help Fifi cook. "Move your feet," she said to the Goon. And the Goon did. He bent his legs up until his knees were near his ears and sat looking like a huge, ungainly grasshopper while Catriona got supper ready. Howard began to see that his mother had found the right way to manage the Goon. He tried it himself when he was setting the table. He told the Goon to get out of the way of the spoon drawer, and the Goon did and grinned at him. "Set for six, Howard," Catriona said. "I expect the Goon would like some liver and bacon, too."

"Would!" the Goon said. He inhaled fried onions and grinned deeply.

Howard began to feel that Mum was not taking a serious enough view of the Goon. When supper was ready, and Quentin's typewriter was still doing bursts of clattering, Catriona said, "Howard, call your father and Awful."

"Not Sykes. Let him keep at it," the Goon said.

Catriona accepted this without even asking why and sent Howard into the study with a tray. Quentin looked up absently from his typewriter and said, "Put it down on those papers." He did not seem alarmed or anxious either.

"Dad," said Howard, "I think Mum's got the wrong idea. She's giving the Goon supper. You don't give hired assassins supper, do you?"

Quentin smiled. "No, but when a wolf follows your sleigh, you give it meat," he said. Howard could tell he was only half-serious. "Leave me in peace, or we'll never get rid of him."

Howard went back to the kitchen, rather exasperated. He found the Goon sheepishly trying to wedge his knees under the table and Awful protesting. "I'm not going to have supper with him!" she was saying. "He threw his knife at me."

"Shouldn't have screamed," said the Goon. The table lifted

13

on top of his knees, and things began to slide off one end. Fifi caught them. She looked as exasperated as Howard felt. The Goon slid Catriona an embarrassed look and doubled his legs around the back of his chair. He was really almost kneeling like that, and he looked very uncomfortable.

"He did, Mum!" Awful shrilled. "And he smells." When Catriona took no notice, Awful announced, "I hate everyone except Fifi."

"What have I done to get hated?" Howard demanded.

"You were scared of the Goon," Awful said.

Howard found himself exchanging a shamed look with the Goon. "Scare myself sometimes," the Goon remarked, cautiously picking up a knife and fork. He was trying to behave properly. He kept glancing nervously at Catriona and Fifi to see how he was doing, and he made strong efforts to keep his mouth shut while he chewed. Howard thought he nearly choked once or twice. Even so, the Goon managed to eat huge amounts. Howard had never seen such a stack of potatoes on anyone's plate before. When he had finished, the Goon retreated quickly to the chair he had sat in before and sat in everyone's way again, picking his teeth with his knife and looking relieved.

"Wouldn't you like to go watch the telly in the other room?" Fifi asked him after she had fallen over his legs six times.

But the Goon shook his little head and sat on. He sat while Fifi cleared away and then went up to her room in the attic. He sat while Catriona washed up. When Catriona went away, too, and the Goon was still sitting, Howard thought he had better stay in the kitchen as well. He felt someone ought to watch him. So Howard fetched out his bag of books, with the rip in it that the Goon had made, and tried to do homework on the kitchen table. He found it hard to concentrate. With the Goon sitting there, he did not feel he could spend half the time designing spaceships, as he usually did. He could feel the Goon's round eyes staring at him and see the knife that had ripped his bag flashing at the corner of his eye. When, at last, Quentin came into the kitchen carrying four typewritten pages, Howard was heartily relieved.

The Goon sprang up, looking as relieved as Howard. He took the pages and examined them. Howard was quite surprised that the Goon seemed able to read.

"That will have to do," Quentin said as the Goon looked questioningly at him. "It's not quite the same as I sent Mountjoy, but it's as near as I could manage from memory."

"Not a copy?" asked the Goon.

"Definitely no copy," Quentin assured him.

The Goon nodded, folded the papers, and stuffed them into the front of his leather jacket. "Get along to Archer then," he said. "See you." And he loomed his way to the back door, tore it open, ducked his little head under the lintel, and went away.

As soon as the door slammed, Catriona and Awful shot into the kitchen. "Has he gone?" said Awful, and Catriona said, "Now tell us what all that was about."

"Nothing—nothing at all really," Quentin said, in a way which everyone knew was much too airy. "Mountjoy's idea of a joke, that's all."

Catriona fixed him with her most powerful look. "Quentin," she said, "that won't do. He talked about Archer, not Mountjoy. Explain."

CHAPTER TWO

"But I can't explain about Archer," said Quentin. He sat in the Goon's chair and stretched. "I only know Mountjoy. Make me a cup of tea, Awful." As Awful set off readily toward the kettle, he added swiftly, "With boiling water and two tea bags and only milk in the cup. Curry, mustard, pepper, and vinegar are strictly forbidden."

"Bother you!" said Awful. One of the things she enjoyed most was making people curried tea.

"What a life!" said Quentin. "I have to bargain even to get a cup of tea. What does it matter to Awful that I am a famous writer and my name is a household word?"

"So is 'drains' a household word," said Awful as she filled the kettle. "Mum, he's putting us off."

"No, I'm not. I'm just arranging my thoughts," Quentin said.

16

"Then stop blathering," said Catriona. "Tell us why on earth he wanted you to write two thousand words."

"He didn't. It must be Mountjoy," said Quentin. He clasped his hands behind his head and stared thoughtfully down at the soft curve of paunch that stuck his sweater out. "Though come to think of it," he murmured, "Mountjoy did mention a superior once, about eight years ago. I'd forgotten that. Anyway, as far as I knew, it was Mountjoy's idea—a sort of joke—to cure my writer's block. Mountjoy's quite respectable, you know. There's nothing underhanded about him. I met him playing golf a few months before we had Howard, when I was suffering terribly from writer's block and telling everyone—"

"I remember," said Catriona. "You told the milkman about it until he refused to come to the house."

"Well, it's a terrible condition," Quentin said plaintively. "You three are lucky not to know what it's like. You haven't a thought in your head, or if you have, you can't somehow get it down on paper, or if you *do* manage to put something down, it goes small and boring and doesn't lead anywhere. And you panic because you can't earn any money, and that makes it worse. It can go on for years, too—"

Howard was just thinking that he was glad he did not intend to be a writer—designing spaceships seemed much easier— when Awful interrupted. "I know," she said. "It's like when they tell me in school, 'Make a drawing of ancient Britons,' and I can't because I'm not in a drawing mood."

"Yes," said Quentin. "Very like that. So you see how relieved I was when Mountjoy rang me up and said come to his office and discuss an idea he had had to break my block. He swore he could do it. And he was right. What I was to do, he said, was to promise to send him every three months two thousand words of any old thing that came into my head. It had to be new, and by me, and not a copy of anything else I'd done, and I was to deliver it to him at the Town Hall. I said, but suppose I couldn't even do that? And Mountjoy laughed and said here was the clever bit. I was to imagine he had the ability

17

to stop the Council from supplying me with water and gas and light and to order them not to empty my trash cans and so on. He said if I made myself scared enough of that, I'd have no difficulty in writing his two thousand words. And he was right. I'm still grateful to Mountjoy. I went home and did him the first two thousand words, and as soon as I had, I began to write books again like a demon. I wrote *Prying Manticora* that same month. And the first draft of *Stark* in—"

"But wait a minute," Catriona said, frowning. "If you've been sending Mountjoy stuff for thirteen years, and he's been passing it on to this Archer, then Archer must have masses of it by now. What does he do with it?"

"Do you think Archer publishes it?" Howard asked. "He could be making a lot of money out of you."

His father shook his head, rather uncomfortably. "He couldn't, Howard. I always write really idiotic things that nobody would want to publish. Most of them aren't even finished. You can't get much into four pages. I'll tell you—last year I sent Mountjoy a solemn discussion about what to do if rabbits suddenly started eating meat. This time it was about old ladies rioting in Corn Street."

"What do you do about that?" Awful asked, bringing Quentin a slopping mug of weak gray tea.

"Dodge their handbags," said Quentin. "Thanks."

"No, stupid, I mean the rabbits," said Awful.

"Set them catching mice, of course," said Quentin. "No, Howard, I'd have noticed if anyone printed any of those things. I assure you, nobody ever has."

"And is this the first time Mountjoy didn't get the words?" Howard asked.

Quentin shook his head again. "It's the first time they've gone astray, but there have been several times when I didn't get around to doing them. Mountjoy never minds—except there was that one time..." Quentin stared at his tea, looking puzzled. "It was just after Awful was born," he said. "You must remember, Catriona. She kept us awake every night for a

18

month, and I was too busy trying to catch up on sleep to write anything. And quite suddenly, everything in the house was cut off. We'd no light, and no heat, no electricity, no water, and the car wouldn't go either—"

"Yes, I do remember," said Catriona. "Howard screaming as well as Awful, because he was cold, and all the washing. Didn't they say it was some sort of freak? I remember we kept having people to mend things, and they said there was nothing wrong. What happened?"

"I went around to see Mountjoy," said Quentin. "It was superstition really. And I remember he looked rather taken aback and muttered something about his superior's not being as patient as he was. Then he laughed and told me to write the words and probably everything would come right. So I did. And all the power came back on while I was doing them. I really can't explain that." He raised the tea to his mouth at last. Awful watched expectantly. "But I really can't explain Archer's Goon eith—" He took the mug away from his mouth again, with a sigh. "Don't tell me, Awful. I forgot to say don't put salt in it. What have you *done* to this mug?"

Quentin held the mug up to the light. There seemed to be big wobbly shapes carved into both sides of it.

"The Goon did that," said Awful. "With his knife and there's no salt in it, only sugar. He threw the knife at me, but it stayed in his hand."

"Don't talk nonsense, Awful," said Catriona. Very sane and severe, she took the mug and looked at it and felt the dents with her finger. "This can't have been done with a knife. These marks are glazed over. It must have come like that from the shop."

"The Goon did do it," said Howard. "I saw him, too."

Quentin took the mug back and held it up to the light again. "Then perhaps he tried to carve *G* for Goon," he suggested jokingly. "It's either a *V* or a *Y* on the other side. Do you think it's *A* for Archer upside down?"

Howard knew from this that his father was not going to treat

19

the matter of the Goon seriously. And he knew his mother was not either when she laughed and said, "Well, Quentin, make sure you do Mountjoy's words in future. We don't want Archer sending any more Goons around."

In a way, it was a weight off Howard's mind. The Goon had scared him. But if neither of his parents was worried, then that made it all right. He went upstairs to his room and sat comfortably among his posters of astronauts and airplanes, designing another spaceship until it was bedtime, and tried not to think of the Goon. But his mind would keep straying to all those words his father kept sending to Archer. What could Archer possibly do with them? Why did he want them badly enough to send the Goon for them?

During the night the set of drums the Goon had carried into the hall started to boom softly. Most of the family would not have noticed had not Catriona been so sensitive to noise. She woke everyone up three times, getting up and going downstairs to slacken them. She thought they must be vibrating to the traffic outside. But they continued to give out a gentle humming throb. Catriona got up again and padded them with handkerchiefs. She got up again and filled them with socks. Finally, she woke everyone up for a fifth time by going and hurling all the spare blankets over them, with a mighty BOOM. Even then, she claimed, she could still hear them throbbing.

"Your mother spent the whole night listening to her own ears," Quentin said irritably, shuffling into the kitchen with his hair on end and his eyes half-shut. "Where are my emergency supplies of tea?"

"Your paunch is sticking out of your pajamas," Awful said. "The Goon did them."

"It was that Goon that last touched them." Fifi yawned.

"What have I done to deserve Awful?" Quentin demanded. "Fifi, forget the Goon and save my life by giving me some tea. Everyone forget the Goon."

Howard willingly forgot the Goon. He went to school and spent the day happily designing spaceships. He forgot the

20

Goon so completely that it was a real shock to him when he came out of school with his friends at the end of the afternoon and found the Goon towering like a lighthouse on the pavement outside. The Goon saw Howard. Recognition came over his little face in slow motion. He turned and came wading toward him above the crowd. Howard went suddenly from being the one who stuck out above the crowd to feeling frail and weak and knee-high. He looked around for help. But all his friends, finding themselves in the path of the Goon, had quickly thought of things they needed to do elsewhere. Somehow they were gone, leaving the Goon towering above Howard.

"Came back," the Goon pointed out, grinning as he loomed.

"So you did," said Howard. "I almost didn't notice. What do you want now?"

"Those words," the Goon said. "They're no good."

"What do you expect *me* to do about it?" said Howard.

"Your dad home today?" asked the Goon.

"Yes," said Howard. "I think so."

"Go there with you and tell him," said the Goon.

Since the Goon was not a person you contradicted, they set out side by side. Howard said resentfully, "Why do you have to go with me? Can't you go by yourself?"

The Goon's little face grinned down at him from beyond the Goon's huge shoulder. "Not scared of me," he said.

"Oh, yes, I am," said Howard. "Just seeing you makes me feel ill."

The Goon grinned again. "Tell you things," he said enticingly. "About Archer and the rest."

"I don't want to know," said Howard. But he found himself asking anxiously almost at once, "Is Archer annoyed the words are no good?"

The Goon nodded and looked triumphant. "Like me really," he said smugly.

"I don't like you. Nobody could," said Howard. "What will Archer do?"

21

"Send me," said the Goon.

"Are you going to make trouble for Dad today?" Howard asked.

"Maybe," said the Goon.

"In that case," said Howard as a sort of experiment, "we'll go somewhere else." He turned around and walked the other way. The Goon turned around and walked beside him. "Where shall we go?" said Howard.

"Want to see Archer? Or one of the others?" the Goon offered.

"Let's see Mr. Mountjoy," said Howard, not really meaning it.

"All right," the Goon said equably.

Considerably to his astonishment, Howard found himself walking briskly to the center of town, up Corn Street and along High Street, with the Goon towering beside him. They came to the Town Hall and climbed the steps briskly, just as if they had real business there. Someone will stop us soon, Howard thought. They pushed open the big door and entered a wide marble hall. Howard thought he saw out of the corner of his eye some men in uniform who could have been policemen, but when he looked, they seemed to have melted away, just as his friends had. His footsteps and the Goon's rang briskly through the hall as they went to a window marked "Inquiries." There was a rather fierce-looking lady sitting at a desk behind the window. Before Howard could speak to her, the Goon found a door beside the window. He calmly tore it open and loomed over the fierce lady's desk.

"What do you want?" asked the lady, tipping her head back ungraciously in order to see the Goon's face.

The Goon smiled affably. "Mountjoy?"

The lady was one of those who take pleasure in denying people things. She took pleasure in saying, "Mr. Mountjoy doesn't see casual callers. You have to have an appointment."

The Goon said, "Extension six-oh-nine. Where's that?"

"Over in the housing department," said the lady. "But—"

22

"Where's that?" said the Goon.

"But I'm not telling you," finished the lady.

The Goon jerked his head at Howard. "Go and look for it," he said.

"You can't do that!" the lady said, scandalized.

The Goon took no notice. He just marched out of the room and across the marble hall to the marble stairs, and Howard hurried behind. The lady shouted after them. When that did no good, she came to the door of her office and shrieked, "Come back!"

Howard very much wanted to come back by then. When the Goon stopped a few stairs up, he hoped they could go away now, before they got arrested. But the Goon simply called across the empty space to her, "Mountjoy?"

"I'm not telling you!" shrieked the lady. "Come back!"

The Goon jerked his head to Howard again, and they went on up the stairs. The next twenty minutes were the most harrowing ones Howard had ever spent. The Goon, smiling his daft smile, simply walked calmly into every room they came to. They went into offices, filing rooms, planning rooms, committee rooms, reference rooms, private rooms, and public rooms. Howard kept thinking: We'll be arrested soon! We can't *do* this! And certainly from time to time, agitated people no bigger than Howard did seem to try to bar the Goon's way; but either the Goon smiled his daft smile at them and put them aside, or he said, "Mountjoy?" and when they shook their heads, he went on. Most people melted away before the Goon got that near.

Like a Centurion tank through butter! Howard thought, hazy with embarrassment. The Goon went, and Howard followed. One room with a large table and a carpet actually had a committee meeting in it, twelve or so people sitting at the table. As the Goon marched in, a man in a dark suit said angrily, "This is the highway board, not a public thoroughfare!" The Goon smiled his daft grin at the man, spotted a door across the room, and homed on it in great strides over the carpet. The angry man picked up a telephone and started to talk indignantly into it. This time, Howard thought as he pattered after the Goon, we *shall* be arrested! He was so embarrassed by then that he hoped it would be soon.

But the Goon seemed unstoppable. He took Howard up some more stairs and then strode down a long corridor with frosted windows, which evidently led to another wing of the Town Hall. He tore open the door at the end. Inside, there was a chain of offices, where people were typing at desks or walking about, consulting plans of buildings. The Goon turned his grin on Howard. "Getting warm." He marched down the chain of rooms, and Howard followed, past the usual small people trying to stop them and the usual indignant faces, and made for a door at the end. A notice on it read "M. J. MOUNTJOY." The Goon's huge hand tore this door open, too. The man inside looked up with a jump.

"Here you are," the Goon said to Howard. "Mountjoy." He beamed proudly at Mountjoy, as if Mountjoy were treasure and the Goon had dug him up.

"That is my name," Mr. Mountjoy said. He looked uncertainly from the Goon to Howard in his school blazer, with his bag of books hung from his shoulder. His eyes went to the tape with which Howard had mended the rip the Goon had made in the bag and then back to the Goon. It was clear he thought they made an odd pair. Mr. Mountjoy himself wore a neat dark suit. He was largish and plumpish, with smooth hair and large, shrewd eyes. It was exactly the kind of man Howard had imagined to go with the smooth, rumbling voice on the telephone.

"Talk to him," the Goon said to Howard.

"Er—" said Howard. "My father's Quentin Sykes—"

Before he got any further, the open door behind them was crammed with anxious people, who all wanted to know if Mr. Mountjoy was all right. They liked Mr. Mountjoy, and they wanted him safe. Howard felt more embarrassed than ever. Several of the men wanted to know if they should turn the Goon out. The Goon turned and looked at them as if this were

24

a very surprising notion. Not so much surprising as impossible, Howard thought.

Mr. Mountjoy straightened his sober tie uneasily. "I'm quite all right, thank you," he said in a soothing rumble. "Please shut the door. Everything is under control." But as the people crowded out of the room, Howard distinctly heard Mr. Mountjoy add, "I hope!" When the door shut, he eased his tie looser, and his eyes went to the Goon, fascinated. "You were saying, young man?" he said to Howard.

"Why do you *really* make my father send you two thousand words every three months?" said Howard.

Mr. Mountjoy smiled. "I don't *make* him do it, young man. It's just a friendly device I thought of to keep him from drying up again." The smile was sincere, and the voice such a friendly, soothing rumble that Howard felt thoroughly ashamed of asking. He turned to go away.

"Not true," the Goon remarked pleasantly.

Mr. Mountjoy gave the Goon an alarmed, fleeting look. "But it *is*. Quentin Sykes hadn't been able to write anything for nearly a year after his second book came out. I liked the book, and I was sorry for the man, so I hit on a way to get him going again. It's a sort of joke between us by now."

"Not true," the Goon remarked, less pleasantly and more firmly.

That changed Howard's mind. "No, I don't think it is," he said. "If it's a joke, why did you stop all the water and electricity in our house one time when he didn't do the words?"

"That had nothing to do with me," Mr. Mountjoy said sincerely. "It may well have been a complete coincidence. If it was my superior—and I admit I have a superior—then he told me nothing about it at all."

"Was it Archer who did it?" asked Howard.

Mr. Mountjoy shrugged and spread his plumpish hands toward Howard, to show he knew nothing about that either. "Who knows? I don't."

25

"And what does Archer do with the words?" said Howard. "Who *is* Archer anyway? Lord mayor or something?"

Mr. Mountjoy laughed, shook his head, and began spreading his hands again, to show he really did not know anything. But before his hands were half-spread, the Goon's enormous hand came down from behind Howard's shoulder. It landed across Mr. Mountjoy's gesturing hands and trapped both of them down on Mr. Mountjoy's desk. "Tell him," said the Goon.

Mr. Mountjoy pulled at his hands, but like Awful before him, he found that made no impression on the Goon at all. He became hurt and astonished. "Really! My dear sir! Please let me go."

"Talk," said the Goon.

"I deplore your choice of friends," Mr. Mountjoy said to Howard. "Does your father know the company you keep?"

The Goon looked bored. "Have to stay here all night," he said to Howard. He propped himself on the fist that was holding down Mr. Mountjoy's hands and yawned.

Mr. Mountjoy gave a strangled squeak and struggled a little. "Let go! You're squashing my hands, and I'll have you know I'm a keen pianist!" His voice was nearly a yelp. "All right. I'll tell you the little bit I know! But you're to let go first!"

The Goon unpropped himself. "Can always do it again," he told Howard reassuringly.

Mr. Mountjoy rubbed his hands together and felt each of his fingers, morbidly, as if he had thought one or two might be missing. "I've no idea what Archer wants with the blessed words!" he said peevishly. "I don't even know if it's Archer I send them to. All I've ever heard is his voice on the telephone. It could be any of them."

"Any of who?" Howard said, mystified.

"Any of the seven people who really run this town," said Mr. Mountjoy. "Archer's one. The others are Dillian, Venturus, Torquil, Erskine, and—what are their names? Oh, yes. Hathaway and Shine. They're all brothers."

26

"How do you know?" demanded the Goon.

"I made it my business to find out," Mr. Mountjoy said. "Wouldn't you, if one of them made you do something this peculiar for them?"

"Shouldn't have done," said the Goon. "Won't like that. Know. Working for Archer."

"Then what are you doing here?" Mr. Mountjoy said. "I concede that you may not have much brain. You don't appear to have room for one. But this is an odd place to be if I work for Archer, too."

"Doing him a favor," said the Goon, pointing a parsnip-sized thumb at Howard. He said to Howard, "Know I'm your friend now. Want to know any more?"

"Um—yes," said Howard. "How does he send the words to whoever it is?"

"I address them to a post office box number and send a typist out to post them," said Mr. Mountjoy. "I really know nothing more. I have tried to find out who collects them, and I have failed."

"So you don't know how this last lot went missing?" said Howard.

"It never reached me," said Mr. Mountjoy. "Now do you mind taking your large friend and going away? I have work to do."

"Pleasure," said the Goon. He put both hands on the desk and leaned toward Mr. Mountjoy. "Tell us the back way out."

"I bear you no malice," Mr. Mountjoy said hastily. "The door at the end. Marked 'Emergency Stairs.'" He picked up a folder labeled "Center development: Polytechnic" and pretended to be very busy reading it.

The Goon jerked his head at Howard in the way Howard was now used to and progressed out into the offices again. Heads lifted from typewriters and frozen faces watched them as they progressed right down to the end of the rooms. Here, sure enough, was a door with wire mesh set into the glass of it. "Fire Door," it said in red letters, "Emergency Stairs." The

27

Goon slung it open, and they went out onto a long flight of concrete stairs.

The Goon raced down these stairs surprisingly quickly and quietly. Howard's knees trembled rather as he followed. He was scared now. They kept galloping down past other wire-and-glass doors, and some of these were bumping open and shut. Howard could see the dark shapes of people milling about behind them, and at least twice he heard some of the things they said. "Walked straight through the highway board!" a woman said behind the first. Lower down, someone was calling out, "They went up that way, Officer!" Howard put his head down and bounded two stairs at a time to keep up with the Goon. Scared as he was, he was rather impressed. The Goon certainly got results.

At the bottom of the stairs a heavy swing door let them out into a backyard crowded with gigantic rubbish bins on wheels. Here Howard, as he threaded his way after the the Goon, remembered to his annoyance that he had forgotten to ask Mr. Mountjoy how Archer—or whichever brother it was—had first got hold of Mr. Mountjoy and made him work for him. But it was clearly too late to go back and ask that now.

The yard led to a parking lot and the parking lot led to a side street. At the main road the Goon stuck his head around the corner and looked toward the front of the Town Hall, about fifty yards away. Three police cars were parked beside the steps, with their lights flashing and their doors open. The Goon grinned and turned the other way. "Dillian nearly got us," he remarked.

"Dillian?" asked Howard, trotting to keep up.

"Dillian farms law and order," said the Goon.

"Oh," said Howard. "Let's go see Archer now."

But the Goon said, "Got to see your dad about the words," and Howard found himself hurrying toward home instead. When the Goon decided to go anywhere, he set that way like a strong current, and there seemed nothing Howard could do about it.

28

CHAPTER THREE

Five minutes later Howard and the Goon turned right past the corner shop into Upper Park Street. Howard was rather glad to see it. He liked the rows of tall, comfortable houses and the big tree outside number 8. He was even glad to see the hopscotch that Awful and her friends kept chalking on the sidewalk—when Awful was not quarreling with those friends, that was. But the thing which made him gladdest of all was to see his own house—number 10—without a police car standing outside it. He had been dreading that. Mr. Mountjoy had only to say who Howard's father was.

Dad was in the kitchen with Fifi and Awful, eating peanut butter sandwiches. All their faces fixed in dismay as the Goon ducked his little head and came through the back door after Howard.

Quentin said, "Not again!" and Fifi said, "The Goon returns. Mr. Sykes, he haunts us!"

Awful glowered. "It's all Howard's fault," she said.

"What's that noise?" said the Goon.

It was the drums, throbbing gently from under the mound of blankets in the hall. Quentin sighed. "They've been doing that all day."

"Fix them," said the Goon, and progressed through the kitchen into the hall. Howard paused to take a peanut butter sandwich, so he was too late to see what the Goon did to the drums. By the time he got there the blankets had been tossed aside, and the Goon was standing with his fists on his hips, staring at the slack and silent drums oozing socks and handkerchiefs. He grinned at Howard. "Torquil," he said.

"Torquil what?" asked Howard.

"Did that," said the Goon, and marched back to the kitchen. There he stood and stared at Quentin the same way he had stared at the drums.

"Don't tell me," said Quentin. "Let me guess. Archer is not satisfied. He has counted the words and found there were only one thousand and ninety-nine."

The Goon shook his head, grinning as usual. "Two thousand and four," he said.

"Well, I thought I'd better end the last sentence," Quentin said. "Mountjoy never insisted on an exact number."

The Goon said, "Mountjoy must have told you something else then." He dived a hand into the front of his leather jacket and brought out the four typed pages, now gray and used-looking and bent. He thrust them at Quentin at the end of a yard or so of arm. "Take a look. What's wrong?"

Quentin took the pages and unfolded them. He separated them one from another, enough to glance at each. "This seems all right. My usual drivel. Old ladies riot in Corn Street. I couldn't remember quite what I put in the lot Archer never got, but this is the gist—" He stopped as he realized. "Oh," he said glumly. "It's supposed not to be anything I've done before. But

30

how the devil did Archer know?" He looked up at the Goon. The Goon's head nodded, so fast that it almost jittered. The daft grin spread on his face. He looked so irritating that Howard was not surprised when Quentin exploded. "Damn it!" Quentin shouted. He hurled the papers into the bread and peanut butter. "I've already *done* the words for this quarter! How can I help it if some fool in the Town Hall loses it? Why should I bother my brains for more nonsense just because you and Archer say so? Why should I put up with being bullied in my own house?"

He raged for some time. His face grew red, and his hair flew. Fifi was frightened. She sat staring at Quentin with both hands to her mouth, pressed back in her chair as far away from him as possible. The Goon grinned, and so did Awful, who loved Quentin raging. Howard lifted up the typewritten papers and helped himself to more bread and peanut butter while he waited for his father to finish.

"And I don't care if I never write Archer another word!" Quentin finished. "That's final."

"Go on," said Awful. "Your paunch bounces when you shout!"

"My lips are now sealed," said Quentin. "Probably forever. My paunch may never bounce again."

Fifi gave a feeble giggle at this, and the Goon said, "Archer wants a new two thousand."

"Well, he won't get it," Quentin said. He folded his arms over his paunch and stared at the Goon.

The Goon returned the stare. "Stay here till you do it," he observed.

"Then you'd better get yourself a camp bed and a change of clothes," said Quentin. "You'll be here for good. I'm not doing it."

"Why not?" said the Goon.

Quentin ground his teeth. Everyone heard them grate. But he said quite calmly, "Perhaps you didn't grasp what I've just been saying. I object to being pushed around. And I've got a

31

new book coming on." Howard and Awful both groaned at this. Quentin looked at them coldly, "How else," he said, "shall I earn your bread and peanut butter?"

"You look through me and fuss about noise when you're writing a book," Howard explained.

"And you go all grumpy and dreamy and forget to go shopping," said Awful.

"You must learn to live with it," said their father. "And with the Goon, too, by the looks of things, since I am going to write that book whatever he does." And he looked at the Goon challengingly.

The Goon's answer was to go over to the chair where they had first seen him and sit in it. He extended his great legs with the huge boots on the end of them, and the kitchen was immediately full of him. He fetched out his knife and began cleaning his nails. It was hard to believe he had ever moved.

"Make yourself quite at home," Quentin said to him. "As the years pass, we shall all get used to you." An idea struck him, and he turned to Fifi. "Do you think people can claim tax relief for a resident Goon?"

Fifi was backing into the hall, signaling to Howard to come, too. "I don't know," she said helplessly. Howard and Awful followed her, wondering what was the matter. They found her backing into the front room. "This is terrible," Fifi whispered. She looked really upset. "It's all my fault. I was busy when your dad gave me those words to take to the Town Hall, so I gave them to Maisie Potter to take because she was going that way."

"Then you'd better get hold of Miss Potter," said Howard, "or we'll have the Goon for good."

"Perhaps Miss Potter stole them," said Awful. It was automatic with Awful to turn the television on whenever she came into the front room. She did it now. When the picture came on, she sprang back with one of her most piercing yells. "Look, look, look!"

Howard and Fifi looked. Instead of a picture on the screen,

32

there were four white words on a black background. They said: "ARCHER IS WATCHING YOU." It seemed as if Archer were backing the Goon up.

Fifi uttered a wail of guilt and fled to the hall, where she stood astride the drums and phoned the Poly in a whisper, so that Quentin should not hear. But the Poly had closed for the night by then. Fifi tried telephoning Miss Potter at home then, but Miss Potter was out. Miss Potter went on being out. Fifi spent the rest of the evening sneaking into the hall to stand astride the drums and dial Miss Potter's number, but Miss Potter kept on being out. Awful meanwhile turned the television on and off and switched from channel to channel. No matter what she did, the only thing the screen showed were those four words: "ARCHER IS WATCHING YOU." In the kitchen Quentin sat with his arms folded, staring obstinately at the Goon. And the Goon sat attending to his nails and filling the floor with leg.

Catriona came in quite soon after that. She was not tired that day. She stood in the doorway with an armful of sheet music and said, "Where's Awful? I can't hear the television. And who's breathing so heavily? . . . Oh, it's you, Quentin!" The scratching of knife on nail caused her head to turn and her eyes to travel up yards of leg to the Goon's little face. "Why have you come back?"

The Goon grinned. Quentin snapped, "He grows here. I think he's a form of dry rot."

"Then he can make himself useful," Catriona said. She gave the Goon the kind, firm, unavoidable look that seemed to work so well on him. "Take this music up to the landing for me, and then come down and help me get supper. Oh, and do you play the piano?"

The Goon shook his head earnestly. He looked really alarmed.

"What a pity," said Catriona. "Everyone should learn the piano. I wanted you to help Awful practice. Howard, why aren't you doing your violin practice? Hurry up, both of you."

33

As Howard and the Goon both leaped to their feet, Quentin said, "You've forgotten me. You haven't asked why I'm not doing anything."

"I know about you," Catriona said. "I can see that you're refusing to write another two thousand words. You should have done that thirteen years ago. Hurry up, Howard!"

Howard went gloomily to look for his violin. That was the bother with Mum's not being tired. He and Awful both had to practice. Dad always politely allowed them to forget. He opened the cupboard under the stairs where his violin probably was and found the Goon tiptoeing gigantically after him, looking woebegone.

"Don't know how to cook," the Goon said.

"She'll tell you how," Howard said heartlessly. "She's in her good mood."

The Goon's round eyes popped. "Good mood?"

Howard nodded. "Good mood." The Goon's way of talking was catching. He dragged his violin out from under a heap of Wellington boots and took it away upstairs, feeling really hopeful. An hour or so of Mum in her good mood might persuade even the Goon to leave.

Howard was not much good at playing the violin, but he was good at getting practice done. He set his alarm clock for twenty minutes later and spent four of the minutes sort of tuning strings. Then he put the violin under his chin and disconnected his mind. He let the bow rasp and wail, while he designed a totally new spaceship for carrying heavy goods, articulated so that it could thread its way among asteroids and powered by a revolutionary FTL drive. That did not take long, so he spent another few minutes looking at himself in the mirror as he played, trying to see himself as the pilot of that spaceship. Although he was so tall, his face was annoyingly round and boyish. But the violin at least gave him several manly chins—though not as many as Dad had—and he thought that now that he had grown his straight tawnyish hair into a long fringe, his eyes stared out keenly beneath it. He could almost imagine

34

those eyes playing over banks of instruments and dials or gazing out on hitherto unknown suns.

After ten minutes he was able to stop playing. Mum had told Awful to do her piano practice. Howard knew from experience that the resulting screams drowned everything else. He listened and from time to time drew the bow across the strings—so that he could truthfully say he had been playing the whole time—and felt more hopeful than ever. The Goon had proved sensitive to noise from Awful. Surely he would not be able to stand much more?

Finally, Awful's screams died away to a sultry sobbing. Howard scribbled the bow about for another half minute. Then his alarm went off, and he was able to go downstairs. He passed Fifi dialing Miss Potter again in the hall. In the kitchen Quentin was still sitting, still looking obstinate. Awful was lying on the floor, gulping. "Shan't practice. Won't practice. Want television. I shall die, and then you'll be sorry!" And the Goon, far from being driven away, was at the sink, laboriously carving potatoes down to the size of marbles and sweating with the effort.

"*Very* good!" Catriona told the Goon kindly.

"Now just peel the peel, and we might have enough to eat," Howard said. The Goon gave him a wondering stare.

"Don't tax his mind, Howard. He's on overload already," Quentin said.

"Want *television*!" bawled Awful.

Howard went away into the hall. It was funny, he thought, that Mum could control the Goon perfectly, yet she could never make Awful do anything at all. "Any luck?" he asked Fifi as she put down the phone.

"No," Fifi said despairingly. "I'll have to wait and try to catch her after the lecture tomorrow. Oh, Howard! I do feel so guilty!"

"She's probably just forgotten you asked her to do it," Howard said.

"She never forgets anything—not Maisie Potter!" said Fifi.

35

"That's why I asked her to do it. Howard, I'm afraid the Goon might stick his knife into your dad!"

"Not while Mum's here," said Howard. "Anyway, I don't think Dad's frightened of the Goon. He's just annoyed."

By the time supper was ready Awful had sobbed herself into the state where you feel ill. When she got like that, she could often make herself sick. She crawled under the table and made hopeful vomiting noises. She knew that would put everyone off supper anyway.

"Stop it, Awful!" everyone shouted. "Stop her, Howard!"

Howard got down onto his knees and looked into Awful's angry, swollen face. "Do stop it," he said. "You can have my colored pencils if you stop."

"Don't want them," said Awful. "I want to be disgustingly sick."

The table above them lifted and sloped sharply. Howard found the Goon had got down on his knees too, half under the table. Fifi was catching knives and glasses as they slid off. "Bet you can't be sick," the Goon said to Awful. "Go on. Interested."

Awful glowered at him.

"Let me try?" suggested the Goon. "Both do it. Bet I win."

Awful's swollen face began to look interested. She shrugged crossly. The Goon stuck his head out from under the table and looked at Quentin.

"Mind if we use the bathroom? Competition."

The little head staring across the table looked rather as if it were on a plate. Quentin shut his eyes. "Do what you like. I don't deserve any of this!"

"Come on," the Goon said to Awful.

Awful scrambled out willingly. "I'm going to win," she announced as they left.

Five minutes later they came back. Awful looked smug, and the Goon looked green. "Who won?" asked Howard.

"She did," said the Goon. He seemed subdued and not very hungry. Awful, on the other hand, was thoroughly pleased

36

and amiable and ate a great deal. Howard was exasperated. If even Awful at her very worst could not send the Goon away, what would? The Goon ate the small amount he seemed able to manage with painstaking good manners and kept his feet wrapped dutifully around the back of his chair, so as not to lift the table.

And as if this were not enough, Catriona was grateful to the Goon for putting Awful in a good mood again. She began thinking of him as a proper visitor and wondering where he should sleep. "I wish we had a spare room," she said. "But we haven't, with Fifi here."

Fifi and Howard were not the only ones who found this a bit much. "Get this quite clear," Quentin said. "If he decides to stay, it's his bad luck. He can sleep on the kitchen floor for all I care!"

"Quentin! That's unfeeling!" said Catriona.

Howard made haste to get away again upstairs, where he barricaded himself into his room. He knew what would happen if he did not. His mother would give the Goon Howard's room and make Howard share with Awful. And Howard was not making that sacrifice—not for the Goon! All the same, he was surprised to find, while he was wedging a chair under his doorknob, that he felt a little guilty. The Goon had helped him find Mountjoy and had made Mountjoy answer his questions. He seemed to want Howard to like him. "But I don't like him *this* much!" Howard said, and made sure the chair was quite firm. Then he designed several more spaceships to take his mind off the Goon.

When he came down in the morning, he found the problem solved. The Goon was doubled into the sofa in the front room, wrapped in the blankets that had been over the drums. The Goon had really settled in. He had moved the sofa around so that he could watch breakfast television and was basking there with a big grin on his face and a mug of tea in his hand as he watched. As Howard came in, however, the picture fizzed and vanished. Howard just caught the words "ARCHER IS WATCH-

37

ING YOU" before the Goon's long arm shot out and turned the television off.

"Keeps doing that," the Goon said in an injured way.

"Perhaps Archer doesn't trust you," Howard said.

"Doing my best," the Goon protested. "Staying here till your dad does the words."

"You're going the wrong way about it," Howard explained. "I know Dad. You've got his back up by hanging around trying to bully him like this. The way to do it is to pretend to be very nice and say it doesn't matter. Then Dad would get a bad conscience and do the words like a shot."

"Got to do it my way," the Goon said.

"Then don't blame me if you're still here next Christmas," said Howard. The Goon grinned at that, as if he thought it was a good idea, annoying Howard considerably.

On the way to school Howard noticed that someone had chalked the name ARCHER beside Awful's hopscotch. It was chalked on the wall of the corner shop, too, and when Howard got to school, the name ARCHER stared at him again, done in white spray paint on the wall of the labs. There was a long, boring talk about vandals in Assembly because of it. Howard was annoyed for a while because it was Dad's business, not his. But he forgot about it in English because he was busy making a careful, soothing drawing of his articulated spaceship.

Fifi was waiting for him when he came out of school, waving and looking anxious. In a way, it was as bad as the Goon. Howard's friends all made chortling noises, pretending they thought Fifi was his girl friend. He went over to her as slowly as he could. But that only made Fifi run to meet him. "What's up?" he said.

"Don't look so glad to see me, will you?" Fifi said. "Someone might notice. Miss Maisie Potter's up, that's what. She didn't come near the Poly today, and that's not like her. I want you to come around to her house with me."

"Do you think she's ill?" said Howard.

"I think she's avoiding me," said Fifi. "She saw the Goon that night, remember. I think it's fishy." She clung to Howard's arm, causing a further set of chortles from Howard's friends. "Be ever so nice and come with me, Howard. I don't like to face her with stealing on my own."

"Oh, all right," Howard said hastily. They walked down the street together, pursued by chortles.

As soon as they were out of hearing, Fifi said, "The Goon's still there, you know. Sitting. Grinning. You dad's just sitting, too—sitting it out. He hasn't even tried to write his new book. I keep thinking of that knife."

Howard sighed. He had hoped the Goon would have got tired of waiting by now.

Fifi wrapped her scarf around her neck and flung the end bravely over her shoulder. "Frankly, Howard, I'm wondering if I should go to the police. Your dad won't. But someone should."

"It may not do any good," said Howard. "Dillian runs law and order."

"Dillian?" said Fifi. "Who's Dillian?"

"Archer's brother," said Howard. "Mr. Mountjoy said there were seven of them, and they run—"

He was interrupted by well-known piercing shouts and pounding feet. Awful was racing after them, having seen them crossing the end of the street where her school was. "Where are you two going and not taking me?" she demanded when she caught up. "You're supposed to look after me."

Fifi sighed rather. "We're going to Miss Potter's to get the words back. It's a long way."

"I'm coming, too," Awful announced, as they had known she would.

"Then be good," said Howard.

"I'll be how I want," Awful retorted. But she was afraid of making them angry enough to send her home, so she skipped along beside them almost quietly and did nothing worse than make a rude sign at two little girls across the street. "Our

39

school was written over last night," she said. "It says 'ARCHER' on all the walls."

"So does mine," said Howard.

"Let's go see Archer," Awful suggested. "You could set me on him."

"Oh, no!" said Fifi. "He must be worse than the Goon."

This sobered Awful somewhat. She skipped along without talking, while they went past the Poly and through the shopping center and on up Shotwick Hill. "Where are we going?" she complained at the top of Shotwick Hill.

"I warned you," Fifi said. "She lives up Pleasant Hill way. Woodland Terrace."

"It's posh up there," Awful objected. "And a long way. And," she added, "I wish I hadn't come now."

The way was all uphill. Long before they got to Woodland Terrace, Awful was shuffling and dragging and moaning that she was tired. She said she hated the houses here. Even the ordinary houses were beautifully painted and very neat. Most of the houses were more like red-brick castles than ordinary houses, and they got bigger and redder and more castlelike, with bigger gardens and more trees, the higher they went into Pleasant Hill. It was quite a surprise to find Woodland Terrace was a row of small houses. Awful perked up when she found Miss Potter's house actually had gnomes in its little front garden.

"She would have gnomes!" Fifi said contemptuously as she rang the bell at the little stained-glass front door.

Miss Potter, when she opened the door, had a towel around her head and her glasses hanging from her neck on a chain. She hurriedly put the glasses on in order to stare. For an instant she looked really dismayed. "Oh," she said, "what a surprise!" and forced a smile to her ribby face.

"That typescript I gave you to drop into the Town Hall . . ." Fifi began.

"What about it?" Miss Potter said, much too quickly.

"My father needs it urgently," said Howard.

Miss Potter looked at him and then backed away, in a way that made Howard feel like the Goon. "Oh, but I—" she said, and took hold of the front door to shut in in their faces. And that would have been that, but for Awful. Awful wanted to see what the house was like inside, and she was never shy. She slipped in under Miss Potter's skinny elbow and walked into the hall. In order not to shut Awful into the house, Miss Potter had to leave the door open. She stood holding it and looking meaningfully from Awful to Howard and Fifi. When none of them moved, she said, with cross politeness, "Won't you all come in?"

They went into the small dark house. It had a sad, damp smell and a lot of clocks ticking. Awful made a face because her curiosity was already satisfied. Miss Potter ran ahead of them into a spotless little living room and cleared two small books and a neat note pad from a shiny table. "You'll have to excuse everything being so untidy," she said. "I've been working hard all day, and I wasn't expecting visitors. I'm so nervous about that paper Mr. Sykes set me, Fifi! I can't think of anything else!"

"Think about that typescript," said Fifi. "Have you still got it?"

"How about some tea and cookies?" Miss Potter said brightly.

"Yes, please," said Awful.

But Howard and Fifi both said, "No, thanks," at the same time, and Fifi added, "Typescript, Maisie." Awful glowered.

Miss Potter put a hand to the towel around her head distractedly. "Oh, yes. Now let me think . . ."

Awful was annoyed at not being allowed tea and cookies. She said loudly and gloomily, "She's putting you off. She's stolen it."

"I have not!" Miss Potter exclaimed indignantly. "I've only— that is—Well, if you must know, I lent it to someone."

"Whatever for?" said Fifi. "When you knew Mr. Sykes—"

"I can get it back," Miss Potter protested. "My friend only

41

lives just up the road. She only wanted a peep at it." And with a distinct look of relief she added, "I'll—I'll get it back and give it to you tomorrow without fail, Fifi."

It seemed to Howard that Miss Potter was getting more and more shifty. Fifi evidently thought so, too, because she said sternly, "No, that won't do, Maisie. Tell us where your friend lives, and we'll go get it now."

"Oh, I can't do that!" Miss Potter cried out. "She doesn't like strangers. She won't know who you are. She—she doesn't care for children. I'll go see her myself this evening, I promise!"

Fifi looked frustrated. Howard found he did not believe a word about this friend of Miss Potter's. He thought of the Goon and the Goon's techniques. He said, "We're staying here until you give us that typescript. My father needs it. It's his property."

This produced a new flurry of excuses from Miss Potter. "But I can't bother my friend in the middle of the afternoon like this! And just look at these awful old clothes I'm in!"

"We'll wait while you change," said Fifi.

"Besides," added Miss Potter, becoming truly inspired, "my hair's wet."

"Wear a hat," said Awful. "Doesn't she tell a lot of lies?"

At this, Miss Potter made a noise of exasperation. "Very well," she said, tossing her toweled head angrily. "We'll all go see my friend. But I insist on going upstairs to change first." She turned and marched out of the neat living room. Howard hastily nudged Awful and gave her the look which meant she could be as awful as she liked. It did not seem to him that Awful needed much encouraging just then. Nor did she. She grinned fiendishly and scampered after Miss Potter. He heard her following Miss Potter upstairs, saying, "I want to see your bedroom. I like seeing bedrooms."

"Oh, Howard," Fifi whispered. "She'll never forgive me!"

Howard comforted his conscience by telling it that Miss Potter probably deserved it for stealing the words and telling lies

42

about friends. "Quick," he whispered back. "I bet the words are here somewhere."

Quietly and hastily he and Fifi tiptoed about, searching the neat little room. They opened drawers and cupboards, looked in the empty wastepaper basket, and ended lifting up clocks and shaking out empty vases. There was nothing. Miss Potter did not seem to keep even old letters. They tiptoed to the only other room, which proved to be Miss Potter's kitchen, and searched cupboards there, too. Fifi looked in the oven and the fridge, while Howard sorted through the two plastic bags and the cabbage stalk, which was all that was in Miss Potter's garbage pail. Again nothing. All the while, they could hear footsteps moving about upstairs and Awful's voice loudly saying things like "Why do you have so many kinds of makeup? They don't make you any prettier." Or, "Why do you keep your nightie in this silly teddy bear?" It made Fifi giggle.

Howard thought Miss Potter must have the words upstairs, probably in the teddy with her nightdress, and he was just hoping that Awful would have the sense to look when he heard Awful saying, in a very loud, warning way, "You *did* change quickly! Don't you like little girls watching you?" Fifi was giggling helplessly. Howard took her arm and towed her back to the living room just in time.

Miss Potter came bouncing tightly down the stairs in a neat pleated skirt, with a neat scarf over her head, and her lips were tightly pressed together. She looked furious. "Fifi, you should teach that child some manners!" she said. "Do you think you could wait outside while I find my keys?"

Awful stuck her head over the banister, grinning wider than the Goon. She whispered, in a great loud gust, "Miss Potter wants to telephone. She's got a telephone upstairs, too."

Miss Potter shot Awful a venomous look and followed that up with an artificial-looking jump. "Oh, silly me! I have my keys here all the time! Shall we go?"

They went out of the house. While Miss Potter was locking it

43

with much fussy jangling of keys, Howard tried to decide whether there really was a friend or Miss Potter had just decided on this way to get rid of them. Either way there was nothing they could do but follow Miss Potter uphill and into Pleasant Hill Road itself. "My friend is *such* an admirer of your father's books," Miss Potter explained to Howard as they climbed. "She's been asking me for months now if I couldn't get her just a peep at some of his newest writing. She says she simply *must* read every word he's ever written. She says it's his style that's so marvelous, but I think the important thing is that he's so sympathetic to the woman's point of view. Don't you agree?"

"I don't know," Howard panted. Miss Potter set quite a fast pace. "I've never read any of Dad's books."

"He says we musn't till we're old enough," Awful explained.

Miss Potter struck back smartly at this. "You poor child! Can't you read yet? How sad!"

"You do make catty remarks," Awful said. "Is it because you're an old maid?"

Miss Potter pressed her lips together and walked on up the hill in seething silence. Howard gave Awful the look that was meant to call her off, but he was not sure it worked. They came in silence to the very top of the hill, to the driveway of the largest and reddest house yet. The brick gatepost said 28. Number 28 was like several castles melted together, with brick battlements and towers sprouting off its many corners. The way into it seemed to be through a big glass porch in front. Miss Potter went through the porch door and then undid the mighty studded front door beyond enough to put her head around it.

"Cooee!" she called. "Anyone at home? Dillian, dear, it's me!"

44

CHAPTER FOUR

Dillian! thought Howard. It had never occurred to him that it might be a lady's name. Perhaps there was more than one Dillian, he thought, and it was a name like Hilary or Vivian that did for both men and women. As he thought it, he looked around to see the glass door of the porch swing and click shut.

A voice spoke. It was a sweet, laughing lady's voice, and none of them could see where it was coming from. "Why, it's Maisie!" it said. "Who are your friends, Maisie?"

Miss Potter, still with her head around the great front door, called back, "I've brought Quentin Sykes's dear little children, Dillian, and the student who baby-sits them. May we come in?"

"With pleasure, dear," said the sweet voice, almost chuckling. "Come on in."

Miss Potter pushed open the massive door, and they all trooped through it. They stood blinking. The castle was a palace inside. They were in a vast room, where light blazed from crystal chandeliers onto an acre of shiny floor made of different woods put together in patterns. The light gleamed off the gilding of elegant little armchairs and winked in the drops of a small fountain near the stairs. There were banks of flowers around the fountain and here and there in the rest of the space, as if there were going to be a concert there or a visit from the queen. Golden statues held more lights at the foot of the stairs, which swept around the far side of the room in a grand curve. Everyone tiptoed forward into the gleaming, scented space, quite awed. There was a proud, smug look to Miss Potter as she whispered, "Dillian's home is charming, isn't it?"

Fifi pulled herself together enough to say, "Cozy little place—" and stopped as she saw Dillian coming down the stairs.

Dillian was wearing a shiny white ball gown, which she held up gracefully as she came, to show her little high-heeled silver shoes. Fifi and Howard stared, thinking of fairytale princesses, and Awful thought of Miss Great Britain. Dillian had long golden hair, and her face was beautiful. When she reached the bottom of the stairs and came gracefully toward them, they saw she was even more beautiful than they had thought. She gave them a wonderful smile.

"Maisie! How kind of you to bring them!" she said.

Miss Potter turned a dull red. It was very clear she adored Dillian and would have done a great deal more for her than steal two thousand words. "I—er—I was afraid you might be annoyed, dear," she said.

"Not in the least," said Dillian. "Come and sit down, all of you, and we'll have some tea." She turned and led the way gracefully to the gilded chairs near the fountain, where she sat down in a billow of lovely skirt. She bent and rang a little golden bell that stood on the curb of the fountain. As they followed her, slithering a little on the shiny floor and quite

46

astonished, a footman came from behind the stairs somewhere and bowed to Dillian. Their heads all turned to him. He wore a red velvet coat and a white wig and stockings. "Tea, please, Joseph," Dillian said to him. "Or would you prefer a milk shake?" she asked Awful.

Awful turned her stare from the footman back to Dillian. "No, thanks."

"Bring one in case anyway, Joseph," Dillian said to the footman. "Do sit down, everyone."

Miss Potter fussily pulled gilded chairs about to make a group around Dillian, and they all rather gingerly sat in them. Once they were sitting, they found that the banks of flowers around the fountain hid most of the huge room. They seemed to be in a small space full of scents and gentle drip-drip-dripping from the fountain. It all was so elegant that Fifi tried to hide her striped leg warmers under her chair. Howard could not think what to do with his slashed bag of books. Finally, he hid it and its tape under his chair, and then there seemed nowhere to put his feet. He felt as if he had more leg than the Goon.

"You must bring your father with you next time you come," Dillian said to Howard. "I do so admire his books. But it's just as great an honor having his children here—or do you get very tired of having such a famous father?"

As far as Howard knew, having Quentin for a father was just ordinary life. "I—um—get used to it," he said.

"Of course," Dillian said with great sympathy. "You don't want to be known just for being the son of Quentin Sykes, do you? You want to be yourself."

Howard felt his ears turning red. He hated people talking to him like this. "I . . . suppose so," he said.

"So what are you going to do when you grow up?" Dillian persisted.

Howard began to feel the way you do when someone tickles the bottom of your feet. He had to change the subject or scream. "Design spaceships," he said. "But we really came to

47

ask for my father's two thousand words back." At this, Miss Potter turned and gave him a shocked look. He felt rude. "Er—please," he said.

"Of course, dear," said Dillian. "Spaceships! How interesting! But I suppose you do come under Venturus."

"It's urgent," Howard pressed on. His ears seemed to get hotter with every word. "You see, Archer got angry when he didn't get the words and sent the Goon around. And my father's refused to do another lot. So we need the ones you've got."

He stopped. Dillian's face had gone blank, as if she had not understood a word he was saying. It looked as if there had been a mistake. Perhaps she was not the Dillian Mr. Mountjoy had talked about. Howard's stomach, and even his ears, went quite cold at the thought. Meanwhile, the footman was coming back, gently wheeling a little golden trolley with a tall silver teapot on its top shelf and silver plates of sandwiches on its lower one. Dillian turned to him. "Put it in the middle, Joseph, where people can help themselves."

"You *are* the Dillian who farms law and order, aren't you?" Howard said.

A slight, proud smile flitted across Dillian's lovely mouth. She gave a very small nod. "Not in front of the servants, dear," she murmured. "Maisie, pass the sandwiches around."

The footman picked up the teapot and poured cups of tea like a high priest performing a ceremony. He carried a cup to each of them as if the cup were the Holy Grail and then followed the grail up with two more grails, one with sugar and one with cream. Miss Potter, at the same time, held a plate of sandwiches toward each of them, in an offhand sort of way, to show she was used to it, and made conversation. "Quentin Sykes's books are so sympathetic to women," she said, thrusting the silver plate at Fifi.

The footman presented Fifi with a grail of tea at the same moment. Fifi got utterly confused and tried to pick a sandwich up with the sugar tongs. She went as red as Howard's ears and

48

could not speak for the next twenty minutes. Awful, however, was quite composed. When Miss Potter waved the sandwiches at her, Awful waved them grandly away. And when the footman bent solemnly down and held out a tall pink grail of milk shake to her, Awful waved that away, too. This puzzled Howard. Awful had been the one who wanted tea at Miss Potter's house, and she loved milk shakes. And the sandwiches were delicious, small and tasty and without crusts, the kind that Awful usually thought the height of luxury.

It puzzled Dillian as well. As the footman reverently put the milk shake back on the trolley, she said to Howard, "Doesn't your little brother want anything to eat or drink at all?"

Howard's ears went hot again. Awful looked smug. She loved being mistaken for a boy. "No, I don't," she said firmly, before Howard could explain. Dillian nodded to the footman, and he went away. "Good," said Awful. "Can Howard talk to you *now*?"

Dillian turned to Howard. "Yes. Perhaps he should. So it's Archer who's getting two thousand words every three months from your father?"

Howard nodded. "Didn't he tell you? He's your brother, isn't he?"

The blank look came back to Dillian's face. Howard realized it meant she was angry. "Archer never tells me anything. We haven't spoken for years," she said. "What can Archer be doing with all those pages of writing? Do you know?"

"No," said Howard. This irritated Dillian. She stared down into her teacup, tapping her little silver foot crossly on the shiny floor. Howard grabbed four of the tiny sandwiches to encourage himself. The tapping of Dillian's foot and the tinkling of the fountain were the only sounds between the scented banks of flowers, and it seemed very rude to interrupt. "Why did you want the words?" he said.

"To see what was going on, of course," Dillian said. "I knew one of us was up to something, so I asked dear Maisie to get me a sample." Miss Potter gave a pleased and saintly smile. Dillian

49

flung her golden hair back angrily. "But I'm still none the wiser," she said, "except that I know it's Archer now. Archer!" she said, flinging her hair again. "I'd thought it was Erskine or Shine—they're both horrible—and Torquil thought it was Hathaway trying to get back into things, but we never dreamed it was Archer. How wrong we were! Archer was always far too ambitious!"

Howard swallowed the four sandwiches. Even together they were not a big mouthful. "What's Archer trying to do?"

"Stop the rest of us," Dillian said, with her face blank and angry, "so that he can have everything for himself. We've not been able to move outside this town for the last thirteen years. We're all very angry about it. It's taken us all this time to discover that your father's words must be doing it. Now the question is: how? Your father must do something special when he writes them. Has he told you what?"

"I don't think he knows," said Howard. "He says he just writes drivel—"

"Well, it certainly isn't in his best vein," Dillian said wryly. "If the stuff I've got about old ladies rioting is a fair sample, then it's idiotic. I can't see how Archer can use it for anything."

She tapped with her foot again. Scented silence fell, with the fountain drip-dripping like part of the silence. Miss Potter, who was obviously annoyed at being left out of the talk, held out a plate of sandwiches. Dillian waved them gracefully away. Miss Potter, determined to take part, held out a plate of cakes as small as the sandwiches. Dillian waved those away too. So did Fifi and Awful. Howard took two. "I can't imagine dear Mr. Sykes writing any kind of drivel," Miss Potter said. And when that only made more silence, she said, "How odd, Dillian, dear! I never knew you had any family."

This made Dillian give a comic little shrug. "There are seven of us," she said.

"I do envy you, dear!" said Miss Potter. "Large families are such fun!"

"It's not fun," Dillian said coldly. "We don't get on at all.

50

Torquil's the only one I can bear to talk to. Archer speaks only to Erskine, and Hathaway and Venturus don't speak to any of us, or to each other either. As for Shine—words fail, Maisie!''

All this while Awful had been staring fixedly at Dillian. Now she said, ''Where do you come in the family? Eldest?''

''No, dear,'' said Dillian. ''I come between Shine and Hathaway, almost in the middle.''

Howard took three more cakes. They were delicious, but they seemed to melt down to nothing when he ate them. ''But you all share running the town,'' he said. ''How do you arrange that if you don't talk to one another?''

Dillian waved that away, rather as she had waved away the cakes. ''The farming was arranged at the beginning, when we first came. We each took the things the others didn't want.'' Her lovely mouth pouted rather. ''Of course, it went in order of age, and I got saddled with boring police business and so on. But—'' The pout vanished in a smile and a chuckle. ''But Erskine got drains and sewers, and serve him right! It wasn't supposed to be for good, you see, dear. We were going to expand and move on. Then Archer did whatever he did, and we seem to be stuck here. Now suppose you tell me a little bit more about this arrangement your father has with Archer.'' She leaned forward and smiled at Howard.

Howard smiled dreamily back. The food and the scent of the flowers and the dripping of the fountain were making him feel peaceful and sleepy, and it struck him that Dillian was rather nice. But before he could get around to answering, Awful interrupted. She had still not taken her eyes off Dillian. ''How old are you?'' she demanded.

Dillian gave an annoyed little laugh. ''Now that would be telling, dear.''

Miss Potter was clearly glad to have another chance to express her dislike for Awful. ''You should never, never ask a lady her age,'' she said reprovingly. ''Dear Dillian is ageless. She's the eternal feminine.''

"Don't be sickening," Awful retorted. "I bet she's seventy at least."

Dillian's face went blank and annoyed. Miss Potter was horrified. And Fifi at last recovered enough to mutter, "You shut up, Awful!"

Awful stood up. "I'm going to be bad," she announced. "I may scream. I can feel it coming on."

"Oh, Lord!" said Fifi. "Howard, we'd better go."

Howard stood up, too. He knew Fifi was right. He dragged his bag out from under his gilded chair, which promptly fell over into the nearest bank of flowers. Dillian turned her blank look at him, and he felt as badly behaved as Awful. "Sorry!" he muttered. He picked the chair up and tried to straighten the bent flowers.

"We can't go yet!" Awful insisted loudly. "We haven't got Dad's words. She's trying to make us forget so she can keep them!"

"Awful!" Fifi said sternly. Her face was as pink as the geraniums arranged behind her.

"Don't worry, dear," Dillian said kindly. "Children do get tired and cross. And you know, I nearly did forget it was those words you came about. I was enjoying our talk so much. I'll send for them at once." She bent and rang the little golden bell again. After a moment the footman came through among the flowers again. This time he was carrying a folded sheaf of papers, in both hands, as if they were Magna Carta and might fall to pieces unless they were handled very gently indeed. Unlike the papers the Goon had produced, these were crisp and white and new. The footman handed them to Dillian, who passed them to Howard with a smile. "There, dear. Do just check to see they're the right ones."

Howard felt ashamed of being distrustful, but he did unfold the papers and glance over them. The typing seemed to be Quentin's. He recognized the way half the capital letters soared into the air, so that their tops were cut off. He had no way of knowing quite what his father had written, but near the begin-

52

ning, his eye caught: "and if Corn Street were to fill with old ladies, clubbing policemen with handbags and umbrellas." He folded the paper up again. "This looks all right," he said. "Thanks very much. And thanks for the tea."

"You're welcome, dear," Dillian said, smiling radiantly.

Howard stowed the papers carefully in his blazer pocket and held out his hand for Awful in the way that meant she was to come along at once. Fifi stood up and held out her hand, too. Awful shuffled over to them. "I don't want to stay in this old hole anyway," she said rudely.

"I shall smack you!" Fifi whispered. She and Howard dragged Awful out from among the flowers. Awful let her feet trail and made them tow her across the shiny floor. Howard looked back in embarrassment and saw Miss Potter had taken another cake and settled back smugly in her chair, to show she was staying on. But Dillian gathered her ball dress up and came gracefully to the front door with them. It made Howard sweat with embarrassment at the way Awful was behaving. He dragged Awful through the mighty wooden door, and through the porch, and then down the driveway, knowing Dillian was waving and smiling behind them, and promised himself he would hit Awful as soon as they were in the road.

But Awful escaped just outside the gate because Howard's hand was so slippery with sweat by them, and Fifi let go of her, too, in order to sigh heavily. "Oh!" Fifi said. "I'd give my ears to look like Dillian! Wasn't she glamorous!"

Howard laughed. As they turned and walked downhill, he was distracted from his annoyance with Awful, and even from sweet thoughts of getting rid of the Goon in half an hour, by the sheer contrast between Fifi and Dillian. He looked at Fifi's peaky little face and frizzy light brown hair and laughed again. "You couldn't look like her. She's twice your size for a start."

"I've always wanted to be that tall," Fifi said yearningly.

"Stupids!" Awful called out. She was lurking a safe distance behind Howard. "She's an evil enchantress. And she dyes her hair."

53

"A lot of people dye their hair," Fifi said over her shoulder. "Do come on. There's no such thing as enchantresses."

"Yes, there is!" Awful said indignantly, still hanging behind. "Why do you think I didn't have any tea? Bubbling things are going on inside me, I'm so hungry. But I was right. You and Howard just sat there getting enchanted, and I didn't."

Fifi raised her eyebrows at Howard and sighed. "Come on!" she called back. "Before your mum gets home!"

"Not until Howard makes sure we've really got Dad's words," Awful called. And she dug her hands into her pockets and stood still.

Howard's hand went irritably to check the pocket where he had put the papers. It felt limp and flat. He plunged his hand inside. Apart from half an old pencil and a rubber band, that pocket was empty. Unable to believe it, he felt in his other pockets. Then, frantically, he searched his trouser pockets, too. There were no papers in any of them. "I don't believe it!" he said.

"Maybe you put it in your schoolbag," Fifi suggested.

Howard knelt and turned his bag out on the pavement on the spot, halfway down Pleasant Hill Road. He sorted through everything and shook out all the books. Awful came up and watched, keeping safely on the other side of Fifi. When Howard had found a note about history homework but absolutely nothing else that was typed, she said, "Now do you believe me?"

"They dropped out," Fifi said firmly. "Let's go back and look. Look carefully, both of you."

They went back uphill. Fifi scanned the hedges; Howard looked in the gutter. Awful sauntered behind, still with her hands in her pockets, looking superior. And she seemed to be right. There was nothing that looked remotely like paper all the way to the top of the hill or anywhere on the downward slope beyond. Here Howard suddenly noticed that the house he was searching beside was numbered 104.

"We've come too far," he said to Fifi. "Let's go and look in

54

her driveway. And if it's not there, I'm going to knock on her door and ask her."

They went back up the slope. And before long they found themselves going downhill again. They stopped beside a gate labeled 18.

"This is ridiculous!" said Fifi. "Go back and check the numbers."

Back uphill they trudged again. Awful planted a hand on each gate and called out its number as they went. "Twenty-four. Twenty-six. Thirty. Thirty-two—Howard! It's *gone!*" Even Awful had not expected this. She looked thoroughly depressed. They stood in a huddle, dumbfounded. There was no number 28 now or any room for one between 26 and 30.

"We're on the wrong side of the road," Fifi said at last.

So they crossed the road and looked there. But on that side all house numbers were odd ones, and there was no number 28 between 27 and 29 there either.

At that point Fifi at last admitted that Awful might be right. "The—the old *hag!*" she said angrily. "Let's go home anyway. It's late."

"Before I die of hunger," Awful said pathetically. "Do you believe me now, Howard?"

Howard nodded dismally. He felt thoroughly depressed, almost too miserable, as they trudged home, to be angry at the way Dillian had cheated them. He had hoped to get rid of the Goon and put everything right, and nothing had happened at all. On top of the rest he felt as hungry as if he had had nothing to eat at all. "No wonder Miss Potter's so thin," he said to Fifi. Fifi nodded. He thought she was trying not to cry.

When they got to the bottom of Shotwick Hill, Howard borrowed some money from Fifi and bought Awful a doughnut in the shopping center. He thought she deserved it. She had done valiantly.

The result was that when they finally trudged down the passage to the back door of 10 Upper Park Street, Awful was the only one looking at all happy. In the kitchen Quentin and

55

the Goon were sitting facing each other across a pile of peanut butter sandwiches. They did not look happy either. Both their faces turned toward the door.

"Tea is now officially supper," Quentin said. "Where were you?"

The Goon jerked his face at Quentin. "First time I've seen him worried," he said.

Awful's face lit up at the sight of the sandwiches. She dived on them. The Goon picked the plate up before her dive was finished and held it high in the air. Quentin shouted through the resulting screams, "Not a mouthful until I find out where you've all been!"

"It's all my fault, Mr. Sykes!" Fifi shouted back. She flopped into a chair, still trying not to cry. The Goon put the plate down again. Awful stopped yelling in order to eat sandwiches as if they were her first meal that week. Howard ate the few he managed to snatch before Awful started. Fifi drank a large mug of tea and explained.

"Shouldn't have anything to do with Dillian," the Goon observed. "Bag of tricks. Smiles and steals your trousers."

"Well, we know what's happened to the words now," Quentin said to the Goon. "You can go get them from Dillian."

"Can't," said the Goon. "Told you. Need my trousers."

Quentin smothered an exasperated sigh. "You mean," he said calmly and carefully, "that you still intend to sit over me trying to make me write some more?" The Goon nodded, grinning his widest. "That does it!" Quentin slammed his hand down on the table, so that the empty plate bounced, and sprang to his feet. "Take me to Archer this instant!" he said. "I demand to see him."

The Goon considered. "Take you tomorrow," he said.

"Why not now?" Quentin shouted, losing his calm completely.

"Can't," said the Goon. "Bank not open."

"What on earth," roared Quentin, "has that got to do with—" Wincing at the noise, Catriona came in as he roared. She was

56

tired. She sank into the chair Fifi hurried to get out for her, spilling music and the evening paper onto the table as she sank, and shut her eyes. Everyone became quiet and considerate. Quentin picked up the paper and began to read it. The Goon, to Howard's amusement, tiptoed to the kettle and made the cup of coffee Catriona always needed. He brought it to her with a humble, sheepish grin. Catriona knew it was the Goon. She said, with her eyes still shut, "Quentin—"

"I know, I know," Quentin said. "I'm seeing Archer tomorrow, it seems." He looked at the Goon to confirm it.

The Goon nodded and plucked the newspaper out of Quentin's hands. He took it across to Howard, grinning and pointing to a place on the front page, where it said, "YOUTHS INVADE TOWN HALL." "Mountjoy held his tongue," he said to Howard. "Thought he would."

Howard had barely time to wonder if he was pleased or not to be called a "youth" and lumped in with the Goon when Quentin reached out and plucked the newspaper back. "My worldly goods are yours," he said quietly, out of consideration for Catriona, "but only after I've read them first, my good Goon. When do we see Archer?"

"Hold hard," said Fifi. "I want to see Archer, too. After tonight I've a bone to pick."

"So do I," said Awful.

"And me," said Howard. "And we're at school all the time the bank's open."

The Goon was surprised. "Don't even give you a break for lunch these days?" he asked wonderingly.

"Of course they do!" Awful said scornfully. "And you're not to go without us."

"Meet us, twelve-thirty, outside the High Street bank?" the Goon suggested.

Catriona suddenly opened her eyes. "Are you talking about tomorrow?" she said. "Howard, don't forget I'm coming to your school tomorrow afternoon to hear your school orchestra. Have you done your violin practice?"

57

Howard had forgotten, of course, both things. He felt really annoyed. He always forgot school orchestra if he could, because Mr. Caldwick, who ran it, had a bleating voice that made him want to scream like Awful after ten minutes. And he had forgotten Mum was coming to hear it because it was so embarrassing to have your own mother coming to school as an official. Orchestra always started just before afternoon school, too; that meant he was going to have to be in two places at once if he wanted to see Archer. Archer was the one he was determined not to miss, but he could not tell Mum that. He supposed he had better do his violin practice so she would think he was doing what she said.

While Howard was thinking this, Catriona told Awful to do her practice, too. Awful's mouth opened. The Goon promptly put his fingers in his ears.

"Oh, don't yell. Do it," Howard said wearily. To everyone's surprise, Awful obeyed him and went off to the piano in the front room as good as gold. Just as well, Howard thought, as he went upstairs, or he might have been the one screaming. When he had the violin under his chin and the alarm set, he found it necessary to design a really complicated spaceship, full of unnecessary but soothing twiddles. Dillian had made a fool of him, the house was still full of the Goon, and he had a feeling that tomorrow was going to be a more than usually trying day.

CHAPTER FIVE

The next day was Friday. When Howard woke up to find rain slanting in a bleak wind, he knew he had been right about the day. He came downstairs to find the drums booming again, faintly, and a lot of fizzing from the front room, where the Goon was enjoying his tea and television. A crackling voice announced, "Archer is wa—" before the Goon turned it off.

"Know you are," the Goon's voice said. "So's Torquil."

I'm surprised Dillian isn't, too, Howard thought as he went to get breakfast. There Fifi said to him, "Don't forget the bank at lunch. I'm so nervous I won't go if you're not there."

Before Howard could reply, Catriona rushed briskly through the kitchen, calling out, "Howard, don't forget to take your violin to school."

"Everyone's on at me!" Howard shouted after her as the back door slammed behind her. "Leave me alone!"

He was still grumpy when he set off into the rain with his violin and Awful. In spite of the rain, someone had tried to chalk "ARCHER" all along the walls of Upper Park Street. Perhaps the people who had done it were the group of boys loitering and laughing halfway along the street. As Howard and Awful went past them, the boys crossed the road and loitered along behind them. When they turned the corner, the boys turned that way, too.

"Do you know them?" Awful asked. The boys were all Howard's size and probably older.

"No," said Howard. "But I think they're after us. You go down Zed Alley and by the Poly. And run. I'll hold them up while you go."

"What about you?" Awful asked, hovering.

"I'm bigger than you. Run," said Howard. To tell the truth, he was looking forward to working off some of his bad temper. So Awful turned aside and streaked off down Zed Alley, running in long, pounding strides, with her head down and her arms working. Howard waited while her feet went splashing and stamping down the first zig of the alley. As he heard them go faint when she turned into the zag, he turned around, scowling against the rain, to face the boys. By this time they had realized that Awful had got away. They came at him in a bunch, and three of them tried to dive past and get into the alley. Howard stood in the entrance to the alley, feeling brave and noble, and swung his violin case at the nearest oncoming stomach. There were two minutes of fierce fighting after that, but by the time some of the boys did get past into the alley Howard had heard Awful's feet turn into the last zig and was fairly sure she had got away. He wrenched free himself and ran.

The other boys ran after him. Howard was a fast runner, but he was slowed down by the violin in its heavy black case. The boys were not carrying anything, and they kept catching up. To Howard's annoyance, they chased him all the way to school. He was forced to stop and use the violin as a weapon

60

again at the corner of Union Street and again just outside school. Here someone had been busy with red spray paint and written "ARCHER" in huge letters outside the school gate. The third lot of fighting took place on top of it. By this time Howard was not feeling noble, and his temper seemed to have worked on rather than off. When he finally limped into school, hot and sticky and prickly with running in the rain, his nose was bleeding and he hated the name of Archer.

Howard's nose trickled blood most of the morning. He felt steadily more angry. His whole family was being got at by Archer, and he wanted to do something about it. That morning he had not even the patience to design a spaceship. He simply waited for the bell to go so that he could get away and see Archer. When it did, he leaped up and ran.

The boys were waiting across the street in spite of the rain. There seemed to be nearly twenty of them now. A lot of people who arrived at the gate at the same time as Howard were turning back inside the school. "It's Hind's gang," Howard heard someone say. "I'm going out the back way." Howard was tempted to do the same, but when he looked at his watch, he saw he had not time to go all that way around and still be sure of meeting the Goon. He set off through the gates at a run.

Hind's gang ran slantways across the street to catch him. There was a lot of hooting and angry shouting, and most of them were held up in the traffic; five arrived on the school side in front of Howard. Howard folded his arms across the top of his head and used himself as a battering ram. He was determined not to let Archer or anyone else stop him. He was held, and tore free, and was held again. The boy doing most of the holding was a ginger-haired lad Howard remembered from that morning. Howard hit at him and missed and got hit by someone else. When he finally dragged loose, they had added a bleeding lip to his bleeding nose. Howard mopped it angrily as he ran. They ran after him, but he had no violin to slow him down this time, and he got away quite easily. He arrived at the

61

bank only a minute late, trotting, mopping, and very much out of breath.

The Goon was standing in the bank doorway with Quentin, sheltering from the rain. He gave Howard a look of professional interest. "Fight?" But before Howard could answer, Fifi and Awful trotted up, both of them looking rather the way Howard felt.

"A lot of big boys just set on her!" Fifi said. "It's too bad!"

"Fifi knocked their heads together," said Awful. "I kicked."

The Goon and Howard stared at Fifi. It was hard to imagine her that warlike. Quentin humped his shoulders under his red and black checked overcoat. "The bank will take one look at us and decide this is a holdup," he said.

The Goon grinned and barged his way through the door into the bank. It was a very stately bank inside, hushed and respectable, with orderly lines of quiet people waiting in front of each cashier. The Goon, in his usual way, strode to the front of the nearest line and shouldered the person there out of the way. Everyone in the line looked at him indignantly, but he took no notice and stooped his small head down to speak to the cashier. It was like the Town Hall all over again, Howard thought, and braced himself to be thrown straight out. But the cashier answered the Goon politely and pointed to the other end of the counter. The Goon strode up there and beckoned. Almost at once a respectably dressed young lady in a neat pleated skirt like Miss Potter's came out of a side door and waited for them.

"What did he say?" Fifi wondered as they went over there.

"'This is a stick up,' of course," Quentin said. "It's the only language he knows."

But nothing could have seemed less like a stickup. They followed the young lady through the door and among other young ladies all busy at things like oversized typewriters and then into an inner part where everyone was looking urgently at displays on screens. It was all wonderfully quiet. Nobody seemed surprised to see them being led past. Howard found his anger was drizzling slowly away. Feelings like anger just

62

did not seem to fit here. The thing that worried him most was the fact that none of them looked respectable. His lip was swollen, Fifi and Awful were disheveled, and Quentin's coat was a perfect eyesore. Quentin loved that coat. He had worn it from ever since Howard could first remember. Everyone else in the family hated it. Catriona called it the Tramp's Coat.

Finally, they arrived at a door which said, in gold letters, "J. C. Whyte, Manager." The young lady tapped discreetly on this door, and someone inside said, "Come!" The young lady opened the door and motioned them through.

They went into a nice modern office room with a warm orange-red carpet. J.C. Whyte—if that was his name—had iron gray hair and a quiet, impressive manner, wrapped in a quiet, impressive striped suit. He was talking to a customer when they came in, a big young man in overalls, who looked even more out of place in the office than they did. J.C. Whyte was obviously trying to get rid of the young man because he said, in a final sort of way, "Well, that's the best we can do, considering the recession," and handed the young man a bundle of papers on his way to shake hands with Quentin. "Oh, good morning, Mr. Sykes," he said, as if Quentin were the most important person in the bank.

As Quentin shook hands, the young man in overalls slung the bundle of papers carelessly back onto J.C. Whyte's desk and said, "I'd better take them all out of your way, J.C. He seems to have brought the whole family."

Quentin stared a little. Mr. Whyte said very politely, "If you'd be good enough to go with Mr. Archer, Mr. Sykes."

"Oh," said Quentin. "Yes, of course."

The young man in overalls gave them all an amused look over his shoulder as he led the way to a door at the back of the office. It swung heavily, and when it was open, they could see it was more than a foot thick. Howard could have sworn it was the door to a safe. Inside, he knew it was a safe. Its walls were lined with pigeonholes, so that there was only a narrow passage down the middle. He looked into some as the young man

63

led them through. He saw black cashboxes, brown leather jewel cases, and bundles and bundles of important-looking envelopes. Some of the lower pigeonholes had doors across, perhaps to hide money. But there was not much chance to look because Archer led them straight through to another, much smaller door at the back. This door was just as thick, and they all had to bend to go through it except Awful. Beyond that they came out into a huge place. It was as big as an airplane hangar, brightly lit by dangling electric bulbs.

They all stopped, in a huddle, and stared around. There were installations, machines, cabinets, readouts, winking lights, screens, dials, illuminated plans, displays flashing in all directions, almost as far as they could see. There were machines in the distance quietly at work running on rails, pushing more displays into place. Other machines were humming along the iron girders overhead. Howard's anger vanished completely. He forgot his fat lip. He did not even mind about Dad's coat—it did not look out of place here anyway. All he could feel was amazement and a good deal of rather strong envy.

One of the machines ran along the girders overhead until it stopped just above them. With a gentle humming it lowered what seemed to be a huge scoop. Quentin and Fifi backed nervously away from its shiny red underside. But when it came to floor level and stopped, they saw it was upholstered inside in cream-colored leather, like a huge armchair or the inside of an expensive car. Archer swung himself briskly into it and settled in a cream swivel seat at one end, where there was a display screen and a control panel with banks of colored buttons.

"Come on," he said. "Make yourself comfortable."

They climbed in and sat in the leather seats around the inside. Archer touched a button. The machine hummed, and they found the scoop rising up into the middle of the vast workshop. It was a strange feeling, half-cozy, half-exposed, and very like being on the big dipper in a fairground. Fifi

64

looked more nervous than ever. Awful gazed over the edge, delighted. Quentin folded his arms and pretended he was quite used to this sort of thing. Howard, staring about even more eagerly than Awful, realized at last that the Goon had not come with them. In fact, now that he thought, he could not remember the Goon's coming any farther than the main part of the bank. Archer, of course, was boss here.

Archer swung his seat around to face them. He was not very like Dillian since his hair was dark and his eyes were far bluer than hers. In fact, they were the bluest eyes Howard had ever seen, luminous cornflower blue, with a keenness to them that caused Howard another large jab of envy. For Archer's eyes clearly were eyes that spent their time scanning banks of instruments, just as Howard had always longed to do.

"Why did you want to see me?" Archer asked Quentin. He had a very crisp way of speaking, which Howard found he rather admired.

"I want to know," Quentin said, "why you've made me write you two thousand words every quarter for the past thirteen years."

"I don't know," said Archer. "Because I haven't."

Quentin's mouth opened, then shut again. He rubbed his hair to give himself time to absorb this. "But I understand you control power supplies," he said. "So it must have been you who cut off all my services eight years ago, when I failed to deliver the words."

Archer said, "I do farm power. I knew you were cut off then. But it wasn't me who did it."

"But," said Quentin, "you don't deny sending the Goon around to me when this last lot of words went missing?"

Archer smiled. He had a nice, wry sort of smile. "I admit he came from me. Yes. But the idea was just to intercept one lot of words to find out what was being done with them. I didn't want Dillian getting too far ahead of me. But the words you sent then were the only lot I've ever seen. And they were quite worthless. You know that, don't you?"

65

They stared at him suspiciously. Archer looked back, straight and calm and blue-eyed. He seemed honest as the day. There seemed so little harm in him that Awful said boldly, "Then why do you keep interrupting our telly with 'ARCHER IS WATCHING'?"

"And why did you set that gang on us and chalk 'ARCHER' in the street?" Howard said.

A slot in the instrument panel by Archer's seat began to reel out a long paper tape with numbers on it. Archer ran it through his fingers and read it as he answered. "I don't own any gangs. I never chalk on streets. People always try to put the blame on me. Excuse me a moment." He bent forward to speak into a grille. "Those Mompas futures—buy them in, as many as you can get. And you can begin selling Steeples now."

"Where do you come in the family?" Awful asked, watching with interest.

"I'm the eldest," said Archer. He tore the tape off, crumpled it, and threw it into another slot, which swallowed it with a *whoof*. "Sorry about that," he said. "Now—"

"I thought you must be the eldest," Awful said.

Archer was surprised. "Why?"

"Because Howard always gets blamed for the things I do," said Awful.

Archer looked at Howard and smiled, with his mouth tipped down sympathetically. Howard licked the swelling on his lip and remembered that Archer had had nothing to do with that. Archer had sent the Goon, of course, but even so it was quite hard not to like him. If it were not for the way Quentin was rubbing his hair and watching Archer dubiously, Howard would have decided Archer was one of the nicest people he had met. But Dad did know about people.

"You don't look any older than Dillian," Fifi said to Archer in a hoarse, shy whisper.

"My family doesn't age at the rate you people do," Archer said.

"Where are you from then?" Fifi whispered.

66

Archer was not saying. He gave a private, wry grin. "Elsewhere," he said, and the grin faded off his face as he turned to Quentin. Howard was surprised to see how much less pleasant that left his face. "And here we stick," he said, "because one of us seems to be using your words to pin us to the spot. Whom were you sending your writing to?"

"I don't know," said Quentin. "I only dealt with Mountjoy."

"Then have you any idea what you did to make your words so powerful?" Archer said. "Describe what you were told to do and how you carried out your orders."

"I flatter myself that my words are always powerful," Quentin said. "Yes. I'll describe what I did. But only on condition that you answer a few more of my questions first." Archer seemed astonished at this. He stared at Quentin. Quentin stared back.

"I don't see why I should tell you anything," Archer said at length in a mutinous sort of mutter. His face turned rather red, and it was clear he had his teeth clenched. He swung his chair around suddenly so that he could see over the side of the scoop and began to work buttons and levers in his control panel. There were hollow echoes down below. One of the machines ran on its rails to a row of slim steel installations and began moving them slowly to a new position. Everyone else sat tensely. It gave you a very helpless feeling, aloft in the scoop, with all the controls in Archer's hands. "I love technology," Archer remarked, carefully maneuvering the machine to a new line of rails. "I have machines here that can do anything I want them to. I can tamper with anything in town. I always think it's lucky for the citizens here that I'm not particularly cruel."

Quentin said very carefully and calmly, "In that case, I'd better point out that I'm due at the Polytechnic in half an hour, and my children are supposed to be back in school."

"I know," Archer said, still leaning out and guiding the machine. "But no one could do anything if I kept you here—unless Dillian felt like swapping the words she stole for you, of course."

67

There was a short silence, which felt rather long. Then Fifi said timidly, "But you won't hurt any of us. I can see you won't, Mr. Archer."

The steel instruments now seemed to be where Archer wanted them. He stopped the machine and swung his chair around again where he sat thoughtfully tinkering with other knobs and controls. Below, in the vast shed, displays lit and colored lights flashed as he turned them on and off. Then he said, "Does anyone besides me want a hamburger?"

"Me, please," Howard and Awful said together.

Archer turned around and laughed. He seemed to be in a thoroughly good mood again. "Eight hamburgers then," he said. "I expect you both can eat two." He pressed some more knobs. After a moment a tray slid out from under his control panel, bringing with it a most appetizing smell. Eight brown buns were on it with a steaming hamburger peeping out from each. "I'm not unreasonable," Archer said as he passed them around. "Ask me your questions. And perhaps you'll see then how important it is for me to have a new piece of writing from you."

Everyone bit and chewed enjoyably. Quentin swallowed a huge bite and said, "So we take it that my words somehow have power to impose restrictions on you. What are these restrictions precisely?"

"I can't move from this town," Archer said. "None of us can. Erskine can go out as far as the sewage plant, but the rest of us are stuck inside the city boundaries."

"I can see that must be a great nuisance," Quentin said, chewing thoughtfully. "How did you discover my words were doing it?"

"By looking until I found the unusual thing," Archer said. "We probably all found out that way. I found out eight years ago, when whoever it was cut off your supplies of power. I've kept careful watch ever since, but I still can't find out who's doing it or how."

68

"How do you keep watch?" Howard asked, picking up his second hamburger.

Archer laid down his second hamburger and swung his chair to press some more knobs. The screen at the end of the scoop lit up like a television. It showed a view of the front room at home. Just the low down view from one corner, Howard thought, that you would get if you looked out of the television. Archer pressed another knob. The picture changed to a view of the kitchen, looking down from the ceiling. The light bulb, Howard thought. It changed again to the same sort of overhead view of Quentin's study. "I wish you used a word processor," Archer said to Quentin, "or even an electric typewriter. I'd know at once how it was being done if you did."

"I detest the things," Quentin said. He sounded quite quiet, but Howard could tell he was getting angry.

"That's how you put the words on our telly," Awful said, wiping her fingers on her coat. "I know you did because you didn't say you didn't. I need some chips now to wash down my hamburger."

Archer smiled agreeably. He pushed the tray back under his control panel and pressed knobs again. "And I'll tell you a very odd thing," he said to Quentin, "which you wouldn't know to ask. We've been stuck in this town for twenty-six years really. I've no idea how it was done for the first thirteen years, but when I came to check, all my instruments agreed that it had been going on for twice as long as I thought." The tray slid out again with two newspaper bundles on it. Archer handed one to Awful and one to Howard, although he had not asked. The chips inside were nicely salted and soaked in vinegar. "I thought I was the only one who knew," Archer continued. "But Erskine knew. He told me when he came to see me last week. He said he thought whoever it is was going to try to get rid of us all soon." Archer's face went very unpleasant as he said this. "That's why I needed some words from you," he said.

69

Quentin nodded. "I see. A different question now." He waved his last lump of hamburger around the scoop and outward at the rest of the huge workshop. "All this," he said. "It must take a great deal of money."

Archer grinned across his own last piece of hamburger. "Yes, but I'm a millionaire. It's no problem."

"I thought you must be," said Quentin. "But there must have been a time, more than twenty-six years ago, I suppose, when you weren't a millionaire. How did you get the money to start?"

Howard thought this question was rather an impudence. So did Fifi. They both looked nervously at Archer. But Archer smiled his agreeable wry smile. "I got money from the taxes," he said. "We all farm the taxes. We agreed on that when we first came."

Howard could see that the cool way Archer said this made Quentin very angry. He interrupted hurriedly, "How did Erskine know it was twenty-six years?"

"I didn't ask," said Archer. "Erskine farms drains and water, so I suppose he keeps watch through his pipes."

"This town seems well and truly bugged," Quentin remarked. He still sounded calm, but Howard could tell he was getting angrier every second. "Looking at this stuff you have in this place," he said, "I'm surprised you haven't taken over the world by now."

"Oh, I intend to," Archer said cheerfully. "As soon as I've stopped the person who's stopping me." And he finished his second hamburger, obviously quite unaware that by saying this, he had turned Quentin utterly against him. But Howard knew. He saw it in his father's eyes as Quentin politely asked his next question.

"And who do you suspect is stopping you?"

Archer considered ruefully. He smiled his agreeable smile. "I suspect everyone," he said. "I'd have done it myself if I'd thought of it. It makes sense to stop the rest of them from getting in your way while you take over. I suspect Erskine

70

most, even though I quite like him, because he's almost as clever as I am. Venturus is clever, too, and he farms education, so he could have got on to you through the Poly. Shine is ruthless enough, Torquil and Dillian are selfish enough, and Hathaway hates us all even if he *is* a recluse." Archer thought again. "Torquil now," he said. "Your wife comes under Torquil."

"Mum's got nothing to do with this," Howard said quickly. And Awful did her best to defend Catriona, too, by asking, "Is Torquil the youngest?"

"No, Torquil's after Hathaway—fifth," said Archer. "Erskine's sixth. Venturus is the youngest."

"Is Venturus selfish, too?" Awful asked. "I am."

"Probably. I haven't seen him for years," said Archer.

"Then I like Venturus best," Awful decided.

Archer laughed, but he looked rueful, too. "You could do worse," he said. "I like Venturus next after Erskine."

Quentin stood up and wiped hamburger grease onto his coat. "Come on, Awful. We all must be going." And he said to Archer, "If you would make this gadget put us down?"

Regretfully Howard got up as well and threw the newspaper from his chips at the slot, which swallowed it with a most satisfactory *whoof*. He would have loved to stay, and to miss orchestra practice, and perhaps persuade Archer to show him some of his technology. But he could tell that Quentin was trying to get away without making any promises to Archer, and that did seem the right thing to do. Fifi was looking even more depressed to be going. Perhaps that was because she had not done anything yet about picking a quarrel with Archer. She sat where she was, with her arms around her knees and a mournful smile on her face.

"Wait a minute," said Archer. "You haven't told me your exact orders for writing those words."

"You know as much as I do," Quentin said. "Two thousand of them, not a copy or anything I've done before. Nothing else. Come along, Fifi."

71

"Then you'll do me two thousand by those orders for tomorrow," Archer said, smiling.

"Regard them as done," Quentin said, waving a vague hand.

"Mr. Sykes!" Fifi said reproachfully.

Archer glanced from Fifi to Quentin. He was clearly astonished to see that Quentin had not agreed to do the words. A blush swept across his face. Then the grim look gathered on it. "I warn you, Sykes," he said, "I don't like being made a fool of. The trouble you've had up to now is nothing to the trouble you'll have if you don't do those words."

Quentin sighed. He folded his arms. "Howard," he said, "you have sense. Speak to him from me, as a taxpayer and a citizen of the world. If I tell him, I'll lose my temper."

"He means he won't," Howard explained a little nervously. "He doesn't like your ideas."

The blush swept over Archer's face again. "But I answered all his questions! I thought—"

"Precisely," Quentin said meaningfully.

"He doesn't think you ought to take over the world," Howard interpreted. And seeing the irate astonishment growing on Archer's face, he added, "And he doesn't bully easily."

The red of Archer's face grew brighter still. His eyes blazed blue. "But my plans are all made!" he said. "I'm not going to be stopped by you! Write those words or suffer!"

"No," said Quentin. "I can't square it with—"

Archer hurled himself around in his chair. His hands swept out to a whole clutch of buttons in his console. "Oh, get out of my sight!" he yelled. "I've had enough of all of you!"

The scoop tilted and then seemed to whirl through the air. Howard had a dizzying feeling of being slung by it, as if it were a Roman catapult. Bright light and wet rain washed over him. He found himself standing on wet tarmac, staggering a little, and staggered farther, across some red painted letters that said 'ARCHER,' to hold himself up on what turned out to be the school gate. He stood there, panting, catching up with the fact that Archer's technology was something other than normal technology. Then he wondered where Dad and Awful and Fifi had got to. Just as he had caught up with the fact that he was outside his own school, he heard a bell ringing from inside the buildings.

Howard cursed. He was in time for orchestra practice after all.

CHAPTER SIX

Catriona was already there when Howard slithered into the hall and left his violin case among the stack of odd-shaped bags and cases at the end. She tactfully pretended not to know Howard as he tiptoed gloomily to sit in one of the little wooden chairs arranged by the platform. The violins were always given the small chairs. Howard's legs stuck out like the Goon's, and there was no way he could prevent Mr. Caldwick from noticing him.

Mr. Caldwick left off talking to Catriona and came down from the platform to tell Howard he was late. "It's really most discourteous to keep your mother waiting like this," he bleated as he made sure Howard's violin was in tune.

This, of course, made all the other violins turn around and whisper, "Is that your mum?" Howard could hear the whisper spreading while Mr. Caldwick went back to the platform and made a long bleating speech about how lucky they were to have Mrs. Sykes with them this afternoon. Howard doubled his legs up and tried not to listen. He had enough to think about. He thought about Archer and could not decide if he liked Archer or not. Then he thought about that vast space full of technology and knew what he thought about that. He was about as envious as a person could be. Real technology was better any day than imaginary spaceships, however well designed. Howard thought he could cheerfully go without the alien suns and settle for the banks of instruments. He wished he were Archer like anything.

He came back to reality to hear his mother speaking. "I want you to pretend I'm not here," Catriona was saying, "and play just as you usually do. I shall listen, but I shan't say anything till later. Ready?"

Mr. Caldwick stepped forward and raised his baton. Howard made haste to put his violin under his chin. And they played just as they usually did. It was terrible. Because Catriona was there, Howard found he really noticed for once. Everyone who could played a different wrong note. Howard wondered how it was possible, without the law of averages producing at least one right one. He had not thought there *were* so many notes you could play. And of course, everyone was so busy searching his or her music for his or her wrong note that no one had time to look at Mr. Caldwick's baton at all. The music swiftly became a race to get to the end first. The first violins won the race, by a triumphant short bar, from the cellos, with the trumpets beating the flutes breathlessly into fourth place. The drums came last, because the drummer had lost his place in the music and never hit his drums at all.

Knowing some of the things Catriona said about school orchestras at home, Howard was pleasantly surprised when she came forward and said, "Well, that was quite a good effort. But I think some of you haven't seen quite what this music's supposed to be doing. Let me show you on the piano." She went to the piano, and to Howard's surprise, she did show them.

75

She showed them what each set of instruments was doing, holding the tune, supporting it, or pushing pieces of a new tune through the first one. The shape of the music suddenly became clear. And what was more, after about half of an hour of being shown, everyone became very excited about getting it right. When Catriona told them to try again, violins were put eagerly under chins and wind instruments to mouths. Howard, feeling as eager as the rest, realized that his mother was very good at her job.

They played. This time they were almost tuneful. Some of them even watched the baton. They had got some way, and the drummer had just hit a drum for the first time that afternoon, when there was a strange clattering among the instrument cases behind Howard. Someone seemed to be chanting. Mr. Caldwick looked over there irritibly and froze, staring. Catriona also stared. The music died away as the orchestra, one by one, turned to look and stayed twisted around, staring. Howard turned to look, too. And he stayed twisted around, just like the rest of them, staring. Only the violin under his chin stopped his mouth from dropping open.

A tall and startling figure was walking up the middle of the hall, surrounded by bobbing disco dancers in wild clothes and followed by what seemed to be the cathedral choir. At any rate, there was a line of about two dozen small choirboys walking and singing behind them, and behind that was an agitated man in a black cassock whom Howard recognized as the choirmaster. But his eyes went back to the tall figure in front, dressed like something from "Aladdin and the Lamp." He knew it was Torquil. It could be nobody else.

Torquil was wearing an immense golden turban. Ruby earrings dangled from his ears. He wore a wide red sash, baggy white trousers, and golden slippers with turned-up toes. He twirled a small jeweled baton as he strode.

"Do you think he's a genie?" somebody said beside Howard.

In that case, Howard thought, who was the fool who rubbed the lamp? He supposed Torquil had chosen to dress like that because he was as handsome as Dillian, but what had possessed him to bring twenty disco dancers and the cathedral choir was beyond Howard to guess. He was very annoyed. Torquil had interrupted just as he was enjoying orchestra practice for the first time ever, and he could see that his mother was so confounded by this strange procession of people that she could think of nothing to do or say.

Mr. Caldwick pulled himself together and bleated, "I don't know who you are, sir, but you can just go away!"

Torquil halted at the back of the orchestra. His dark eyes flashed proudly under his glittering turban. "I am Torquil!" he cried out. "I farm music in this town, and I have a perfect right to be here."

"Go away!" bleated Mr. Caldwick. "Take all these people out of here!" The choir had stopped singing by this time because most of the choirboys were staring about and giggling; but the dancers were still dancing away, and the choirmaster was wringing his hands. "The orchestra is trying to practice," Mr. Caldwick bleated. "And you—"

"Oh, be quiet, you old sheep!" said Torquil, and he flourished his jeweled baton at Mr. Caldwick.

Most of the orchestra gasped at hearing Mr. Caldwick called an old sheep, even though many of them usually called him that themselves. The choirboys laughed, and even the busy dancers grinned. Everyone's head swung toward Mr. Caldwick, expecting him to grow wool and drop on all fours. But nothing seemed to happen.

Torquil's baton pointed at Catriona. "I want a few words with you in private," Torquil announced.

By this time Catriona had recovered from her surprise. She said, in the firm matter-of-fact manner that worked so well on the Goon, "Then you'll have to come see me after school. I'm busy now."

The manner made no impression on Torquil at all. His baton whisked round to point at the disco dancers. "Jump about, all of you," he said. The baton whirled on to point at the choir.

77

"Sing," Torquil instructed them. "All of you make a noise. Interrupt." The choir obediently burst into an anthem. The dancers moved in among the chairs of the orchestra, jigging and whirling. Torquil smiled as he turned back to Catriona. "Now you can't be busy till I let you," he called out. "Don't put me off anymore, or I shall be angry." And he strode through the orchestra toward the platform, with the dancers whirling about him. Music stands fell in all directions. A dancer in shiny purple with crimson hair knocked into Howard and then cannoned into his music. Howard watched sheets of music flying, and all the anger he had somehow not managed to feel at Archer rose up in him.

Howard jumped up. He found himself running after Torquil as he strode and gripping his violin by its neck like a club to hit Torquil with. Torquil leaped gracefully up onto the platform. Howard floundered noisily up after him and grabbed Torquil by his silken sleeve. "Stop it!" he said. "Do you hear?"

He was rather frightened when Torquil swung around to glare disdainfully at him. He did not quite dare club him with the violin, even though all Torquil did was to tug to get his sleeve away. Howard hung on angrily. "Let go!" Torquil said. "Are you a boy or a limpet? I only want to speak to Mrs. Sykes."

"Then do it, and stop acting about!" Howard said, and he let go of Torquil's silken sleeve with a shove, rather surprised at his own daring.

Torquil flashed him a contemptuous look and turned to Catriona. "Mrs. Sykes, is there somewhere we can talk without being overheard?"

Catriona looked at Mr. Caldwick to see if he knew. Mr. Caldwick held out both hands piteously and made gasping noises. Howard was puzzled. But Torquil stretched out his baton and tapped Mr. Caldwick smartly on the head with it. "*Glunk* only suggest the storeroom behind the platform," bleated Mr. Caldwick.

"No good. Venturus will hear. He farms schools," said Tor-

78

quil. "Why do you think I brought all these noisy people along?"

"We could go sit in my car," Catriona suggested.

"Good idea," said Torquil.

"Now look here, Mr.—er—Torquil . . ." Mr. Caldwick began.

Torquil tapped him on the head and shut him up again. Then he turned and beckoned the choirmaster. "You. Choirmaster," he said. "You come take this music lesson, or whatever it is, while we're gone. He'll do it twice as well as the sheep," he said to Catriona.

"I know," she said. It was true. The choirmaster was a friend of hers. Howard tried to give the choirmaster a friendly smile as he struggled among the knocked-over music stands to get to the platform. But the choirmaster was evidently as much under the spell of Torquil's baton as Mr. Caldwick. He simply gave Howard an agitated stare. And Howard felt Catriona's hand on his arm. The hand gave a shaky little pull, to tell him Catriona wanted him to come to the car, too. Howard nodded. He did not want Torquil hitting Mum with his baton. Catriona gave his arm a grateful pat before she turned away to get out her car keys.

As the choirmaster scrambled unhappily onto the platform, Torquil waved his baton across everyone else in the hall. The choir stopped singing with a jerk. The dancers stood where they were. The faces of the orchestra all turned to him. "Now you're all to do what he says," Torquil called out, pointing the baton at the choirmaster. "Is that clear?" He jumped off the platform and strode through the hall to the door, calling over his shoulder to Catriona, "They'll all forget everything straight afterward. Not to worry. Where's your car?"

"In the yard outside the main door," Catriona said, hurrying after him.

Howard grabbed up his violin case and ran after them. And to think he had wanted to miss orchestra practice! he thought as he ran. It was almost funny. But not quite.

79

When he caught up, Torquil was standing out in the rain in his finery, prodding Catriona's car with his baton. "Hathaway runs transport," he was saying. "Archer knows machines, and Dillian and Shine could both have it bugged. There. It's safe from all of them. But Erskine could still hear if you chance to have it parked over a drain." He bent down to look under the car and saw Howard. "Oh, the limpet boy's still here."

"Howard is my son," Catriona said. "He's going to sit in the back while we talk."

"Suit yourself," said Torquil. "He'll forget with the rest. Get in then, limpet. I'm getting wet."

Catriona opened the car door. Howard tipped the front seat forward and scrambled in. "Who runs housing?" he asked as he went.

"Um," said Torquil. "I forget. Venturus probably. He got stuck farming all the dull things." He tipped the seat straight and climbed in after Howard. It was a small car. As Torquil sat down, his great golden turban got squashed against the roof and began to slip off sideways. He tried to push it straight, but there was no room. Torquil took it off in the end, with a flourish, as if that were what he had always meant to do. His hair tumbled out from underneath, curly and not as dark as Archer's. Howard thought he looked better without the turban.

As soon as Catriona was settled in the driving seat, Howard asked, "Do you farm anything else besides music?" He was determined to find out as much as possible. Torquil might be able to get him to forget, but it stood to reason that if Torquil wanted to talk to Catriona, she would have to remember what they said. And Howard could always ask her afterward.

"Mine are all the interesting things, like sport and shops," Torquil said. "Now be quiet, or I'll shut you up like the sheep." He turned gracefully to Catriona. "Mrs. Sykes, you must be wondering what I'm going to say."

"No, I'm not," Catriona said, in her very driest way. "I know

80

you're going to ask me about the two thousand words Mr. Mountjoy gets my husband to write every three months."

Howard could see from Torquil's handsome profile that Torquil was annoyed, though he tried not to show it. "Very good, Mrs. Sykes," he said. "Clever guess. And why am I asking?"

"Because you don't know why Mr. Mountjoy wants them, and you want to find out," Catriona said. "Let me tell you straightaway, I haven't a clue why."

Torquil was plainly irritated that she knew all this. He said huffily, "I know why. We all do. What I don't know is *who*. Come now, Mrs. Sykes. Hasn't your husband given you a little hint about who really wants his words?"

"He has not," said Catriona. "He doesn't know."

"But you must have tried to guess," Torquil said wheedlingly. "Give me just a hint about which of us you think it is."

"I've no idea," said Catriona. "Frankly, Torquil, I heard of your existence only three days ago. Before that I didn't even know Quentin had been doing words for Mountjoy all these years." Mum was taking the wrong line with Torquil, Howard thought. He did not like to be unknown. Her plain, sensible manner was rubbing him the wrong way. His profile was looking thoroughly sulky.

"You've had thirteen years to find out in," Catriona went on. "Why is it suddenly so important now?"

"Because Archer's made a move," Torquil said irritably. "He's finalized his plans to farm the world. So has Dillian. She's been organizing all the women in the country all week. I always watch them. Besides," he added, cheering up a bit, "there's been a feeling in the air these last few days. Something important is going to happen. I'm extremely sensitive to that kind of thing."

"Are you indeed?" Catriona said dryly.

"And very easily hurt," announced Torquil.

"I'm sure," Catriona said.

"And I'm getting offended," Torquil said. "In fact, if there

81

weren't something you could do for me, I'd get out of this car this moment!"

"What can I do for you?" Catriona said, drier than ever. Howard longed to tell her to watch it. She was treating Torquil just the way she treated Awful, and it was a mistake with both. Torquil was beginning to tremble with anger.

"I'll tell you," Torquil said. "Your husband is going to write Archer two thousand words, isn't he?"

"I suppose he will in the end," Catriona agreed. Howard wondered, but he did not like to interrupt.

"When he does," said Torquil, "you're to get them and give them to me."

"Now how could I do that?" Catriona asked. "I may not even be in the house when he does them."

Howard could feel the seat Torquil was sitting in shaking. "Well, you're to think of a way!" he ordered. "Use your female cunning. Get the words somehow. Then give them to me. I'm in the Bishop's Lane disco most evenings except Sunday. You'll find me in the cathedral otherwise."

And Torquil, Howard supposed, was taking the wrong line with Catriona. She was getting more and more sensible. "But why should I?" she said.

Torquil's temper cracked. His voice filled the car in a hysterical shriek. "Because I order you to! Because I farm music! Because you'll lose your job if you don't!"

"Lose my job?" Catriona was really alarmed.

"Yes! Lose your job!" Torquil shouted with obvious satisfaction. Then, just as Awful did when she made an impression on Catriona, he calmed down almost at once. "Yes," he said thoughtfully. "Your job can be part of the government cuts. Do you think I can't do it?"

"I . . . don't know," said Catriona.

"I can. Don't risk it. Get me those words," said Torquil. "Go on. Promise." Catriona's mouth opened. "Or the Council makes you redundant," said Torquil.

Catriona sighed. "Very well. I promise. But—"

"Good!" Torquil said. He became very brisk and cheerful now that he had got his way. That was just like Awful, too. "I shall expect to hear from you next week. Make your husband write the words over the weekend. And—" He twisted around in his seat to look at Howard. The baton was ready in his hand. Howard swore to himself that Torquil would not make him forget. He would fight it somehow. But as Howard braced himself, a thought struck Torquil. "Oh, yes. Let's hear from you, limpet. Who do *you* think is using your father's words?"

It was a perfect opportunity to fish for more information. Howard took it. "Well, it can't be you," he said, flattering Torquil, "though you could be bluffing. And so could Dillian. Obviously the one who's doing it doesn't want the rest of you to know. But I don't think it's Archer. He said he wasn't, and I think he was telling the truth. I haven't seen Shine yet—"

"And I don't advise you to, limpet," said Torquil. "Shine farms crime. Go on."

"So Shine is quite likely," said Howard. "I haven't a clue about Hathaway, but it could be Venturus, if he farms housing. Mountjoy was in the housing department." Here he remembered that Quentin had met Mountjoy playing golf, and Torquil farmed sport. He decided not to mention that. He said, "But I think Erskine was the one Archer suspected."

Torquil, to Howard's relief, took the baton back in order to tap thoughtfully at his mouth with it. "Hm. Erskine. That's quite an idea. Erskine's a dark horse. And he's bound to want to climb out of his drains by now."

"Why do you want Mum to get you the words?" Howard asked boldly.

Torquil laughed, showing teeth as handsome as the rest of him. "Simple, my dear limpet! If someone's found a way to keep us all here while they go out and farm the world, I want my share. I badly want to farm America at least. And now—" The baton reached out. "Forget," said Torquil, and rapped Howard's head.

It felt as if someone had clashed a pair of cymbals on both

83

ears. Howard went deaf. There was a moment of numb blankness following that. Howard struggled against it with all his might and then went on struggling, without quite knowing why anymore. He could still see Torquil as a blur of scarlet and white and gold, climbing out of the car. He clung to that. He watched Torquil slam the car door, then, more blurred still through the rainy window, cram the golden turban back on his head and stride away. When he was out of sight, Howard climbed over into the front seat beside Catriona. Both of them sat there limply, watching rain patter and run on the windshield. For a while there was nothing else in Howard's head. But slowly, in the same way that the raindrops ran together into blobs, and the blobs into clots, and then into streams of water, memory began to clot in Howard's brain. He let it clot, without forcing it.

After a while he was helped by seeing Torquil again, blurred and blobbed by the rain on the windshield. Torquil had reformed his procession. He came striding out of the hall into the schoolyard, followed by the dancers and the choir, with the choirmaster hurrying behind. A few strides into the yard Torquil held up his baton. The whole procession vanished. The yard was suddenly empty. Oddly enough, that made Howard quite sure of his memory.

Catriona moaned slightly. "Howard," she said, "can you remember?"

"Yes," said Howard. "All of it."

"Thank goodness for that!" said Catriona. "Otherwise, I'd have trouble believing any of it. What's-his-name did just vanish, did he?"

"Torquil. Yes," said Howard. "And he was dressed like the Arabian Nights."

"Then we're not mad," said Catriona. They sat for a while longer, watching the rain drip across the empty yard. Then Catriona said, "I don't feel up to facing your school orchestra again; it's beyond hope anyway. Shall we just go home?"

"Let's," said Howard.

84

So Catriona started the engine and the wipers, and they rolled down the yard to the gates. As they turned out into the yard, Howard saw that in spite of the rain, two or three boys were loitering on the sidewalk opposite. Another one, with ginger hair, was loitering up to join those. Howard grinned. Let Hind's gang gather. They would have to wait till Monday now to get him! Then a thought struck him.

"Mum," he said, "how about driving around by Awful's school and picking her up, too?"

"Yes, it'll save her getting wet," Catriona agreed, and turned left instead of right.

Sure enough, when they came to Awful's school and joined the line of cars waiting to take children home, there were three wet boys waiting on the other side of the road there, too. While they waited, another thought struck Howard. Archer had thrown him to his school, but he had no way of knowing if Archer had done the same for Awful—or what he had done with Dad and Fifi. As a way of preparing Catriona, in case Awful was not there, he told her about Archer while they waited.

"So Archer's just such another?" was Mum's dry comment.

Howard was going to protest that Archer was not really like Torquil when he saw Awful in the distance come through the school gate, see the boys, and stop. He saw her turn and say something to two girls her own age who were just coming out, too. Both little girls tossed their heads angrily and walked away, leaving Awful standing looking dejected. Poor Awful, Howard thought, as he got out of the car. She *would* quarrel with people. He suspected Torquil was the same. "Over here!" he shouted, waving.

Awful's head came up, like something springing to life. She came racing along to the car. The boys started to move after her, but when they saw Howard and the car, they gave up and turned away. Awful pounded up and dived headfirst into the back seat. "I love coming in the car!" she said, bouncing up and down. "Archer threw me back to school. Did he throw you?"

85

She sat up as Howard got in. "What's wrong? You both look funny."

"Torquil," said Catriona. "Fasten your seat belt, Howard."

"Oh, have you seen him? Is he *very* horrible?" Awful asked eagerly.

Howard said what he thought Torquil was. It made Catriona say as she drove, "Howard! You shouldn't teach her words like those!"

"I know them anyway," said Awful. "Dad says them a lot, too. And I thought he would be because he was the one horrible Dillian liked. Tell me."

The drive home was so short that they were still telling her as they walked up the side passage and Catriona unlocked the kitchen door.

The Goon looked up with a grin as they came in. He was filling the kitchen with leg, just as usual.

"How did you get here?" Howard said.

"Broke in," the Goon observed. He grinned at Catriona beguilingly. "Won't get any burglars with me here. Keep them out."

"You have a nerve!" said Howard. "Where's Dad? And Fifi?"

The Goon did not seem to know. "Poly?" he suggested.

Catriona flopped into a chair. "Well, since you're here, you can make us a cup of tea," she said. The Goon got up at once and did so, slowly, carefully, and humbly. Catriona drank a cup of tea. Then she had the Goon make her two cups of coffee and drank those. Otherwise, she simply sat, waiting for Quentin. Howard supposed she must be anxious. But it was not so. When Quentin did at last come in, Catriona said, "Quentin!" in the voice that sent Howard and Awful sliding for cover to the corners of the room.

Quentin took his coat off and threw it into the third corner. He flung his briefcase into the remaining corner. "What did Archer do with Fifi?" he said irritably. "He slung me all the

86

way to the Poly, but Fifi never turned up. The wretched girl's got half the books I needed for the afternoon!"

"Quentin," said Catriona, "I insist that you go to your study this minute and write four thousand words!"

"Oh, do you?" Quentin said nastily.

The rest of the day was devoted to a family row. It was an epic row, even for the Sykes household, and it went in three parts.

The first part of the row was entirely between Catriona and Quentin. Catriona towered and boomed. She insisted that Quentin write two thousand words for Archer and two thousand words for Torquil. This, as she thundered more and more angrily, was the only possible way to stop them all from being pestered like this. Quentin stood and shouted that nothing would possess him to write any words for anyone anymore. At which Catriona thundered that he was selfish. To which Quentin howled that he was *not* selfish; it was a matter of right and wrong. To which Catriona boomed that he should have thought of right and wrong thirteen years ago. To which Quentin bawled that he had only just found out the *facts*!

Since Quentin was the only person Howard knew who could stand up to Catriona when she was angry, this part went on for some time. Howard was reminded of that saying about an irresistible force's meeting an immovable object. The Goon was clearly fascinated. His mouth opened, and his little head turned from Quentin to Catriona like someone watching a tennis match. When it got too dark for him to see the one who was shouting, the Goon got up and tiptoed heavily to put the light on.

Quentin, at that point, was yelling, "Face the facts, you stupid woman! This town is run by seven megalomaniac wizards!" He blinked at the sudden light and rounded on the Goon. "You!" he bawled. "I hope you're taking this down in shorthand. I want Archer to know!"

The Goon blinked, too, and grinned foolishly. Howard and

87

Awful both looked at the lighted bulb and thought Archer probably knew anyway. Then they looked at the taps over the sink and wondered if Erskine did, too.

"Leave the Goon alone!" thundered Catriona. "He's only doing his job!"

"*Only* doing his job!" Quentin howled scornfully. "People excuse every kind of dirt by calling it only a job! He's a good chap, this Goon. He's getting paid for terrorizing my household, so that's all right!"

"You brought it on yourself!" boomed Catriona. "But you'd no business to bring it on me and the children!"

"What's a megglemaniac?" Awful asked hurriedly, hoping to stop the row there.

It did not stop the row. It just moved it into Phase Two, which was the part when Quentin and Catriona both kept appealing to Howard and Awful to say that they were right and the other one was wrong. Howard did not like their doing that. He seemed to be on both sides at once.

Quentin said, "A megalomaniac is someone who thinks he owns the world. Archer's one. This Torquil seems to be another." And he embarked on a long speech about them, with digressions on Dillian and the Goon. "Look at them all!" he shouted. "Two of them in expensive fancy dress, and Archer wallowing in a shed full of costly hardware! How much does it all cost? Who pays for it? I do. I pay my taxes as a citizen; they use the money for their luxuries. Parasites, all seven of them. And you"—he rounded on the Goon—"you're a parasite's parasite. How do you like being a louse on a louse?"

The Goon wriggled and then scratched his head as if he thought the louse part ought to be taken literally. Catriona again told Quentin to leave the Goon alone. "We're not talking about what *you* pay!" she thundered. "We're talking about what *I* earn! Howard, do you think it's right I should lose my job because your father has fine feelings?"

"It's not fine feelings. It's right and wrong!" Quentin shouted. "Howard, you've spoken to Archer. You heard him coolly announce he's out to rule the world. And he's worried that someone's trying to stop him! I say more power to that person's elbow"

Howard found himself wriggling, like the Goon. "But," he said, "the person who's stopping him wants to farm the world, too."

"Exactly," said his father. "So I write nothing for any of them. Awful, don't you think that's something worth sacrificing your bread and peanut butter for?"

"Not if there's nothing else to eat," Awful said anxiously.

"We all shall be out in the street!" boomed Catriona. "Howard, you know I earn more than he does!"

"Yes, you oughtn't to sacrifice Mum's job," Howard said.

"Am I not sacrificing my own?" Quentin yelled, flinging out a dramatic arm. "Knowing what I know, I shall never dare sit at my typewriter again. What do you think?" he asked the Goon. "Do you really, even with your tiny mind, want Archer to rule the world?"

"Do it better than Dillian or Torquil," the Goon said.

"That's no answer!" said Quentin.

"Need my supper," the Goon said sadly.

"Then go out and get something," Howard said. "Hold up a fish and chip shop. Rob a hot dog stand. I'm starving!"

It was now late enough to be Awful's bedtime. The Goon arose dolefully and turned out the empty pockets of his jeans. He looked plaintively at Quentin. "Don't prey on me," said Quentin. "Go and batten on Archer. Go and—"

But here the back door opened and Fifi came in. This started Phase Three of the row. Fifi had a pale, unfocused look, as if she had a cold or had been watching too much television. Howard and Awful were glad to see her. She was safe, and the row might end now. Even the Goon looked at her as if he thought she might lend him some money.

"Fifi!" said Catriona. "You said you'd be in to get supper!"

"Yes, where were you?" said Quentin.

89

"Oh—walking about," Fifi answered dreamily. "What's the matter? Why are you all looking so upset?"

"Won't do the words," said the Goon. "Didn't like Archer. Holy duty."

Pink swept into Fifi's pale face. "Didn't like Archer!" she almost shrieked. "Oh, Mr. Sykes! Archer's the most wonderful person in the world! Of course, you'll write something for him. You *have* to be joking!"

The Goon's mouth opened. Everyone else stared. Awful suddenly exclaimed, "Oh. Boring. Fifi's in love with Archer. Boring, boring, boring!"

"What if I am?" Fifi said defiantly. "I'm doing no harm." Her voice wobbled a little. "I know he'll never look at me."

Quentin staggered to the table and sat down with his head in his hands. "This was all I needed!" he proclaimed. "Fifi on the other side! We now have a fifth column in our midst!"

"The Goon's that, too," Howard pointed out.

"The Goon is sold by the meter and doesn't argue," said his father.

"Fifi," said Catriona, "help me make him see sense."

So began Phase Three of the row, which was more of a passionate argument than a row. Fifi and Catriona combined against Quentin at first. But Howard was slowly drawn in on Quentin's side. At first he joined in only to make the sides even, but as time went on, he was convinced by Quentin's arguments. It did make sense to stop Archer or one of the others from farming the whole world, if you happened to have a way to do it. And though Mum and Fifi kept saying that Quentin had no right to make the rest of them suffer, Howard began to agree with Quentin more and more that you had to do a thing you knew was right, even if people did suffer. It seemed worth a sacrifice.

Meanwhile, Awful and the Goon formed an alliance, too. They tiptoed to the stove and tried to make something to eat. There were a lot of things neither of them knew. Awful kept pulling Howard's arm and whispering things like "The Goon

90

says you have to break eggs before you fry them. Is that right?" or "If I put a slice of bread under the grill with an egg on it, does it end up as scrambled eggs on toast? Or not?"

Howard was so busy with the argument that he was rather impatient with these questions. So when the Goon pulled at his sleeve sometime later, looking woebegone, Howard did not feel very sympathetic.

"What have you done now?" he said. "Burned some water?"

"No," the Goon said dolefully. "Want Fifi. Archer gets everything."

CHAPTER SEVEN

The sacrifice began the next morning. Howard was awakened by the Goon standing dismally beside his bed.

"Archer's on the telly," said the Goon. "Wants your father."

As Howard got up and went to his parents' bedroom to start the tricky and dangerous task of waking Quentin at eight o'clock on a Saturday morning, he was nearly knocked flying by Fifi racing downstairs to look at Archer. Fifi had got it bad, Howard thought, if she could hear Archer all the way from the ground floor when she was in the attic. He went in and shook Quentin's shoulder and was rewarded with an unshaven growl.

"Archer," said Howard. "On the telly."

"Ellimerroterell!" went Quentin.

But Catriona leaped up and became Howard's ally. "Howard, get his dressing gown. Quentin, I insist you speak to Archer."

Quentin growled more fiercely than ever, but they got him up and marched him to the stairs. "Tea!" wailed Quentin, turning pathetic. "You can't expect me to talk to Archer without a cup of tea first!"

The Goon had thought of that. He met them on the landing with a fistful of steaming mugs, one for each of them and one for Awful, who was up, too, by this time.

"You know," said Quentin as he shambled downstairs, sipping from his mug, "this Goon of ours is getting quite housetrained. If he goes on this way, I might consider hiring him myself as a bodyguard."

"Hurry up!" said Catriona.

They reached the hall. As they passed the set of drums, Torquil's voice came booming out from them. "Mrs. Sykes! Mrs. Sykes, don't forget my two thousand words!"·

Quentin whirled around. The Goon hastily picked up the drums and bundled them, bumping and booming, into the cupboard under the stairs. But he was too late. While he was doing it, Quentin shouted, "I am not writing *any* words! Not for you or anyone else!" And it was clear Torquil had heard. His voice was yelling threats from the cupboard as they all trooped into the front room.

There Fifi was sitting, in the striped clown suit she wore for pajamas, gazing yearningly at the television. In the screen Archer looked up as they came in. He was eating a toasted sandwich, and to judge from glimpses of creamy leather all around him, he was sitting in his scoop.

Quentin opened his mouth to speak. Archer held up the toasted sandwich to stop him. "Don't," he said. "Don't say anything you might regret. I heard all you said last night. Very eloquent you were, too. But you've slept on it now. You must see you were making a great fuss about a very small thing. Just

93

a few pages of writing and an hour or so of your time. That's all I need.''

"No," said Quentin.

Archer smiled, in his wry, winning way. "Oh, come on, Sykes. Where's the harm in it?"

Fifi said, "Mr. Sykes, surely you can see he'd rule the world really well."

"She's right, you know," said Archer. "I'm very fair, and I'm not cruel. I'd do it well. And that's not a thing you can say for any of the rest of my family. One of them will rule the world if I don't. Why don't you help me do it?"

"No," said Quentin. "Not for you, not for anyone. I object to being bullied, I object to being spied on, and I object even more to being ruled. No!"

Archer looked at him with the sandwich halfway to his mouth. "You'll regret that. I warned you. Do you want to reconsider?"

"No," said Quentin.

"All right then," said Archer. "Prepare to regret it." The television screen went blank.

They went back through the hall. Torquil's voice yelled some kind of threat as they passed the cupboard. In the kitchen they discovered that the electricity and gas had been cut off. The Goon had obviously been expecting this. While they had been watching Archer, he had made the biggest teapot full of tea and a large jug of coffee for Catriona. He had done it for Fifi really. Howard saw the Goon's eyes slide wistfully to Fifi, hoping she was noticing his thoughtfulness. But it was Catriona who thanked the Goon. Fifi was busy trying to persuade Quentin not to make Archer too angry. And Quentin's mind seemed to be taken up entirely by the fact that the Goon had forgotten to make any toast.

"Look at this!" he said, flopping a piece of sliced bread back and forth. "Limp white stuff. It doesn't taste of anything even if I put marmalade on both sides of it." At least that is probably what he said, but no one heard the last part of it. Everything

94

was drowned in a sudden bedlam of music. The radio on the windowsill burst into violent organ music, pealing and thundering a toccata and fugue sufficient to make the windows rattle.

Catriona gave a shriek and covered her sensitive ears. Howard picked up the radio and tried to stop the noise. But it was not switched on, and there was no way of even turning the noise down. Howard carried the pealing, thundering radio out into the hall. There the drums were thumping away in the cupboard, and he could hear the strings of his violin twanging faintly in there, too. From Quentin's study, Quentin's tape deck was roaring out the "Ride of the Valkyries," and there was an even worse noise from the front room. The television was playing music full blast, treacly, sentimental music, with lots of swooping and occasional massed choirs. The piano was also playing, probably something very impassioned. Howard could see the notes going up and down by themselves, but most of it was drowned by the television and by awful pipings from the several pieces of a clarinet that Catriona had left on top of the piano.

Torquil, Howard thought. I hope Archer's getting an earful, too.

Fifi and Awful came to help him, and they managed to reduce the din a little. They threw the radio, the tape deck, and the pieces of clarinet into the cupboard with the drums and threw the sofa cushions on top to deaden the sound. Then they draped the Goon's blankets over the television. At this point the piano really made itself heard. It was playing "Chopsticks." Howard shut the lid down. It did not stop the "Chopsticks," but it stopped them seeing the creepy way the notes went up and down by themselves. At least they could hear one another now, if they shouted.

For five minutes it was almost peaceful. Then a brass band arrived and began marching up and down the street outside.

"And look," said Awful, pointing across the street over the

95

heads of the marching band. Awful was the only one whose voice was sure to be heard.

Howard looked. He had been too optimistic about Hind's gang. They were standing on the other side of the road, all twenty of them. Most of them were lounging with their hands in their pockets, listening to the band, but the ginger boy was industriously writing "ARCHER" with spray paint on every empty piece of wall. Fifi stared indignantly. Then she seized a note pad and wrote, "Those boys are victimizing Archer!!!" She took the pad into the kitchen, where Quentin, Catriona, and the Goon were sitting with tissues stuffed into their ears, and showed it to Quentin.

Quentin hurled the pad across the room. "Women!" he bawled. It was almost quiet in there by contrast. "Oh, my heart bleeds for Archer! What about us?"

A heavy knocking on the front door interrupted the things Fifi was trying to shout in reply.

"Go see what that is, Howard," Catriona said, looking strained and desperate.

Howard went and opened the front door. He stared. The very polite-looking man outside was dressed in a quilted robe with hanging sleeves. As Howard opened the door, the man took the flat, squashy hat off his head and bowed, so that the feather in this hat swept the toes of his wide-fronted slippers. He said something, but it was drowned in the music inside the house and by "Land of Hope and Glory" marching past outside.

A new idea of Torquil's, I suppose, Howard thought. "You'd better come in!" he shouted.

The man nodded and stepped into the hall. Howard shut the front door, which shut out "Land of Hope and Glory" at least, and realized that the music indoors had stopped. Torquil wanted them to hear this.

In the ringing silence the polite man said, "Young master, I bear a letter to your father and am enjoined to wait for an answer."

96

He had a very strange accent. Eh? thought Howard. "Dad!" he shouted.

Quentin came out of the kitchen with his dressing gown looped around his paunch and tissue sticking out of both ears. When he saw the polite man—who was obviously trying hard not to stare—Quentin looked resigned. He cautiously took the tissue out of one ear. "Now what do *you* want?" he said.

The man bowed and swept his toes with his hat again. "Master Quentin Sykes?" he asked. Quentin nodded suspiciously. "Master Sykes," said the man, "I am to give you a letter from Hathaway, my patron, and wait with you for your answer."

Awful's face and Fifi's and Catriona's at once appeared around the kitchen door, and the Goon's face wedged itself in above them, all goggling. The hall remained silent. Torquil must have been listening, too.

Quentin sighed. "Let's have it then."

The messenger carefully felt in a pouch hung from his belt and brought out a long, folded yellowish letter, with a large red wax seal to hold it together. He handed it to Quentin with another bow.

Quentin turned it over to the place where there was square black writing. "'Maftr. Quentin Fykes,'" he read. "Parchment, too. Very amusing." With another suspicious look at the polite man, he turned the letter over again and cracked the red wax that held it together. He spread it out with a leathery rattle. The square black writing inside was obviously hard to read. Quentin held the letter up and frowned at it. "'Inafmuchas,'" he murmured. "Oh, this is the best yet! Listen to this, all of you!" And he read:

Inafmuchas we have heard that others do much beleaguer you by threats and promifes, we do this fubmit you fo that you may here learn and be apprifed wherein lies your true duty and allegiance. It is to Hathaway and always has been and formerly was. To Hathaway, once quarterly, have you long fent two thoufand words in writing, and this you

97

muft continue in, as by cuftom you ever did. This we fend you by our own meffenger, enjoining and adjuring you to place in his hand and none other the faid writings and by that one Act confirm the Bond between yourfelf and your

Betrayed but lenient

HATHAWAY

"Eh?" said the Goon.

"Translation," said Quentin, "for those not burdened with brains. Hathaway says it's him I always send the words to and to go on doing it. But isn't there an 'or else'?" he asked the polite messenger.

The man bowed again. "My patron does not make threats, sir. But I am enjoined to press the matter on you by observing that the forbearance you have hitherto known will not extend beyond today."

"That is, give it to him today, or watch out," Quentin translated to the Goon.

Outside, the brass band finished with "Land of Hope and Glory" and switched to "Amazing Grace." This, for some reason, was the last straw for Quentin. He tore the tissue out of his other ear and jumped on it.

"This is too much!" he roared. "I have now had enough! I have passed the bounds of sanity. This!" He held the letter up and rattled it in the messenger's face. "Know what I'm going to do with this lunatic object?" The messenger backed nervously against the front door and shook his head. "You'll see!" shouted Quentin. "So will the others. *Torquil!*" he roared. "Are you listening? *Archer!* Can you see?"

He ran to the hall stand and wrenched open the drawer in it. This drawer was known as the Everything-But drawer because there was always everything in it but the thing you were looking for. Things—string, the insides of watches, hair grips, paper clips, and a button badge saying "I Love Milton Keynes"— flew across the hall as Quentin rummaged feverishly in it, but

98

finally he came up, red-faced and panting, with three bent drawing pins, a carpet tack, and a hammer.

Everyone, including the messenger, followed Quentin, mystified, as he marched into the front room, flapping the letter. There Quentin hurled the blankets off the now-silent television and proceeded to nail the letter to the front of it, across the screen. There was silence while he did it, broken only by banging, a yelp from Quentin when he hammered his thumb, and "Amazing Grace" from outside the window. "Now we don't have to look at Archer," he said. "There. This is now on public exhibition. Everyone who enters this house is to be shown this. Its precise meaning is to be explained in detail whether people want to know or not. Do you know what it means?" he demanded, rounding on the messenger.

The messenger clutched his hat and backed away. "Sir, it is a letter from Hathaway—"

"No, it is not!" Quentin howled. "It is the public death certificate of Quentin Sykes, the writer! Know what I'm going to do now?"

They all shook their heads.

"Come with me," said Quentin. Everyone obediently followed him to the hall and watched him rummage in the Everything-But drawer again. This time he found the padlock and chain that had gone with Awful's bike before it was stolen. He set off with them to his study. Once more everyone followed.

"Watch, Archer!" he shouted. "Listen, Torquil! See, all the rest of you! I am about to padlock my typewriter." He wove the chain in and out of the typewriter keys and snapped the padlock shut around the space bar. "There," he said to the messenger. "Is Hathaway expecting a written reply?"

"Sir, there are to be two thousand words written . . ." the messenger began.

"Then you'll have to give him this instead," said Quentin. "I shall never, ever put another word on paper." He picked up the chained typewriter and dumped it in the messenger's arms.

99

"There you are," he said. "Take this to Hathaway. Tell him to write two thousand words on it himself. If there's any magic in it, he can find it that way. Now get out of my house!"

As Howard let the shaken-looking messenger out through the front door, the brass band finished "Amazing Grace" and started on "Be Kind to Your Web-Footed Friends."

"Wasn't that a bit extreme, Quentin?" Catriona said.

"No, it was not," said Quentin. "Now perhaps they'll all see that I'm in earnest." He folded his arms on his paunch and looked nastily at the Goon. "There's no need for you to stay here any longer."

The Goon shook his head. He gave the usual grin. "Stay and face the music," he said. Howard and Awful stared. It really did seem as if the Goon had made a joke.

The music came back in bursts for the rest of the day. They never knew when it was going to come or for how long. Torquil varied the kind of music artfully, too. Sometimes it was pop music, which neither Howard nor Awful minded much; sometimes it was opera, which they did. Sometimes it was Gilbert and Sullivan, which only the Goon seemed to appreciate. Sometimes it was religious chanting mixed with Viennese waltzes. Quite often it was every kind mixed. You never knew what you were going to have to hear next.

Archer similarly kept everyone guessing about whether the gas or the electricity was going to be on or off. Howard, Awful, and the Goon got very good at rushing to the stove as soon as the kitchen light came on. If Archer had turned the gas on, too, and if they were very quick and had everything ready, there was sometimes just time to fry an egg before the gas went off again.

In the middle of the day the brass band marched away to have lunch, but it was replaced almost at once by the Salvation Army. By this time the house was very cold as well as noisy. The heating boiler had been on and off so often that it began making strange sounds and smelling of burning. Quentin and Howard turned it out to be on the safe side. They all put on

100

extra sweaters, except the Goon, who had no other clothes. The Goon helped himself to Quentin's Tramp's Coat and went about with a foot or so of arm sticking out beyond its little red and black checked sleeves.

Hind's gang still lurked on the other side of the Upper Park Street. Some of them probably went away for lunch, too, but there were always at least ten of them standing there. This meant that neither Howard nor Awful could get out of the house. Howard began to wonder if they were another idea of Torquil's. But they did not seem Torquil's kind of thing.

In the afternoon the neighbors on both sides telephoned to complain of the music in number 10. As the neighbor in number 8 said, quite politely, they could stand the Salvation Army *or* the "Ride of the Valkyries," but not both at once.

Howard had the idea of digging a hole in the back garden and burying all the musical implements. Fine, said Quentin. But they were not to touch the television. That was to remain as a memorial to his lost art. So Howard and Awful carried the drums, the radio, the tape deck, the violin, and the pieces of clarinet out into the garden and piled them in a thumping, yodeling, twanging, roaring heap on the lawn while they tried to persuade the Goon to dig them a hole deep enough for the drums. But the Goon refused to move from where Fifi was. He had taken to following Fifi about, sighing dismally. And Fifi refused to have anything to do with Howard's idea.

"I think Mr. Sykes deserves it for what he's done to Archer," she said.

"What have I done to Archer?" Quentin asked. "Told him no for the first time in his misbegotten life."

This argument was interrupted by the neighbors in the houses behind phoning to complain about the noise in the Sykeses' garden. Howard and Awful went and fetched all the things in. And the phone rang again. Howard answered it wearily.

It was Dillian. Howard winced at her sweet, chuckling voice. He wanted to tell her angrily that she had made a fool of him

101

and to give the words back, but it was difficult to do in the face of Dillian's sweetness and politeness. "Howard, dear," she said, "will you give your father a message from me? Tell him I hear that Archer, Torquil, and Hathaway are all wanting him to write words for them. Poor man! He must feel so pestered! But tell him I shall be very cross if he's naughty enough to do what they want. Have you got that, dear?"

"Yes," Howard said gruffly. "And he's not. He's just given his typewriter away."

"How wise of him!" said Dillian. "Tell him I'm very pleased."

Howard was determined that he would not please Dillian by telling his father this. Unfortunately Torquil must have wanted to listen in. The music stopped in time for Quentin to overhear the word "typewriter." He shouted to know who it was. So Howard had to tell him.

Quentin took it more calmly than Howard expected. "The glamorous Dillian?" he said. "Naturally she's pleased. She's the one who's got the missing words. So she's put her oar in now. That makes four of them. I wonder when I'm going to hear from the others—which are they?"

"Shine, Erskine, and Venturus," said Awful. "I'm keeping count."

"Yes, them," said Quentin, and he turned his face to the ceiling. "Calling all eavesdroppers!" he shouted. "This is a message to all bug-eared monsters! Where are you, Shine? Venturus, don't you want your chance to rule the world, too? Don't miss this unique offer!" He got up and ran to the sink. "Erskine!" he shouted down the plughole. "Erskine, are you sleeping there below? Why are you three all holding back?"

The only answer was the "Dam Busters' March" from the hall cupboard and the front room. Catriona remarked that she thought Torquil and Archer were doing quite well on their own. And this was true. By evening everyone was hungry, shivering, and half-deaf.

"Go and cook in the garden?" suggested the Goon.

102

"Bless you, Goon!" said Catriona. "Why didn't I think of that before? I think this noise must have destroyed my brain!"

They lit a campfire on the lawn and sat around it, wrapped in coats and blankets, toasting sausages on forks. From there the music almost sounded romantic. "Today's been fun," Awful announced. "I like it when things go wrong."

"Lucky you!" said Fifi. "I shall move out if Mr. Sykes doesn't change his mind soon."

The Goon sighed and stared at Fifi's firelit face. "Going to get worse," he confided to Howard.

He was right. They had a wretched night. All of them were too cold, and Torquil gave them a squirt of various music every quarter of an hour or so. Eventually the Goon uttered a great howl and marched upstairs to Howard's room, where he lay on the floor, filling it to overflowing and shivering pathetically.

The next day Archer allowed them almost no electricity or gas at all. Torquil went on squirting them with music indoors. Out of doors he sent them a steel band on a truck, which drove up and down Upper Park Street the whole morning, making sounds Howard thought he might have liked had they not been mingled with Verdi's *Requiem* indoors. They gave up trying to eat in the kitchen and lit campfires in the garden instead. The Goon was good at lighting fires, but that was the only thing he would do, apart from sitting staring gloomily at Fifi.

"He's beginning to frighten me," said Fifi. "Do make him stop."

Howard and Awful coaxed the Goon through the house into the front room. There was no chance of being overheard here because of the tireless tinkling of the piano and the music blaring from behind Hathaway's letter on the television. Through the window they had an excellent view of Hind's gang, standing listening to the steel band. The ginger boy had given up writing "ARCHER" by then, probably because there were no more spaces left to write it on. Still, Howard thought, you can get used to everything. He could even hear through the noise today.

103

"See here," he said to the Goon, "you're going the wrong way about it with Fifi. If you really want her to like you, pretend you're not interested. Play hard to get."

"Easy to get, though," the Goon pointed out. "Fifi knows."

"But girls are strange," Howard said. "Aren't they, Awful?"

"I'm not," said Awful. "I don't love anybody."

"We're not talking about *you*!" Howard said. "Honestly, sometimes I think you're as selfish as—as Torquil!" Awful became very quiet at this and spent a long time moodily poking her toe into a frayed place in the carpet. "Fifi's frightened of the way you stare at her," Howard told the Goon. "Try not to keep looking at her at least."

"Eyes keep turning that way," the Goon explained. "Like looking."

Howard had a burst of inspiration. "Yes, but," he said, "Archer never looked at her once."

The results of this conversation were not quite what Howard intended. It took the Goon most of the rest of the day to work out how not to look at Fifi. When she came near, he simply turned his back on her. "What have I done to him?" Fifi kept whispering. And Awful, instead of taking revenge on Howard for what he had said to her, seemed to be trying to prove that she was not as selfish as Torquil. She was unnervingly kind to everyone, even the Goon. By lunchtime Catriona was anxiously feeling Awful's forehead. "Are you sure you're all right, darling? You've been so quiet this weekend." Howard tried to persuade Catriona that Awful was quiet because she was enjoying the crisis. Ordinary life was not exciting enough for Awful. But Catriona still thought Awful might be ill.

Quentin said he had had enough. The only thing to do was to go out for a drive in the car. "Not you," he said to the Goon. "Even if I wanted to waste gasoline on you, there isn't room for all that leg." They left the Goon standing in the side passage like a dog that has been told to stay at home and piled into the car. Naturally it would not start. "Is this Archer, too?" Quentin wondered.

104

"Hathaway farms transport," Howard remembered.

"Then we'll go for a walk instead," said Quentin. He climbed out of the car and hailed the Goon. "We're walking. Give me back my coat."

The Goon shook his head. "Freezing," he said pathetically.

Quentin took Howard's anorak instead, and Howard had to make do with a third sweater. Their motley party set off down the road. The truck with the steel band did a three-point turn and followed after. Hind's gang followed after that, kicking a tin can to avert the boredom of it.

"I feel like the lord mayor's procession," said Quentin. "But for once in my life I'm getting the attention which is my due. Tell me about Hathaway," he said to the Goon.

The Goon thought. "Don't know much. Runs transport. Recluse. Lives in the past."

"Maybe that explains why there are never any buses," Fifi said.

"And the potholes in Park Street," added Catriona.

They walked down nearly as far as the Town Hall, with the steel band and Hind's gang following faithfully. Quentin turned into Corn Street, and the rest of the procession came, too. There Quentin winked at Howard and dived into the tangle of little, gray, narrow lanes around the cathedral. At the bottom he led them into Chorister Lane, where there were posts to keep traffic out. The truck tried to turn after them and stalled when the driver saw it could not be done. And Hind's gang was stuck behind the truck.

"Quick!" said Quentin. "Before he sends the cathedral choir after us!"

They ran and then walked fast, up Chorister Lane, past the rather prim modern shops there called Kiddicloes and Boddikare, and around under the cathedral. There Quentin led them at a trot through the museum yard, past the park, to the deserted Polytechnic. The diggers excavating for the new building had all been parked over on the far side. They threaded between them and came to Zed Alley.

105

"That was a lot of work just to shake off one steel band," Catriona said. "But I expect the walk did us good."

"Put your car right for you," offered the Goon.

"Oh, if you would!" said Catriona. "I'd been wondering what I'd do tomorrow."

For the rest of the afternoon Howard helped the Goon tinker with the car. Hind's gang filtered back after a while and stood watching sarcastically. But it seemed as if even ten to one, they did not want to tangle with the Goon. They just stood. The steel band seemed to have given up. The Goon proved to be good with cars. He seemed to think that it was quite easy to undo whatever jinx had been put on it.

"Hathaway," he said. "No good if it was Archer. Genius. Artist."

They got the car to work. Then they went indoors to find that Catriona had taken the hammers out of the piano. Fifi and Awful had packed the drums, the radio, the tape deck, and any other instrument they could find into sleeping bags and put them back under the sofa cushions in the cupboard. The only thing making a noise now was the television. Outside in the garden Quentin was frying chops for supper. It looked as if they were holding their own against Torquil, Archer, and Hathaway.

But that was before they knew what Torquil, Archer, and Hathaway could really do. The following week was dreadful.

CHAPTER EIGHT

On Monday they were awakened at dawn by workmen drilling holes in Upper Park Street. Catriona wailed and tied her head up in a thick woolly scarf. It was clear to everyone that this was Hathaway's contribution. They looked out to find that a little red and white striped hut had gone up in the middle of the road. The rest of the street was marked out with red cones and strips of plastic with fluttering orange tags. Among these, swarms of men in earguards were busily running drills from half a dozen yellow bean-shaped machines labeled "Plant Hire."

"They plant them," Quentin bellowed above the din, "and they grow into giant pneumatic drills."

The Goon looked puzzled at this notion. Howard and Awful smiled politely. They knew it was the kind of remark writers felt themselves bound to make from time to time.

Before long there was so much noise and so many holes in the road that the vanload of folk singers Torquil had sent that day were forced to back down into Park Street and drive away. Hind's gang, when it began to gather, had to hop and jump among red cones and piles of tarry rubble. Howard's heart sank rather when he saw them because today he and Awful were going to have to go to school.

"At least there still seems to be plenty of water," Fifi said as she staggered with a bucket into the frosty garden. There was no power at all that day. "How long before one of them cuts that off?"

"As soon as Erskine gets around to asking me for two thousand words," Quentin said. He was sitting cross-legged like a rather chilly Buddha, helping the Goon light the campfire. "How silly they all are—Torquil and Hathaway particularly. How could anyone write anything with all this noise going on?"

"Why not?" demanded Fifi. "It's so stupid! You don't have to put up with any of this. The moment you wrote the words for Archer, he'd put everything right in half an hour!"

"So you think," said Quentin. And he remained utterly obstinate, in spite of all the things that happened that week.

To Howard's relief, Catriona's car still worked. He had been afraid she might lose her job that way, whatever Quentin or Torquil decided to do. Catriona was heartily relieved, too. She waved cheerfully as she threaded her way among the red cones and the drilling workmen.

"Walk you and Awful to school," said the Goon. "Keep Shine off your back." He nodded at the fifteen boys waiting across the broken-up road.

"Thanks," Howard said gratefully. And he was still grateful to the Goon, even though Hind's gang followed behind as they walked, making loud, jeering remarks about people who needed the Goon as nursemaid and calling rude things about the way the Goon's arms stuck out from Quentin's red and black checked coat.

108

"Used to it," the Goon said placidly.

"Are they really from Shine?" asked Awful.

"Have to be," said the Goon, "the way they keep after you."

"What's Shine like?" asked Awful.

"Vicious," said the Goon. He thought. "Plays fairer than Dillian. Acts up like Torquil sometimes. Likes shooting people."

Awful skipped along, happily ignoring the shouts from Hind's gang. "I might like Shine," she decided. "What's Erskine like?"

The Goon gave that tremendous thought. "Don't know. Smelly."

"Now tell me about Venturus," said Awful.

The Goon seemed to find that hard to do, too. "Bit like Archer," he said at last. "Brains and all."

That seemed to satisfy Awful. She skipped happily into school, leaving Hind's gang to follow Howard and the Goon. They looked very frustrated when they found that the Goon went all the way to Howard's school with Howard. But they seemed to have a hearty respect for the Goon. All they did was call more remarks. But they did not give up. They were waiting outside at the end of the afternoon.

So was the Goon. He loomed into sight, dragging Awful by one hand, just as Howard had decided he had better make a rush for it. Hind's gang cast the Goon resentful looks and melted away. And that was really the last Howard saw of them for some days, although he did not know it then.

He came home to find most of Upper Park Street dug away. Quentin was sitting in the cold dark kitchen, looking more obstinate than ever. Torquil had doubled the noise from the television that day, to make up for the folk singers. Nobody could go in the front room from then on. There was a fair amount of noise coming from under the sleeping bags and cushions in the hall cupboard, too.

That was not all. That evening they ran out of matches to light the campfire. Quentin and Awful went down to the cor-

109

ner shop for more, but they found the shop was shut. They went on to the next shop. That was shut, too. "It's Torquil," said Awful. "Howard says he farms shops." But Quentin did not believe her. He said they had gone out too late. He borrowed matches from number 8 and said he would go shopping early on Tuesday. They needed more food by then. The fridge was melting and dripping, and the things in it were smelling strange.

On Tuesday Hathaway's men drilled right down to the pipes and cables under the road, and there was almost no way to get to the houses. Park Street was jammed with the parked cars of Upper Park Street. Catriona had to leave hers at the Poly. That day both she and Quentin had tried to draw money from different banks. They came home with glum faces. Archer had stopped both their accounts.

"No money," Quentin said. He was exasperated and still unbelieving. Determined not to be beaten, he went to the shopping precinct with his credit card. And he could not get into any of the supermarkets there. "I don't understand it!" he said. "There were people inside, all buying things, but the doors wouldn't open and the 'CLOSED' notice was up."

"Torquil," said the Goon.

"I suppose I must believe you," Quentin said angrily.

They had to borrow food. They borrowed up and down Upper Park Street and from everyone else they knew. Quentin borrowed from the Poly buffet, and Fifi borrowed from the students. Fifi was very good at it. She even borrowed some bacon and a big tin of cookies from Miss Potter. Howard would have felt more grateful to Miss Potter if Miss Potter had not sent a forgiving little note with the cookies. "Children are trying at times," Miss Potter wrote. "It is not what they did to me that I mind, but the way they behaved to dear Dillian. But Dillian has forgiven them, angel that she is, and I can do no less."

"*Grrrrrr!*" said Awful, which went for Howard, too.

"I'm only doing this to bring you to your senses, Mr. Sykes,"

110

Fifi said, dumping the tin of cookies in front of Quentin. "Nothing would possess me to go near Maisie Potter otherwise. You can't go on like this. You must see that."

"Fifi," said Quentin, "if I give in to Archer, I shall have money and electricity, no doubt; but Torquil would not let me spend my money, and Hathaway would probably dig up my house. Besides, I'm getting interested. I want to know what they'll do next."

Howard found he agreed with Fifi. He spoke to Catriona privately about it, standing in the bathroom, where the floor was vibrating from the television below and the drilling from outside. "Mum," he said, "can't you persuade him? I know I said it was worth it, but it's getting terrible. And you're not even trying to persuade him now."

"I know," said Catriona. "But I made a mistake getting angry with him. It just made him obstinate. All I can do now is wait for him to come around. I hope Torquil realizes that. I'm scared about my job, Howard. You must know I do most of the earning in this house. If your father earns enough to pay the taxes, it's the most he ever does."

"I've been thinking," said Howard, "about how I would feel if I were Torquil. And I'd be a bit stuck. If he gets you the sack, then he can't threaten you, and you won't come under him anymore. I think he'll just have to keep on the way he is doing—unless he gets angry, of course."

"Since I know the kind of person Torquil is," said Catriona, "it's his getting angry I'm afraid of."

On Wednesday Hathaway's men began noisily filling up the road. But before they had got very far, some of them went back to the beginning and began drilling it up again. All the people Howard went to borrow food from that evening complained about it bitterly. Howard was getting good at borrowing food by then. Since Hind's gang had given up, he could go out quite freely. But the Goon did not believe Hind's gang had given up. He insisted on taking Howard and Awful to school every morning and met them in the afternoon when they came out.

111

On Wednesday, also, Dillian took a hand again. When the Goon met Howard that afternoon, he said, "Police searched your house today. Took away your dad's papers."

That must mean, Howard thought, that Dillian had still not found out how the words were being used. That was quite a relief. "I suppose she was making sure Dad hadn't written anything for Archer or anyone," he said.

"Could have wanted words to compare," said the Goon.

"Was Dad very angry?" Awful asked hopefully.

The Goon considered. "No. Laughed. Chatted."

That told them both that Quentin was still as obstinate as ever. They sighed. Home was thoroughly uncomfortable by then. The house was more like a campsite than anything else, where everyone had his or her own peculiar arrangements for keeping warm or keeping out Torquil's music and Hathaway's noise. The Goon slept on the floor of Howard's room with a pillow tied around his head with string. Catriona had borrowed some jeweled earplugs from a friend. When she had them in, she went around with a deaf, happy smile, and people had to nudge her when they wanted to talk to her. Awful and Howard both slept under their mattresses instead of on top of them. Fifi lived in a kind of tent made of blankets in the middle of her attic, and during the day she crammed a pair of leg warmers on her head, over her hat, to keep out the noise.

"Never mind," said Quentin. "Think how cheaply we're living." When Howard asked him about the police, he laughed. "Poor fellows!" he said. "They didn't know why they were there! We got quite friendly over it. I even asked them to arrest the Goon—he was washing my shirts at the time—but they didn't seem to think they could. They said he didn't have a record, which I must say surprised me."

The Goon looked smug. "Never got caught." His eyes slid hopefully to see if Fifi admired him for this. Fifi did not notice.

"But what did they take?" asked Howard.

"Only my old typescripts," Quentin said airily. "Nothing I need. I was thinking of burning them in the cooking fire

112

tonight anyway." There was a general groan. They were getting seriously short of things to burn in the fire. They had burned the broken kitchen chair that morning. "Don't worry," said Quentin. "There's still the garden fence. We can use that tomorrow and burn Howard's violin case tonight."

The Goon uttered a sound that could have been a howl of impatience. He arose and strode to the hall cupboard, where he fought his way past the muffled drums and the loudly playing bundles of radio and clarinet, beyond the pile of Wellington boots, to the very back. There he discovered a door to a cellar that no one had known was there and disappeared down into it. Shortly he emerged with armfuls of damp timber which he dropped in a heap in the hall. When he had done that, he threw the noisy things down into the cellar and shut the door on them.

"Throw the telly, too?" he asked Quentin hopefully.

"No. That remains as my memorial," said Quentin. "You, my lad, are becoming far too much at home here. It's occurred to me to wonder if Archer really needs you."

"The Goon is a tower of strength," said Catriona. At this the Goon's eyes slid hopefully to Fifi, but Fifi was looking at Quentin.

"So he is," Quentin agreed. "And a support to us all in our affliction, which is not at all what Archer seems to have intended."

The trouble was, as Howard said to Awful, the Goon was a tower of affliction, too. He was becoming seriously mournful over Fifi. And Fifi had now got to the point where she took the Goon for granted and never really noticed him at all. She stepped across his legs without looking, the way you do with a piece of furniture. There were times when the Goon filled the house with the hugeness of his dejection. It got Awful and Howard down, but Fifi never noticed that either. That day the Goon dismally drew a large heart in purple crayon on the kitchen table and sat throwing his knife at it, over and over

113

again. The heart was shortly covered with dents, but it made no impression on Fifi's heart in any way.

"Don't do that! It's dangerous!" she said the few times she noticed.

The Goon sighed. The hugeness of his sighs was phenomenal.

By Thursday Hathaway's men had reduced Upper Park Street to a patchwork of holes and new surface. Then they marked it out into new squares and commenced drilling all over again.

"Don't complain," Quentin said to Catriona. "It's giving those men valuable practice. I've always wondered where road menders trained."

Howard, by this time, had had enough. The constant trials at home made it hard to concentrate at school. When he started to draw a spaceship, he found he kept breaking off to think angry thoughts about Hathaway and Shine and Archer—not to speak of Dillian and Torquil. "Do you think it would be an idea to go see Hathaway?" he asked the Goon on the way home from school.

"Don't know how to find Hathaway," the Goon said gloomily.

"How about Shine then?" said Howard.

"Don't go near Shine," said the Goon. "Dangerous."

"But I think someone ought to speak to Hathaway," Howard said. "He's the one who was getting Dad's words, after all."

The Goon gave one of his sighs. "Did no good seeing Archer."

They turned into Upper Park Street, where Hathaway's men were still hard at work, to find that Torquil had managed to send in a troop of bagpipers. They were skirling away, marching in single file, with their kilts swinging smartly as they picked their way around the edges of the various holes and in and out of red cones and strips of plastic. And though it had not been possible for any cars to get in or out of the street for three days now, a traffic warden was walking slowly up and

114

down. Dillian must have sent her, Howard thought, to the skirling of "Loch Lomond;" that must have meant that taking Dad's old typescripts had not been any help.

As Howard turned to follow Awful and the Goon to the back door, he saw a car actually turn into the road. He stood and watched, expecting the driver to back out again as he realized his mistake. It was a big silver-colored Rolls-Royce. At the sight of it the traffic warden unhooked a walkie-talkie and began speaking into it urgently. Alerted by that, Howard waited. Instead of backing out, the Rolls burst through a line of fluttering red plastic, knocked over two red cones, and came on down the road. It surged around the side of the first hole and then swung around and surged around the next, just missing the pipers, who were coming around the same hole in the opposite direction.

"What is it?" Awful called.

Howard said, "I think it has to be Archer." In fact, he was hoping it would prove to be Shine or Venturus. It could hardly be Erskine, he supposed, because Erskine was more likely to be driving a sewage tanker. The Rolls raced alongside the ditch in the middle of the road and slithered across the new tar outside number 10 to a gentle stop. Howard saw it was Archer. The Goon uttered a howl at the sight, of either rage or despair, and dashed on up the passage to the garden. Archer swung himself briskly out of the beautiful car, looking like a mechanic, but not quite, and stood gazing with his eyebrows up, amused, at the dug-up road, the traffic warden, and the pipers.

"I see my family has been busy," he said to Howard. "Can I come in? I've got something for your father."

"If you like," Howard said. "It isn't very comfortable by now."

Archer grinned his wry grin. "I know. One moment." He leaned into the car and dragged out a gleaming brand-new red typewriter. "Lead the way," he said.

When Howard, followed by Archer carrying the typewriter, came into the kitchen, he could see Awful had already told

115

them Archer was coming. Quentin was sitting at the table, wearing four sweaters, two scarves, Catriona's old raincoat, and a woolly hat, most of which Howard knew he had put on just that minute. He was pretending to be very busy playing ticktacktoe with Awful on the back of an old envelope. Fifi, with her leg warmers bobbing like a gnome hat above her rather too pink face, was arranging the last of Miss Potter's cookies on a plate. Outside in the garden there were clouds of smoke where the Goon lurked with his broken heart. Catriona was not back yet. Howard was glad. Bagpipes always drove her nearly mad.

"Mr. Sykes," said Archer.

"We can't offer you a cup of tea, you know," Quentin said without looking up.

Archer laughed and put the typewriter down on the table. The electric light came on overhead. Fifi gave a cry of delight and rushed to the stove. The gas was on, too. "Tea or coffee?" she said.

"Coffee, please," said Archer. He looked sideways at Fifi, and his face grew rather pink, too. Awful watched with interest.

"Very clever," growled Quentin. "What do you want?"

"To give you a new typewriter," said Archer. "Since you sent Hathaway your old one, you obviously need another."

Quentin gave a sidelong look at the typewriter, even more sideways than the look Archer was having at Fifi. "How is it bugged?" he said.

"It isn't," Archer said, honest as the day and rather hurt at the idea. But Quentin caught his eye and stared at him. The pink of Archer's face grew to red. "To be quite honest," he said irritably, "I've done to it what I think was done to your old one. That's all. I wish you hadn't given the old one to Hathaway. Why did you?"

"So that he could do his own words, of course," said Quentin. "I presume he has the wit to file through the chain? You

116

must have heard me say that at the time. You should be grateful. Now you know who was getting the words."

Archer frowned. "Yes—if Hathaway was telling the truth. Hathaway's so hard to get hold of, that's the trouble. Finding him and stopping him are going to be more difficult than I realized. But once you've done me some more words, I shall have the upper hand at least."

Quentin turned away. "Awful," he said, "you put two crosses in while I wasn't looking."

"Only little ones," said Awful.

"Are you still refusing to do me the words?" Archer said.

"Have a cookie," Fifi interrupted hurriedly. "The coffee won't be long."

Archer gave up for a moment and took a cookie. So did Howard. Apart from the distant skirling of "Scotland the Brave," that was the only sound until Fifi put mugs of coffee on the table.

"Torquil's stopped the telly!" Awful said, realizing.

"He wants to hear what Archer's saying," said Howard.

Archer shrugged. He was looking at Fifi again. "Let him hear," he said. It was clear he had a low opinion of Torquil.

Awful smiled her most fiendish smile. "But Archer's not saying anything!" she said innocently. "He's boring. He's gawking at Fifi and falling in love. Boring, boring, boring—" Howard tried to kick Awful's leg and missed. "Well, it *is* boring!" said Awful.

By this time it was hard to tell whether Archer's face or Fifi's was the redder. "Awful," Fifi said. "One more word from you and I'll—I'll set the Goon on you!"

There was a confused silence. Quentin picked up his coffee and pretended to notice Archer again. "Oh. Haven't you gone yet?"

Archer was still very red. He looked as if he wished he *had* gone. "Mr. Sykes," he said, "write me two thousand words on this typewriter, and I'll pay you a million pounds for them."

117

Quentin stared at him. It was not a pleasant look. "I wondered when you'd get around to that," he said. "Took you awhile, didn't it? Funny the way all you millionaires are really mean at heart."

"But I—" Archer was truly surprised and did not seem to know what to say. "But I didn't think you'd *want* money! The offer was just to convince you that I'm in earnest."

Quentin folded his arms on his paunch, in the way Howard was learning to dread. He went on staring at Archer. "Do you know," he said, "I'd rather see Awful rule the world than you? You just haven't a clue, have you? I know you're in earnest. So am I. Go away and stop bothering me!"

Archer looked at Awful. Red flooded his face again. Somehow he controlled his anger enough to say, probably to Howard, "I don't know how else to persuade him. You can have your electricity back. I'll unstop your bank accounts too. I'll leave the typewriter in case he changes his mind." Muttering helplessly what sounded like "That's all I can think of," Archer turned to leave. Fifi bowed over her coffee, looking miserable. Then, as if this were another thing he did not have much clue about, Archer turned awkwardly back. "Er, Fifi," he said. "Would you like to come out and—er—have a drink or something? I've got my car outside."

"Oh, yes, please!" Fifi knocked her coffee over in her rush to go with Archer. The door slammed, and they were gone.

Howard and Awful were still mopping up coffee when the Goon loomed in the doorway. "Archer took Fifi off," he said miserably.

"Yes, but he left the gas on," said Howard.

"I'll get him some coffee," Awful offered. "I won't put anything in but coffee."

In spite of this generosity from Awful, the Goon slumped inconsolably in his usual chair and sat staring at the legs he was filling the floor with. From time to time he said, "Archer gets everything."

Quentin sat at the table, staring at the dented purple heart on

118

it, almost as inconsolable. "I think we shall have to leave town," he said. "Probably by the town drain since everyone but Erskine seems bound to try and stop us."

They both were still sitting when Catriona came in, white and distraught and covering her ears against the skirling of "Amazing Grace." That seemed to be Torquil's favorite tune. "Howard, please! Find my earplugs!"

Awful followed Howard as he went to look for the earplugs, wanting to know what they could do about the poor Goon. "I don't know!" Howard said crossly. "I'm not a marriage bureau. Look, Awful, how about us trying to find Hathaway?"

"Where?" said Awful.

"Somewhere old-fashioned and hard to find, by the sound of it," Howard said.

"You mean, somewhere like those twisty lanes by the cathedral?" Awful asked.

"Let's go and look everywhere old we can think of," said Howard. "I'll just get Mum's earplugs."

CHAPTER NINE

Nobody really noticed Howard and Awful leave. The other three were too sunk in their separate miseries. The traffic warden had left. The pipers were picking their way around the largest hole and did not see them either. Awful and Howard threaded their way down the street, among the cones, the lanterns, the tarry heaps, and the strips of plastic, until they were level with the red and white striped tent. Hathaway's men were just packing up for the night.

"Let's ask them," Awful suggested.

So Howard jumped a tarry ditch to get near. "Excuse me," he said politely. "Can you tell us where Hathaway lives?"

They looked around at him blankly. "Who's Hathaway?" said one.

"He's the one who told you to dig up this road," Howard explained.

120

The men looked at one another and shook their heads. "Don't think so," said another of them. "We get our orders from the highway office."

"Mind you, I think they've gone around the twist this time," said a third. "But none of them's called Hathaway."

"Name rings a bell, though," said a fourth man. He thought. "Now where have I heard that name?" Howard waited patiently. He had got used to doing that with the Goon. But the man shook his head in the end. "No. Won't come. Tell you what, though," he offered. "I'll keep thinking. It'll come back. I'll let you know when I remember. See you going by all the time."

"Thanks," Howard said, and jumped back across the ditch to Awful.

"Let's look anyway," said Awful.

They cut through Zed Alley and across by the Poly, where the diggers, too, were just packing up for the night. But here, unlike Upper Park Street, the work seemed to be getting somewhere. There was now the skeleton of the new building, outlined in steel girders.

"That's because Hathaway isn't running it," said Awful.

Beyond that they took the shortcut through the museum yard and under the walls of the cathedral, which led them to the steep plunge down Chorister Lane. Halfway down the lane Awful said doubtfully, "It looks a bit modern here to me." Howard felt she was right. He had been thinking of the lane as old and gray. True, there were the modern shops called Kiddicloes and Boddikare, but they had always seemed chaste and tasteful to match the antiquated houses around. But it was evening, and the lights were coming on. Kiddicloes and Boddikare both had huge blue and green signs that flashed on and off. Another lighted up as Howard and Awful passed it. "PALM BEACH," it said, in white and red. It seemed to be a club of some kind. "I didn't know they had those here," Awful said.

"They have them down by the disco in Bishop's Lane," Howard pointed out.

121

Another sign lit up as they passed. This one said "THE EVIL WEEVIL" in green. Before they reached the posts at the bottom of Chorister Lane, there were six more, flashing on and off, and when they came down into the tangle of narrow streets at the bottom, the whole place seemed alive with colored signs, spinning, crawling, hopping, all colors that light could be. Music was coming from many of the upstairs windows. Howard had not realized the town had such a night life. There were so many lights that the evening sky looked dark midnight blue.

"We could go see Torquil instead," Awful suggested as they passed the disco. "You could explain about Dad."

"Only if we can't find Hathaway," said Howard. He turned out of Bishop's Lane, toward Palace Lane. He knew that was old and quiet and respectable because the bishop lived there, in the palace at the top—which was more like a large house than a palace.

But when they turned into that lane, they saw it winding uphill ahead, chock-full of lighted signs, blue, green, orange, red, purple, advertising every kind of place of amusement. At the top, where Howard knew the bishop lived, a huge red sign was blinking on and off. "MITRE CLUB," it said. "GAMBLING."

"This is wrong," said Awful. "It's usually all gray."

Howard was suddenly alarmed. He seized Awful by her wrist and turned to go back.

Behind him, someone shouted, "Hey! That's them! Get them!" Running feet padded softly and swiftly on both sides of the lane. Before Howard could drag Awful more than a yard or so, they were surrounded by Hind's gang and backed up against a shopfront. Twenty or so jeering faces looked into theirs. "Bit of luck at last!" said the boy with the ginger hair. "Lost your nursemaid, have you?"

Howard stowed Awful behind him and talked fast. He did not think anything would stop them from being beaten up, but it was worth a try. "Of course, we've lost him," he said. "We had to lose him. You lot never came near us with him around. We were looking for you."

122

Hind's gang shouted with laughter. "What are you going to do with us now you've got us?" someone called.

"Get you to take us to Shine," said Howard. "We want to see Shine."

They laughed even more at that. "Hey! He *wants* to see Shine!"

"Your wish is granted," said the ginger boy. "Bring them along."

Hands reached out and grabbed Howard, four to an arm, and as many more grabbed Awful. Feet shuffled and padded, and the hands tugged. Hind's gang ran, and Howard and Awful were forced to run, too, or be dragged over on their faces. Hind's gang ran all around them, barging and shoving and tugging, hustling them back down Palace Lane in the most uncomfortable possible way. Everyone's face turned blue, then green, then red as they turned into the next lane. At least they weren't being beaten up yet, Howard thought. But he had a feeling he had only put that off.

Somewhere in the lane after that they came level with a small door next to a fried chicken shop. There was a small red-lit sign over this door.

THE ORIENT

MEDITATION TAUGHT

Someone's foot banged this door open. Hind's gang stormed in through it, dragging Howard and Awful, jamming the two of them in anyhow among themselves, so that they all could trample together down the dark passage beyond. Bruised and breathless, Howard and Awful were dragged out into a quiet yard.

Even the gang went quiet here. People really were meditating. Howard blinked. It was quite light in the yard. The lighted signs in the street outside had made him think it was dark. Here, in a gentle sunset light, bearded men and women with long hair sat against the walls wearing yellow robes and staring into the distance. None of them took the slightest notice of the crowd of boys with Howard and Awful in their midst.

123

"Shine?" asked the ginger boy loudly.

Nobody answered. But after a second one of the men sitting against the far wall silently stood up. He opened a door in the wall beside him and went away through it. Nobody else moved. Howard was just thinking that nothing else was going to happen when the door opened and the man in the yellow robe came out again. He sat down against the wall without a word. But he left the door open.

"Come on," said the ginger boy. Howard and Awful were tugged over to the door. It seemed to be dark inside. "Do you want us as well, Shine?" called the ginger boy.

"No," said a voice from inside. "Wait in the yard." It was a voice as rich as Mr. Mountjoy's, but not so deep.

"Go on in," said the ginger boy. He looked jeeringly at Howard. The rest of the gang stood around the door in a cluster. There was not much Howard could do but take Awful's wrist again and fumble his way into the dim space beyond. It smelled of dust and oil, and it was big. Howard's first thought was that the whole family seemed to like a lot of space.

Almost the only light in there came from rows of black and white television screens over in the left-hand wall. At first it was hard to see anything else in their bluish glimmer. And their eyes were drawn to the screens anyway, because something was going on in all of them. Fights were going on in two of them. In several others, people were meeting and passing one another packages or money. Some were street scenes, with cars and people going back and forth. One was a view of the yard outside, where the gang were standing looking bored and the people by the walls were still meditating away. And in one, a thief was in the act of climbing up a house to break in through the open bedroom window. Howard and Awful were fascinated by that one. The thief was inching his way up a drainpipe, past a big metal box labeled "Burglar Alarm," and the drainpipe was loose. The man was having to be very careful. Awful could not take her eyes off him. But Howard managed to tear his eyes away as soon as the burglar's hands were safely

124

grasping the bedroom windowsill, in order to look at the rest of the place.

The low blue light glinted off things on the walls, hung there by orderly hundreds: guns of all kinds, drills and different lengths of crowbar, racks of blackjacks and knives, lines of explosives, gas cylinders, and heavy cutting equipment. Lower in the distance, several cars glimmered. People were quietly moving around down there, working on the cars. It was just as well that Howard and Awful had been too interested in the screens to move. This part of the room was only a concrete platform a few feet wide. Shine was sitting on the edge of this platform cleaning a gun, almost beside Howard's feet.

She looked up when she felt Howard notice her. "Have you quite finished goggling?" she asked sarcastically. She was the opposite of Dillian in almost every way. Her hair was dark, and she was vastly fat. She was dressed entirely in black leather, which made her look fatter still since the leather stretched and strained in all directions in order to get around her. Howard could hear it creaking as she looked up at him. Shine's face, in spite of its two chins, was quite like Archer's except that, as far as Howard could see, her eyes were dark like Torquil's. "Enjoying my little den?" she asked in her deep voice, jerking her chins at the rest of the room.

"What I can see of it," Howard said.

"Good," said Shine. "Because you'll be getting to know it rather well. I'm not going to let you go in a hurry now I've got you."

This caused Awful to lose interest in the burglar on the screen. "Now *you* want Dad to do you two thousand words," she said.

"More than that." Shine went back to carefully cleaning her gun. "I'll want him to go on doing them," she said. "I know a good thing when I see it even if Archer doesn't. Your dad's going to be so scared about you two that he's going to fall over his own fingers to write words for me. I can't think why Archer didn't realize that."

125

Howard and Awful looked at one another's subdued blue faces. Being beaten up would have been better after all. "Why do you keep blaming Archer?" Awful said. "It wasn't him getting the words. It was Hathaway."

Shine polished her gun carefully with a soft cloth. "So they both say," she said. "I admit Hathaway's sneaky enough, but I'm not convinced. And I always blame Archer if I can. It keeps him annoyed and muddled and out of my hair."

"Are you next eldest, after Archer?" Awful asked.

"Yes. Want to make anything of it?" Shine asked. Her leather creaked strenuously as she polished.

"I just asked," Awful said hurriedly. "I do that with Howard, too."

Shine glanced up at Howard. "He must be a fool to let you, just like Archer. Sit down, boy. And you, girl. You'll be here a long time. Take the weight off your feet." That amused her. She gave a vast, booming guffaw. "By the time you leave you may even be my size!"

Howard lowered himself into a sort of squat on the cold concrete. Shine bulked beside him like a huge leather walrus. "Dad won't write any words," he said. "He's gone obstinate. The more you lot bully him, the worse he gets."

"Huh," grunted Shine. She laid the cleaned gun down and picked up another. "He'll think again when we start sending pieces of you in parcels." The leather on her beefy arms strained as she broke open the new gun. "Better hope he doesn't stay obstinate," she said.

Howard did hope so, fervently. He looked up at the screen that showed the view of the yard. The gang was still waiting there, the other people still meditating. He did not think there was any way he and Awful could run for it—or not at the moment. The best thing seemed to be to try to keep Shine in a good mood. "So if you don't think it's Hathaway," he said conversationally, "which one do you think it really is?"

"Which one of us hasn't been after your father?" Shine countered. "You tell *me*."

126

"I think it's *you*," Awful muttered.

Perhaps it was lucky Shine did not hear her. A buzzer sounded sharply. Shine looked up at the viewscreens. "Dave!" she shouted. "Dave! Time to go! The folks are coming back." In the screen which had so fasincated Awful, the face of the burglar appeared anxiously at the bedroom window. "Not that way!" Shine yelled. "Gor, love a duck! You haven't *time*! Go out the back door, you fool. Get out while they're coming in the front!" She turned to Awful. "Honestly some of these burglars are so stupid! That's the trouble with farming crime. Every idiot thinks he can steal. I'm thinking of asking for their grades in future—I might get some with a clue that way. What were we talking about?"

Howard shrugged and pretended to forget. He did not see why he should tell Shine that Venturus and Erskine were the other two who had not been after Quentin. He squatted on the concrete, watching Shine clean guns, and left the talking to Awful.

"Are you wanting to farm the world, too?" Awful asked.

Shine chuckled. "Only as much of it as I can manage. That's more than this one little town, I can tell you, but I think I'll leave Archer to farm the world. Glad to. I'll even help him get there if he wants. You see, girlie, unlike Archer, I know how much I can do. People can hang on to only as much as they know how to hold. What I know is crime. I always did have this way of having to do things *against* someone else. I prefer to be against Archer. So he can have the world; I'll take the world's crime."

Awful nodded and went on asking things. Shine did not seem to mind. She went on cleaning guns and answering quite equably. She told Awful that the cars were bulletproof ones, for when Shine went out on a job personally. She explained how guns worked. And she said she had already gone a long way, even without being able to move from town, toward taking over the crime in various countries.

"Though it's not the same if a person can't be on the spot,"

127

Shine said. "That's bugged me for thirteen years now, and I'm getting really fed up. Take last week now. I could have had India. If I'd been able to go there, I could have had the whole setup for a song. Man there went bankrupt. But it went to a Swede because I'm stuck here, thanks to your daddy's words."

There were various interruptions to Awful's questions. Once Hind's gang got bored, and Shine had to shout to them to leave the meditators alone. Once she roared at one of the fights on the screens, "That'll do, boys! I want him jelly, not pulp!" And once the man in the yellow robe let in two annoyed young men, who told Shine angrily that they couldn't cut through to that safe whatever they tried. "Told you so," Shine said. "I said you'd need the heavy laser. Go get it." A square of light fell suddenly on the part of the wall where the laser was. "Wait!" Shine said, as the men jumped crossly down off the platform to get it. "You'll need to steal a van to carry all that lot in." She turned, in a great creaking of leather, and looked at the screens. She pointed. "Take that one, on the corner of Bishop's Lane."

The men looked. "But it's a police van!" one said.

"Right," said Shine. "I feel like annoying my little sister. Take it."

"Did you make all the lights in the lanes?" Awful asked while the men were getting the laser.

"Most of them," said Shine. "Round here's Shine Town, and I wanted you to know it. Screens picked you up when you came down Chorister Lane."

"Shine Town!" Awful said, laughing.

Howard had been sitting all this time with his chin on his knees and his behind freezing on the cold concrete, turning over in his mind about ninety impossible ways of escaping from Shine—everything from grabbing the equipment the two young men were crossly lugging outside to simply jumping up and running—but he came back to reality when Awful laughed. It seemed to him that Awful and Shine were getting

128

on rather too well. Perhaps it was not so surprising if you knew Awful.

"I wish I farmed crime," Awful said wistfully.

Shine gave her deep chuckle. "How about you?" she asked Howard. "Fancy a life of crime, laddie?"

A week ago Howard would have nodded. But criminals were people who took what they wanted or tried to make you give it to them if they couldn't take it. He had spent a week now being one of the people they tried to take things from. It made you think. He shook his head and tried to smile politely. All the same, Shine did seem to lead an exciting life. . . . Howard shook his head again, almost angrily. Thoughts of riches and splendid car chases flooded into his head. And the marvelous idea that he might get to be Shine's trusted lieutenant. She would send him out to take over India for her, and he had always wanted to see India.

"Think about it, laddie," said Shine, and bent, creaking, over the latest gun.

"*I'm* thinking about it," said Awful, kneeling beside Shine.

"Sure you are, girlie," said Shine.

She knows we both are! Howard thought. It went through him like a shock. Shine was trying to recruit them both.

"Sure I am," Shine said frankly, just as if Howard had spoken. "Get you on my side, and I don't need to keep you here. I can send you home to get around your Daddy for me. It's better than turning him obstinate. I go for results."

Poor Dad! Howard thought. Fifi onto him for Archer, Mum onto him for Torquil, and now us for Shine! As well as all the rest! Wonderful notions from Shine came pouring through his mind. India. Flying out to India in a private jet. Ordering gangsters about. The marvelous excitement of planning a robbery. The even more marvelous excitement of carrying the crime out. Waiting in the getaway car, holding your breath. The others coming flying up, guns smoking, and dumping gold ingots in the trunk. Then you tramp on the gas and scream away with

129

six police cars after you. Oh, no, Howard thought. She doesn't mean it. She just wants us to get around Dad. He set himself to resist, to refuse to attend to Shine. It was ten times more difficult than resisting Torquil's wand. Shine just went on pressing ideas into Howard's head—lovely ideas, that was the trouble—harder and harder. Howard tried to press back. It was rather like arm wrestling. And anyone, he thought frantically, who tried to arm wrestle Shine was a flaming idiot! Look at the size of her arms! And her mind was even stronger. As you do in arm wrestling, Howard felt himself going, going.

There was a way, he told himself desperately. There was something you did with your mind. You switched it around into a new shape. He almost knew. It was like the way he almost knew how to wriggle his ears. But he could not find the right movement to switch with, any more than he could quite find his ear muscles. And Shine was pressing harder still. Howard's mind was bowed right down, almost to the ground. *He found it.*

Howard bounced back. But there was nothing pressing him. It was so sudden and he was bouncing so hard that he almost knocked himself out.

"Shine, darling," said Dillian's voice.

Dizzily Howard looked up and saw all the viewscreens showing Dillian's lovely face. Shine was creaking like an armchair as she climbed angrily to her feet. She had forgotten Howard for the moment. "Get off my screens, goodie-goodie!" she said. "I don't want to look at you!"

"Then you shouldn't pinch my police vans," Dillian said. "That was awfully *silly* of you, Shine, dear. It made me notice what you were up to."

"So I'm robbing one of Archer's banks! Why should you care?" said Shine. "Go and tell your sugary little tales to Archer. Goodie-goodie!"

"Oh, no, dear," said Dillian. "I never interfere between you and Archer. That's not what I meant. I'm talking about Quentin Sykes's little children, whom you have there with you."

130

Shine puffed out a bad word. "What about them?" She began loading the gun she had been cleaning.

"You do puff these days, Shine, dear," said Dillian. "You really should be careful. You're so overweight!"

"I said, what about those kids?" Shine snarled, snapping in cartridges.

"You're not to harm them, dear," said Dillian. "And if you try to use them against Quentin Sykes in any way, you'll be raided again, and this time I may be forced to put you in prison."

"Oh, go to heaven, you golden goose!" Shine shouted, and fired her gun at the screens.

One screen exploded. The others went blank. Howard clapped his hands over his ears. Even so, through the bang and the crash, the choking smoke and the roaring of Shine, he could still hear Dillian's silvery laughter. Shine was bellowing, "Repair squad! Screens!" and strings of bad words which gave Awful the giggles.

"Where were we?" Shine said when the smoke was clearing. A number of people in overalls ran toward the screens. "Take number 14 out," said Shine. "Put a spare in quick. I want to see that raid. And stop laughing," she said to Awful. "You've seen what happens when I lose my temper. What were we talking about before I did?"

"Hathaway," said Howard.

"That little coward!" Shine said, strutting about so that her chins shook. "No, we weren't. Don't put me off, or I'll *really* lose my temper! Stand up, both of you!"

They scrambled hurriedly to their feet. Shine strutted at them with her hands on her hips. She was mountainous. Howard and Awful backed away.

Then, at the moment when Howard was sure that Shine was going to do someting awful to them, the door to the yard swung open beside him. Torquil shoved aside the yellow-robed man and marched in. Awful stared. Torquil, this time, was dressed like an Egyptian pharaoh, in a slender white robe

131

and a wide metallic-looking wig that was stuck behind both ears. Gems flashed from the big circular golden collar across his shoulders, and from the golden crown like a knotted snake that he wore over the wig. He had painted his eyes with black and green and gold, so that they looked twice as big as they should.

"Oh, good grief! Now it's you!" said Shine. "I shall take up good works if this goes on. What do you want? A pyramid?"

"I've just met Archer," Torquil said breathlessly. He seemed very excited. His painted eyes flashed in what little light there was left.

"Then you could have done me a favor by keeping Archer talking," said Shine. "I'm trying to rob one of his banks."

"No, no!" Torquil said. "I've just had the most perfect, marvelous idea. It's about Archer. You know he's—" His large outlined eyes peered from Shine to Howard to Awful. "I wish you'd have more light in here. Who's this listening?"

Shine flapped her hand in a resigned way. A dusty little light came on overhead, and they all blinked at one another. Shine was fatter even than Howard had thought.

"Lucky I asked!" said Torquil. "I can't tell you in front of him. He's limpet boy Sykes. And I think she's his sister. Send them home or something. This is too good to wait, Shine! It's an idea right up your street!"

"Send them home!" exclaimed Shine. "Who are you ordering about? Little brother, you've let that crown of yours go to your head. I've had word out for these two for ten days, and I'm not going to lose them now that I've got them."

Torquil twirled the golden scepter in his hand impatiently. "Do something with them, or I shan't tell you. Do you, or do you not, want to have Archer at your mercy? I can always go to Dillian." He smoothed his white pleated robe and turned to the door.

"Oh, all right," growled Shine. "The gang has been promised it anyway." She snapped her fingers. The door swung wide open. "Hind!" she shouted. "Ginger Hind! You can have

132

these two for half an hour. Don't kill them, though. I need them. Here you are."

Howard and Awful found themselves helplessly stumbling forward into the yard. It was almost dark out there now, lit greenish orange by the signs in the streets beyond. The meditating people were gray lumps along the walls. Hind's gang members were dark outlines, frighteningly many of them, galloping eagerly toward Howard and Awful. Nobody wasted time on words. Hind's gang grabbed. Howard put his head down and charged for the passage to the street. Beside him, Awful made her worst scream and charged, too, with her arms and legs going like windmills.

It was hopeless, of course. Awful's screams cut off in the first second, and down she went under a pile of bodies. Howard went down two seconds later. As everyone piled on top of him, Howard had a lurid glimpse of one of them looking tall as a house, all legs, and long arms dangling huge fists, and no head to speak of. He shut his eyes and fought.

And felt Hind's gang scrambling off him instead of on. Someone gave a panic-stricken squeal. There was the dull, cracking thump of heads' being brought together. This was followed by frantically running feet and a sense of clear space around him. Howard opened his eyes unbelievingly and looked up at two legs, towering away into darkness.

"Told you not to go near Shine," said the Goon.

Howard scrambled sheepishly to his feet. Awful bounced up and wrapped her arms around the Goon's nearest leg.

"Leave off!" said the Goon. He grasped each of them by an arm and ran them across the yard to the passage. Howard glanced back as they went and saw that the meditators had moved at last. They were standing in a scared-looking huddle against the far wall.

"I knew you'd come!" Awful gasped as they pounded down the passage. "I saw Torquil wink!"

"Made a mistake if you did," said the Goon. They shot out

133

through the door into the street. "Down here," said the Goon. "Your mum's with the car." He ran them down the sidewalk and around the corner. There, sure enough, was their car, with one of its doors ready open and Catriona looking anxiously over her shoulder as they came. The Goon rammed Howard and Awful into the back seat and doubled himself double quick into the front one. The door slammed. "Go quick," said the Goon. "Shine farms all this part."

Catriona drove off so fast that the tires actually squealed. "I have been so worried!" she said. "Don't ever do that again! What were you doing anyway?"

"Looking for Hathaway," Howard said rather sulkily.

"Won't be here," said the Goon. "Lives in the past. Told you."

"And I think you might thank the Goon," Catriona said as they screamed past the Town Hall. "He was the one who knew where to go."

"Thanks," Howard said, and meant it. He turned anxiously to Awful. He was afraid she might still be under Shine's spell.

Awful swore she was not. "I don't want to be under someone," she said indignantly. "I want to be the top one. And Shine was horrible, fat and horrible! But Torquil's funny. I wanted to laugh, the way he was dressed up. And he *did* wink, I know he did!"

They had to walk from the corner because of Hathaway's roadworks, but home, when they reached it, was once more pleasantly warm and brightly lit. Quentin was frying borrowed fish fingers over the gas. He was as relieved to see them as Catriona had been. Howard thought that he had never properly appreciated before ordinary things like light and heat and parents and fish fingers.

"Archer's left the power on?" he said.

"Yes. He'll be trying something else, I expect," said Quentin. "Torquil, however, is still charming our ears from the cellar

134

and the telly. And Hathaway has only packed up for the night."

Hathaway, thought Howard. "Dad, where would you live if you lived in the past?"

"Atlantis," said Quentin. "Oh, I see what you mean. In an antiques shop, I suppose."

CHAPTER TEN

On Friday morning Hathaway's men woke them all at dawn again, drilling a large ditch all the way along the front of the house. The Goon groaned, clutched the pillow tied around his head, and rolled over, so that his legs overflowed from filling Howard's floor onto the landing outside. Fifi hopped over them as she went downstairs, singing.

Fifi must have come in very late the night before, but she was as bright as a button. When Howard stumbled down to breakfast, she was bustling about, looking pink and pretty. "Casting down their golden crowns around the glassy sea!" she caroled. She always sang hymns when she was happy.

"Oh, don't you start!" Quentin grumbled. "Torquil's quite enough."

The Goon sighed, hard enough to blow cornflakes about.

When Howard and Awful left to go to school, they found

they had to do a long jump in order to leave the house. Hathaway's ditch began at the bottom of the front doorstep. It was rather longer than the width of the house, and it was about seven feet wide. All of Hathaway's men were down in it, drilling and digging busily through layers of tar and yellow mud.

Howard wondered how Mum had managed to get out. He himself leaped across, using his violin for balance. Awful's legs were too short for her to jump. But the Goon solved that by grasping both of Awful's elbows and striding across with her dangling in front of him. The Goon's legs were the only ones in the neighborhood long enough to step over the ditch. The postman solved the matter another way. He borrowed a fishing rod from number 11. As Howard picked himself and his violin out of the road, the postman was standing beside him, dangling a packet of letters toward the front door.

"Post!" he shouted, unreeling the line.

Quentin came to the front door in his dressing gown to get the letters. "They say an Englishman's home is his castle!" he bawled above the drilling. "Now we have a moat to prove it!"

As Quentin went in and the postman went back to number 11 to return the fishing rod, one of the men in the moat beckoned to Howard. "I remembered," he shouted. "Hathaway. Shakespeare's wife. She was called Anne Hathaway."

"Thanks," yelled Howard. He was acutely disappointed. He realized, as he and Awful set off to school with the Goon, that he had really been hoping the man knew about Hathaway.

Hind's gang was loitering in Park Street. They followed behind at a very safe distance from the Goon. To Awful's delight, the ginger-haired boy had a black eye. But Howard was not sure he liked the venomous way that eye looked at him. Shine was obviously still after them, but it rather looked as if Ginger Hind were after Howard on his own account, too.

Howard did not let that bother him. He spent most of that day thinking about how to find Hathaway. He was determined to find him. Or her. It was always possible that Hathaway would turn out to be another sister, like Shine. Anyway,

137

Hathaway was the one who could solve all their problems. Since Hathaway was the one Dad had been sending the words to, then Hathaway knew a way to get rid of the other brothers and sisters. So the thing to do was to find him (or her) and get around her (or him). It might not be easy. The others were not easy to get around. On the other hand, Howard thought, he hadn't really made an effort to be nice to any of them so far.

At lunchtime Howard's thoughts carried him to the school library, where the second year had set up a project on the town. There was a map, and models, and drawings, and careful pages of history. And more careful pages about industry and new buildings. Howard looked at it all. It was the first time he had found the project remotely interesting. Someone had even done a drawing of what the new building at the Poly would be like. An Egyptian temple, Howard thought, and he grinned, thinking of Torquil.

He looked most carefully at the map. Pleasant Hill and all those parts to the west must belong to Dillian. Torquil must begin at the shopping precinct and stretch eastward to the disco, down and then up again to the cathedral. Archer must have the center of town, the High Street, the Town Hall, and out as far as Upper Park Street to the west. In fact, Archer had to have most of the middle, except for the old bit by the cathedral where Shine and Torquil seemed to overlap. Give Shine everything southeast from there, and where did that leave Venturus? Erskine had to have out to the east, where the sewage farm was. So that left Venturus with the new housing estate to the south. But Venturus must have all the schools and the Poly as well. And Erskine's drains and Archer's power must crisscross the whole town. In fact, they seemed to overlap everywhere, particularly in the center, leaving nowhere at all for Hathaway.

Howard gave that up and looked for the sewage farm instead. There it was, right at the eastern edge of the map, beyond the part marked "Industry." Who ran industry? Beside the sewage farm, Howard read "Site of old Castle." That was a

138

disappointment. Howard remembered Archer's saying that only Erskine could go out that far. So even if Hathaway had wanted to live beside a sewage plant, he probably couldn't. Howard gave up that idea and turned his attention back inside the black line of "Old City Boundary" and to the center, where the whole family overlapped.

Here there was an irregular shape which said "Site of Old Abbey." It took in some of the park, a piece of the Poly, the library, the museum, and the cathedral. But to Howard's relief, it stopped short of the winding lanes of Shine Town. It looked as if he would not need to go there again. "Somewhere there, I bet," he said, and went off to orchestra practice, rather pleased with himself.

Somehow Howard had half expected Torquil to turn up again. But there was no sign of him. Howard scraped and sawed, more or less along with the rest of the orchestra and almost in time to Mr. Caldwick's baton, and went on thinking how to find Hathaway. Torquil had to farm the cathedral, of course, because of the organ and the choir. Count that out. Even so, the rest of the "Site of Old Abbey" was awfully near Torquil and Shine and not so far away from Archer's bank. Would Hathaway want that if he were a recluse?

But there was this about families, Howard thought, obediently turning to the orchestra's next piece of music. Families might hate one another, but something nevertheless made them stick together. Look at the things Dad always said about Auntie Mildred. Yet Auntie Mildred always came for Christmas. Mum would say dryly, "Well, blood is thicker than water."

That made Howard think about yesterday. Had Torquil really winked at Awful, as Awful swore he had? The way Torquil's eyes had been marked out in paint, Awful could hardly have made a mistake. And there had been first Dillian, then Torquil, and then the Goon had turned up. And the Goon was from Archer. Torquil had just met Archer. What was going on? Oh, I give up! Howard thought, and tried to take off instead in

139

his favorite spaceship for Proxima Centauri. But even there he had no peace. He found he was wondering irritably why Archer didn't build a spaceship instead of spying on Dad. It was such a waste of all that technology.

The end of school put an end to Howard's thoughts. The Goon was waiting outside, looming beside Awful. Ginger Hind was waiting, too, across the street, all on his own, glaring at Howard from his black eye and his good one. Hind was getting to be a real problem, Howard thought, though at least he was on his own now. He followed them all the way back home, watched them jump Hathaway's moat, and went on standing there, glowering. But Upper Park Street looked unusually empty all the same. There was no one there from Dillian. Torquil had not sent any kind of band today. And Ginger Hind seemed to have been deserted by the rest of his gang. Could it be, Howard wondered, that some of them were getting tired of pestering them?

In the kitchen Quentin sat staring. A letter lay in front of him, on the purple heart on the table.

"Been like that all day," said the Goon.

"Take a look at that letter!" said Fifi. She was making tea, all dressed up as if she were going to a party. "Mr. Sykes wouldn't go to the Poly. I had to ring up and say he was ill."

Howard picked up the letter which seemed to have had such a startling effect on his father. Quentin did not seem to notice. The letter was from the city treasurer. Howard read it.

Dear Mr. Sykes,

It has come to our attention that we have not been in receipt of any remittance from you in respect of taxes since April 1970. The sum at present outstanding, with due allowance for the various increases in the city tax and for the compound interest charged on all sums overdue over the thirteen-year period, is now £23,000.56½. We hope you

140

will see your way to an early remittance of the said sum before we are forced to put the matter in legal hands.

Yrs. faithfully,
C. Wiggins
City Treasurer

"Dad!" Howard exclaimed. "You never owe twenty-three thousand pounds!"

"Plus fifty-six and a half pence," Quentin said. "Don't forget that." He turned around and looked guiltily up at Howard. "Don't tell your mother. That was why I was doing the words all these years. Mountjoy said they would be instead of paying taxes. I was a fool to believe him, wasn't I?"

"How will you pay?" said Howard.

"Sell this house," said his father. "Go away. Leave me. I'm a broken man."

Howard took the borrowed peanut butter sandwich Fifi handed him and went into the hall. He paused there to find some shredded old tissues in his pockets and stuff some in both ears. Then he went into the front room. The television was thundering out olde tyme dance music today. Howard could feel the Gay Gordons vibrating the floor and see the blankets over it quivering. He moved the blankets and had a careful look at Hathaway's letter.

It was real parchment. When Howard touched it, he knew it was a kind of leather, not plastic or paper. The red wax looked old and cracked. And the writing had faded a lot, even under the blankets, to a dark brown. It could have been written with one of those square pens used at school in art for lettering. But it could just as possibly have been done with a quill pen. Howard nodded. He put back the blanket and went out into the hall again.

The Goon was standing dejectedly in the middle of it. "Archer's come for Fifi," he said dismally.

Howard took the tissue out of his ears and opened the

141

kitchen door. Archer was standing behind Quentin's chair, reading the letter. He was wearing a suit for once and looked as smart as Fifi did. "Did Shine rob one of your banks last night?" Howard asked him.

Archer turned around, laughing. No one could have looked nicer. "No way!" he said. "The vaults are all booby-trapped. The boys who tried are in hospital." Then he turned to Quentin. "This letter has absolutely nothing to do with me," he said. "I swear." Howard thought Archer was telling the truth. He was quite serious and not trying to seem nice. Quentin groaned. Archer said, thinking, "Hathaway farms records and archives. It could be him."

"Or it could even be C. Wiggins on his own," Quentin said miserably.

Catriona came in through the back door as he said it. "What's happened *now*?" she said. She gave Archer a weary, freezing look.

Howard shut the door hastily. It made him feel bad to see how thin and pale Mum had got this last week. And there was going to be another row. His parents would wait till Archer was gone, and then they would start shouting again. He could see it in both their faces. He turned to the Goon. "Will you come with me to the museum?"

"Archer settled in?" the Goon asked morbidly.

"There's going to be another row," said Howard.

The Goon blenched. "Front door then," he said.

But no one sneaked off that easily with Awful in the house. As the Goon tore open the front door and they stood on the brink of Hathaway's moat, with Archer's Rolls parked on the other side of it, the back door slammed, and Awful whizzed down the passage to the moat. "You're not going without me," she said. Howard supposed he should be thankful that she only said it, instead of yelling it.

"Come on then," said the Goon. He slid himself along the front of the house and picked Awful up by her elbows as before. Because Archer's Rolls was parked exactly at the edge of

142

the moat, even the Goon had to jump down into the moat first in order to get around it. Howard waded through the yellow mud at the bottom and climbed out beyond the car. Ginger Hind began to lope meaningfully toward him across the tarry heaps and holes. Howard leaned on the hood of the Rolls. Come on then, he thought. There's only one of you.

The Goon stood in the moat, dangling Awful, and looked up at the car. "Let his tires down?" he suggested.

"No," said Awful. "Hurry up before Ginger Hind gets Howard."

The Goon dumped Awful on the road and climbed out, sighing. Ginger Hind, when he saw the Goon rising length by length out of the moat, stopped in his tracks and kicked a red cone over in annoyance.

Howard was annoyed, too. He had lost a chance to get rid of Ginger Hind. "Don't you even go home to eat?" he said to him. All he got was a black-eyed glare. Ginger Hind stuffed his hands into his pockets and followed them, down Zed Alley and across the Poly forecourt. Here Howard saw that the skeleton building of girders was now in scaffolding, making an outline sketch of the Egyptian temple building he had seen in the drawing at lunchtime.

Ginger Hind prowled after them all the way to the museum yard. There he stared in surprise as Howard actually turned toward the door marked "Entrance." To most people, Howard included, the museum yard was just a way through to the lanes below the cathedral.

The Goon hung back. "Want to go *in*?" he said. He seemed as surprised as Ginger Hind.

"I need to for a school project," Howard said, for Ginger Hind's benefit. He did not want Shine to know he was looking for Hathaway.

Ginger Hind gave him a look of deep contempt. The Goon hitched himself against one of the stone lions outside the museum and folded his long arms. "Don't like museums," he

143

said. "Old stuff. Bones and bits of jug. Too clean. Should all be on a rubbish heap."

So they went in without the Goon and also, to Howard's relief, without Ginger Hind, who either shared the Goon's opinion of museums or, more likely, did not dare go past the Goon to follow Howard and Awful. Howard thought: I shall have to get that Hind menace on his own again before long. Awful laughed, much too loud for the hushed, bricky atmosphere of the museum. "The Goon hates museums!" she said. "He said such a lot. Shall we go to the Egypt bit and look at Torquils?"

"We'll see." Howard went up to the attendant standing under a notice saying "SAXON EXHIBITION THIS WAY."

Awful skipped along behind him. "Saxons are boring," she said. "They burned cakes and talked about Jesus."

"Excuse me," Howard said to the attendant. "Could I speak to Mr. Hathaway, please?"

The attendant looked at his watch. He did not seem to be in the least surprised to be asked. Howard's heart began bumping. "Yes, I think so," the attendant said. "He usually arranges to see people around now. Is it both of you?"

"Yes, please," said Howard. His heart seemed to beat in his ears as loud as Torquil's drums because he had got it right!

The attendant said, "This way then," and took them around the corner, through the dark canvas corridors of the Saxon exhibition. They passed beautifully lighted displays of coins and buckles and pieces of jug, which made Howard think of the Goon, and some skeletons that had been dug up under the Town Hall, which Awful spared a moment to look at. One had an old spear shaft sticking through its ribs, which impressed her rather. They turned right past a Saxon king in full dress, looking very magnificent and lofty as if he had not known the first thing about burning cakes, and came out around the back into a dusty space full of cases of dead butterflies. The attendant pointed to a white door beyond the butterflies. "In there.

144

Give three knocks, and go through." And he went away and left them to do it.

The door was marked "CURATOR" in plain black letters. Howard and Awful tiptoed past the cases of butterflies. Howard raised his hand to knock.

"Are you scared?" asked Awful.

"No," lied Howard.

"Nor am I then," said Awful.

Howard knocked. Three times. Then he turned the handle and opened the door. There was a dreadful, birdlike, squawking noise and a lot of flapping. He nearly shut it again.

"Funny," said Awful. "That sounded like a chicken." She pushed the door open out of Howard's hands and went in to see. Howard followed.

CHAPTER ELEVEN

It was a chicken. They found themselves out of doors, in a walled space with cobbles in the ground, which seemed to be a sort of farmyard. The evening seemed to have turned much milder and warmer, and this was bringing out a strong smell of manure. There were hens all over the place, running toward a girl of about Howard's age who was scattering corn for them. One of them had got in the way of the door in its hurry. As Howard shut the door behind him, a man came out of the doorway to the right, leading a horse. When he saw Awful and Howard, he stopped, grinned, and called something to the girl. He had such a thick accent that they could not understand a word. But the girl understood. She looked up and bit her lip in order not to laugh.

"Can I be of help to you?" she asked. She had an accent, too, and her voice wobbled with laughter.

They had a right to laugh! Howard thought indignantly. The girl had a long dress on and a silly little cap sitting on her hair. The man was actually wearing a smock, like a joke yokel. He supposed they were actors, hired for another display like the Saxon one, but he did not see why they should have a joke at his expense. "We—er—we'd like to see Hathaway, please," he said as politely as he could. It came out a little curt.

"Come with me," the girl said. She shot a grin at the man and dumped the corn out of her apron in a heap on the cobbles. Leaving the hens to squawk and squabble over it, she led the way to another arched doorway in the opposite wall. She made rather heavy going of it because she had clogs on.

There was a garden beyond the wall, a very well-kept garden made mostly of trees or shrubs trained and clipped around neat paths. It was not surprising it was so neat, Howard thought, as the girl led them through. There were so many people at work on it. Men with shears kept bobbing up from behind hedges to stare at them. Two girls in long skirts came running with rakes to rake a path, and they stared, too. And small boys kept popping up everywhere, giggling. Under a tree that had been trained into a sort of roof, two men were sitting writing with quill pens. One of them was Hathaway's polite messenger. He recognized them. The dismay which came over his face was almost comic.

"I—I trust your father keeps well?" he said.

"It's all right," said Awful. "He isn't here."

"God be praised!" said the messenger. He really meant it.

Awful was biting her lip, too, as they came to the house. It ran along one side of the garden, and it was big. It puzzled Howard because, in a way, it was like Dillian's house, made of red bricks in a thoroughly old-fashioned style. It had a great many diamond-paned windows and brick battlements along the top, in a way that ought to have been old. But it shone with newness. The thick oak of the open door was yellow with newness.

A lady dashed out of the door, saying, "What's this, Anne?"

147

At least when Howard really thought about what she said, he knew it was "What is't, Nan?" but he could not quite bring himself to believe it. The lady was wearing a cap which covered more of her hair than the girl's and made her face look too narrow, and she had on a long, rather beautiful dress of greenish brocade. Howard kept trying to tell himself, uneasily, that she was just dressed up like this for a museum display.

"They're for Father," the girl said in a very much stronger accent. She gave the lady a droll look. "Our strangest yet, think you not?"

"Hush, Anne," said the lady. "Will told me on't." And she said to Howard and Awful, "Welcome to Abbey House. Please to follow me. I will bring you where Hathaway is."

As soon as the lady took them into the house, Howard knew it was not a museum display. He knew, even before they went past some diamond-paned windows that looked out from the other side of the house. There he found himself looking out at the cathedral. One end of it was covered in rather insecure-looking wooden scaffolding, and workmen in strange clothes were climbing up and down long ladders rebuilding the west end, which Howard knew had been added around the reign of Henry VIII. All the people going past on this side of the house were dressed like the people in the garden. But this just confirmed what Howard knew. The house inside was real. He could see it was. The boy's hoop thrown on the floor, the silk cloak tossed over the new yellow oak of the banister, the thick stools, and the leather jug someone had tried to jam out of sight in a corner—all were there because people were really using them. When the Goon said Hathaway lived in the past, he had meant exactly that.

Howard had got used to this idea by the time the lady threw open a pale oak door and said, "Hathaway, here are strange guests again!" So the sight of Dad's typewriter wrapped in chains and lying on the table in that room was almost shocking. It looked thoroughly out of place, even though the room was evidently a study, too.

148

Hathaway was sitting with his elbows on the table, staring gloomily at the typewriter, but when he saw Howard and Awful, he sat up and turned his chair around. Color came into his rather pale face. "Bess!" he said to the lady. And the two of them began to talk so rapidly in the strong accent of the past that neither Howard nor Awful could catch one word in ten. They looked at Hathaway while he talked. His eyes were greenish, and he was fair like Dillian, though like many fair men, the neat little beard he wore was gingerish. He was quite the smallest of any of the family they had so far seen, almost normal size, in fact, probably only a few inches taller than Howard. Altogether he had a narrow, thin, frail look, which seemed to fit well with the padded brocade clothes he wore.

The rapid talk ended with the lady's saying, "I'll look to't," and blowing Hathaway a kiss as she went out. Hathaway turned eagerly to Howard and Awful. "Is it possible you come to me from your father?" he said. He was speaking in a way they could understand, but Howard could see it was not the way he usually spoke.

"No," he said, "Sorry. We came off our own bat."

Hathaway looked guarded at that. "Enterprising," he said. "Why?"

"To ask you things, of course. Stupid," Awful said.

Hathaway smiled. Awful scowled back. That seemed to amuse Hathaway. "See here, little madam," he said. "Your father sent my secretary home in tears. It is I who should scowl at you."

"Dad had a lot to put up with," Howard explained quickly. "He'd had Archer and Torquil already that morning. And Dillian had pinched his words."

Hathaway's greenish eyes lifted to examine Howard. "I know that," he said. "I do keep in touch to that extent. So what have you come to ask me?"

"Stop digging up our road, you beast!" Awful said in her most outspoken way. It sounded to Howard as if she were getting ready to behave as badly as she had with Miss Potter.

149

But when he looked, he saw that Awful liked Hathaway. She was talking to him the way she talked to Dad. She was expecting Hathaway to understand. Howard thought it was lucky that Hathaway did not happen to have a paunch, or Awful would have been making rude remarks about it before long.

Hathaway did understand Awful perfectly, Howard was glad to see. He kept a straight face and asked innocently, "And what is wrong with your road?"

"There's a moat outside our house," Awful said truculently.

Hathaway's straight face became amused and slightly guilty.

"All right," Howard said. "I suppose it is funny! But along with all the rest, it just isn't anymore! And what about the men who keep having to dig it up and fill it in?" He was, he realized, talking to Hathaway as he would talk to Dad, too. He went on hurriedly, trying to sound more polite. "But what I really came about was Dad's two thousand words." Hathaway nodded, because he knew that. "Obvious, isn't it?" said Howard. "Now look . . ." It was no good. He forgot to be polite again. Quite suddenly he found himself as eloquent as Quentin and walked up and down the room, shouting things about Dillian, cursing Torquil and Shine, complaining about Archer, explaining about Quentin and Mum, and generally going on about Hind's gang, the music, the electricity, the borrowed food, and the roadworks.

Awful stood holding the edge of the table, watching him wonderingly. Hathaway leaned his bearded chin on his hand and listened with what seemed to be amused, dry attention. After a moment, however, when he saw Howard was not going to stop quickly, he reached to a shelf behind him and fetched down an hourglass, which he turned sand side up and stood on the table. Then he went back to listening. Howard did not know if the hourglass was Hathaway's idea of a joke, but he did not let it put him off. He had a lot to say. And it was such a relief to tell it to someone who understood. Hathaway understood. Through the look of dry attention, other looks kept flickering: faint guilt, sympathy, dislike of

150

Shine and Dillian, annoyance at Archer, and even some humorous admiration for the way the Sykes family had been coping.

"And today was the last straw for Dad," Howard was concluding when the door beside him opened. The girl who had been feeding the chickens came around it with a tray, swiveling on one clogged foot because she had the tray balanced on her knee in order to open the door. Howard knew how easy it is to drop everything when you do that. Since he was beside the door, he took the tray away from her.

"I thank you," she said, and bobbed a sort of curtsy. Then she took back the tray firmly and carried it to the table. There were mugs and a jug and a wooden plate of cakes on it. The girl made a great business of pushing aside the hourglass and the typewriter to set them out, so that she could take a great many quick, sharp looks at Awful and at Howard.

"And why are you acting as servant?" Hathaway said to her, seeing it. "My daughter Anne," he said to Howard and Awful. "Nan, you are in luck today with your spying on my people from the future. Here are Howard and Anthea, who could be your own descendants."

This made Howard feel very odd. Anne laughed and tossed her capped head. "And not princes!" she said. "There's been a sad falling off in my line. I intend marrying a king. All my offspring shall be royalty."

"We came in disguise," Awful invented. "We left our crowns at home."

"Then that explains all," Anne said, not believing a word. "Wear them next time, and I shall wear mine." Hathaway made her a little shooing motion. "I'll not pour the wine?" Anne asked, pleadingly. Hathaway shook his head. Anne clumped out of the room, casting regretful, curious glances over her shoulder.

"She does what she's told!" Awful exclaimed in surprise.

"Not very often," said Hathaway. "I think she didn't want to let me down in front of you. Sit down. Have some wine."

151

"Her name isn't really Anne Hathaway!" Howard said as he pulled a heavy stool over to the table.

Hathaway shook his head. "No. The name I use here is Moneypenny. She is Anne Moneypenny."

"But Moneypenny's Mum's old name!" Awful said, rather feeling that Hathaway had stolen it. And Howard felt odder than ever. He knew now that the thing that had made him so sure that Bess was dressed up for a museum display was that Bess was really quite like Catriona to look at.

Hathaway laughed as he poured wine into the mugs. "I remember it was. I think it may have some bearing on all this." He pushed the mugs toward them. "Have some spiced wine while I check." He turned around toward his bookshelf.

"Don't drink too much," Howard warned Awful while Hathaway's back was turned. There had been a terrible time last Christmas when Awful got at Dad's Christmas whiskey.

There was no danger of that. Awful took one sip and was nearly sick. She hated spices. When Hathaway turned back, holding a large book bound in pale grayish leather, Awful's face was twisted into a mixture of disgust—because of the taste—and accusation—because it was all Howard's fault—and disappointment—because she had wanted to like the wine. "Oh, dear!" said Hathaway. "We have to drink wine or beer here because the water's not clean. Take a cake instead."

But Awful did not like the cakes either. They were very dry, with seeds in. Howard was not sure he liked them much himself. Hathaway, as he leafed through the book, pushed Awful's mug aside in order to turn the wooden dish of cakes around. "Try the ones this side," he murmured. "You may like them better. Here we are—Anne's marriage, William's descent." The green eyes looked at Howard over the edge of the book rather apologetically. "I haven't looked at the records of my own children before," he said. "Ever since I found that Anne will marry a man called Sykes and move away from town, I have preferred not to know."

"Sykes!" said Howard. He took another cake to steady him-

152

self. This cake was much nicer, with no seeds and a taste of chocolate.

"Yes," Hathaway said rather sadly. "But whether he is your ancestor, I have no means of knowing. I am confined to this town, as you know, and my records can be of only this town. But Will's descent may throw some light." He ran his finger down the page. "Will stays and becomes a wealthy man. There are Moneypennys the whole way down to your day. Moneypenny girls married with the Mountjoys, the Caldwicks, a Wiggins here—most local families. Here is one in the nineteenth century marrying a Hind—"

"No!" Howard and Awful said together. Awful was surprised enough to pick up her mug and drink without thinking. Her eyebrows went up. "This is nice now! It tastes of strawberry!"

Howard thought he saw a little smile on Hathaway's face as Hathaway bent over the book, but all he said was "Ah. This is it. Catriona Moneypenny does descend from William. Marries Quentin Jocelin Sykes in 1967. Children—" Hathaway's green eyes flicked to Howard for a moment in a startled way and then back to the book. "Howard Graham and Anthea Mildred Dolores," he said.

"Why did you look at Howard like that?" Awful demanded.

"Like what?" said Hawathay.

"Surprised," said Awful. "Is it something children shouldn't know?"

Hathaway's face flushed a little. He looked worried. "No, no," he said. "It's only—well, if your parents haven't told you, it would not be right for me—"

"What?" said Howard.

Hathaway seemed more worried still. "Now you're thinking all sorts of terrible things," he said. "It's nothing. Truly. Have they never told you that you were adopted?"

"No," said Howard, and for a moment the ground felt as if it were falling away underneath him. Suddenly he did not seem to be who he thought he was. He did not know who he was.

153

He saw Hathaway looking at him with concern, but he did not want to look at him or at anyone else.

"Oh, I know *that*!" Awful said, scornful and relieved. "Mum told me once when I bit her. She said she wished she could have chosen me like she chose Howard. She"— Awful had the grace to go red here—"she said she'd have chosen someone else."

"I wish you'd *said*!" Howard said.

"Sorry." Awful hung her head. "Mum told me not to. She knew you'd be upset."

"Drink some more wine," said Hathaway. "I know a little how you feel. My family always swore I was a changeling." Howard swigged off the spicy wine. He was not sure it helped. Meanwhile, Hathaway glanced at the sand filtering through the waist of the hourglass. "You haven't much longer here," he said, "I can keep people from your time as they are for an hour, but beyond that I don't let anyone risk himself."

"Why?" said Awful.

Hathaway smiled in a quiet, rueful way, which had just a trace of Archer's smile in it. "Because the longer anyone stays in the past, the older he becomes in his own present day. You won't want to go home a grown woman, will you?" Awful stared at him, not believing it. "It's true," said Hathaway. "I found out the hard way. After two years here I was an old, old man in your time—and I don't age as fast as you would. After all the years I've spent here now, I think I would not be alive in your time at all."

"But don't you *mind*?" said Awful. "How long have you been here?"

Hathaway shrugged. "I've been here nearly thirty years now. I don't mind much. Some things I miss, but I'm pretty happily settled here, as you see. And I've got things well organized, so that I can keep in touch and run the things in your century that I said I would. Mind you"—he laughed a little—"I wouldn't have stayed in the past for those two years if I'd

154

known. It always puzzles me how Venturus manages, living in the future as he does."

"Living in the future?" said Awful. "People can't. It hasn't happened yet."

"I don't think he lives as far ahead as I live back," Hathaway said. "Only a hundred years or so. But of course, I haven't seen him for years."

"But why did you come to the past?" persisted Awful. By now she had absentmindedly drunk most of her strawberry wine and was feeling very chirpy—with a large furry feeling that she loved Hathaway greatly, particularly now she knew he was a sort of grandfather of hers.

"Why did I?" Hathaway reached out musingly and moved Awful's wine mug a long way away from her. "You might say I'm the odd one out in my family, but that's not quite true. I always got on with the three younger ones rather well. I suppose it was after I had such a flaming row with Torquil—"

"He quarrels just like me," Awful said, sitting very upright, with her eyes shining. "I don't mean it either. I wish people understood."

Hathaway smiled. "That will be enough from you, young madam." He clearly did not want to discuss Torquil. He turned to Howard. "There are things I have to say to your brother now. Howard, what purpose do those two thousand words serve?"

Howard came out of his daze of strangeness, rather shamed to see that Hathaway had kindly been allowing him time to feel better. "I thought you knew," he said. "You're the one who got Dad to do them, after all."

"Oh, no," said Hathaway. "It wasn't me. I said it because, upon thought, it seemed the speediest way to get hold of a sample. If I'd known what your father was like—"

"Archer thought one of you had doctored the typewriter," said Howard.

"This?" Hathaway reached a hand to the typewriter Anne

155

had pushed to the end of the table. "No. It's just an ordinary typewriter. So"—he looked almost beseechingly at Howard—"how is it being done? Why are we being confined in space and time like this?"

"In time?" said Howard. "You aren't. Well, at least—"

"I forget. The others probably don't know," said Hathaway. "Sitting here in the past, in the sixteenth century, I *know* that twenty-six years have gone by since we were first confined to the town. Up in your century, it only seems thirteen years—you have had the same thirteen years twice."

"Erskine knew," said Howard. "And Archer suspected. The others didn't say."

"You're stuck in the town, too?" Awful asked, catching up with the talk a little late. Everything had slowed down for her.

Hathaway nodded. "Some of it is merely annoying," he said. "If Bess goes to see her father out at the castle, the children can go, but I have to make my excuses. But I long to go abroad." He looked sad and wistful. "What truly saddens me is that I can never see Anne again after she marries and leaves here."

Awful asked, with a look of low cunning, "Don't you want to farm the world?"

"This world? In this century?" Hathaway laughed. "A man is lucky if he can rule one country here! Besides, what do you do with the world when you have it? Archer seems mad to me. No, I certainly have no such ambitions."

Howard was sure Hathaway meant this. He felt angry on Hathaway's behalf, as well as for Mum and Dad and himself. The person causing all this seemed so spiteful. "I'm going to find out who it is," he said. "Somehow. Who do *you* think it is?"

Hathaway pushed aside the book and the plate of cakes and leaned his elbows on the table thoughtfully. "I think it is some-one unexpected," he said. "We'd have found them out if it were one of the obvious ones, like Shine or Torquil. If I were one of my brothers and sisters, I'd think it was me. But since I know it *isn't* me, well, it could be Dillian. She hasn't done

156

anything with the words she stole, and she could have stolen them as a blind. If she did, that was foolish because it alerted all the rest. And from what I know of Dillian, I think she would be angrier than most at being confined. She hates farming law and order, you know. She's always yearned to be lawless, like Shine." Hathaway glanced at the hourglass. The sand was well below its last quarter, filtering away fast. "I'm considering our characters," he said. "And it interests me that neither Erskine nor Venturus has threatened your father. It's almost as if they *want* you to suspect them. That suggests to me that they're covering up for a third person. And I think that person has to be Archer. Venturus, being the youngest, admires Archer almost to the point of worship. He tries to imitate Archer—"

The way Hathaway said this made Howard feel that Hathaway was trying to tell him something else, something behind the actual words. But he had not a clue to what it could be. "Archer swore it wasn't him," he said. "I thought he was being honest."

"Everyone blames Archer," Awful said in vast, weary wisdom, as if she were at least ninety.

"I know," Hathaway said, with a soft, apologetic movement. He looked at Howard earnestly. "But you wouldn't believe how often Archer has played on that—doing his honest, injured, wry act. Who *me*? You know. And so he *is* honest, but with Archer you have to watch what he *doesn't* say. And if he hasn't told you definitely that Erskine and Venturus are not doing his dirty work for him, then the person you want is Archer."

That look of Hathaway's made Howard surer than ever that Hathaway was trying to tell him something else, but he still could not see what it was. What he said about Archer was enough to worry about in itself. "How could anyone stop Archer?" he said. "He seems so powerful."

"Erskine might," said Hathaway. "Erskine's the only one of us who can really stand up to Archer. I'll try to get a message to Erskine, but I strongly advise you and your father to see

157

Erskine, too." He looked at the hourglass again and pushed his chair back. "You must be going now."

Awful scrambled from her stool with slow dignity. Howard, as he got up, remembered the letter from the city treasurer. "By the way," he said, "are you the one who found out Dad hasn't paid his taxes? He got a bill for thousands of pounds this morning."

Hathaway went red. It was almost the way Archer did. Surprise and annoyance and some guilt swept across his face. "I was going to do that!" he said. "It would have been my next move. Someone else got in first. That's really annoying! Now what can we do about that?"

"It's the last straw for Dad," Howard said.

Hathaway crossed to the door and opened it. Howard followed, admiring the way Hathaway's padded blue robe swung comfortably about him. Living in the past had its points. Dad would have loved that robe as a dressing gown. "It's difficult," Hathaway said, going with them into the rest of the house. "It's easier to start the Council on a thing like that than to stop it. I'll think about it. And I suppose you'll want me to call off the road menders?"

"Yes, please," said Howard.

"I'll do it at once," said Hathaway.

They went through the house. Awful trod with unnatural dignity behind. The house was full of bustle and voices. Somebody was singing in the distance and clattering dishes. There was a smell of food cooking, mixing with wax and smoke and scents coming in through the open door to the garden.

"I like this house," Howard said.

Bess was standing by the open door to say good-bye. She heard Howard and sank into a deep curtsy, smiling with pride and pleasure. Howard did his best to bow back. Awful bent her head majestically. It was all she dared do.

Outside, in the gathering evening, Anne and the little boy were hiding in the garden, watching them. There was only one little boy, Howard realized. He had just kept appearing all over

158

the place. As Hathaway took them through the garden to the farmyard, Anne and William kept pace with them behind hedges and shrubs. Howard could hear them rustling and giggling. It was not meant to be rude. William was too shy to come out.

"It would be easier to provide your father with the money he owes," Hathaway remarked as they came to the barnyard, "than to stop the Council from asking for it."

Howard remembered a book he had read. "Couldn't you bury some money where our garden's going to be, and I could dig it up tomorrow?"

Hathaway laughed. "Yes, if I could stop someone else from finding it during the four centuries in between! No. There must be a better way. I'll consider."

The man in the smock was grooming the horse in the middle of the yard. The hens had all gone to roost. Howard could hear hennish croonings in the background, while Hathaway exchanged a couple of jokes with the man. It was all in the thick accent of the past, which Howard found impossible to follow. They crossed the cobbles to the museum door. On this side it was a small white door in the wall, less than half the size of the big main gate beside it.

Hathaway opened the door for them. "Come to me again," he said, "if you get into difficulties. I'll help in any way I can." Again, the way he said this gave Howard a strong feeling that there was something else Hathaway knew, which he was trying to tell him without saying directly.

"Thanks," Howard said, to both parts of it, the said and the unsaid. He was still wondering what Hathaway meant when he found himself in the dingy little space with the dead butterflies. The door marked "CURATOR" was just shutting behind them.

CHAPTER TWELVE

Hathaway really had no need to make threats or dig up the road, Howard thought. If he could have come to see Quentin himself, Dad would surely have been on Hathaway's side. Hathaway was—

Suspicion hit Howard. He stopped between two cases of butterflies, frowning. Shine had tried to get them on her side. Shine had said Hathaway was sneaky. Could he have worked quietly away inside Howard's head as they talked? He thought over their visit and wished he knew. Hathaway, in his quieter way, had been as plain and straightforward as Archer. And that worried Howard. He had been alerted to the things that were wrong with Archer by the look on Quentin's face. He wished Quentin had been with him this time, to tell him about Hathaway. He was not at all sure he could be right on his own.

Hathaway had been reasonable and understanding. Far from trying to keep them in the past, he had made sure they spent only the hour there that was safe. He had agreed to call off the road menders. The one unpleasant thing he had done—which was something Howard did not want to think about yet—was to tell Howard he was an adopted child. And that had surprised Hathaway, too. But that all could have been part of it, Howard told himself worriedly. How could you judge people like Hathaway, Shine, or Archer in the normal way? He felt confused and lonely and desperately wanted Mum or Dad to advise him.

Wait a minute! Mum always said that you could tell what people were like by their houses. Howard found himself thinking of the pleasant, lived-in house and the people busy in the garden. It could not have been more different from Archer's workshop, Dillian's palace, or Shine's dark den. Hathaway really did seem different from the others. And it was quite natural that they would not understand him and despised him for it.

Howard walked on into the Saxon exhibition, very much relieved. Awful, who had been valiantly sober up to then, stomped after him unsteadily. Beside the skeletons, she announced, "Nobody loves me!"

"Don't talk nonsense!" said Howard.

"I'm not norking tonsense!" Awful retorted.

In the foyer she found it necessary to lie down and laugh.

"Do get up, Awful," said Howard. But Awful lay on her back, kicking her feet up, and seemed to be laughing and crying at once. Howard looked around to find the attendant standing beside him, looking reproachful.

"Would you mind moving her?" he said to Howard. "We're just closing."

Howard tried to make Awful get up, but all she did was roll over on her face. "I'm going to be sick," she said.

"No, you're not. Not in here," Howard said. He got hold of Awful under her arms and heaved her up. Awful had some-

161

how gone unusually heavy. Her legs trailed. Howard heaved and dragged her across the foyer and managed to back out through the swing door with her. Awful found this very funny. She laughed all the way.

Outside, it was nearly dark and very much colder than it had been in Hathaway's time. To Howard's relief, the Goon was still leaning on one of the stone lions. Ginger Hind was leaning on the other stone lion, glowering at the Goon; that was not so good, but there was not much Howard could do about it. Both their heads turned in surprise as Howard backed out, towing Awful.

"Something wrong," stated the Goon.

"Awful's got herself drunk," Howard explained.

"Sell wine in museums these days?" the Goon asked, puzzled.

"No." Howard ignored the malicious grin growing on Ginger's face. "We saw Hathaway, and he gave us both some wine. Do you think you could carry her? She's gone heavy."

"Know I can carry her," said the Goon. He stepped over and scooped Awful up with no trouble at all. "Didn't know Hathaway lived here," he remarked as he did so.

Awful suddenly noticed what was happening. "Put me down!" she screamed, kicking and struggling mightily. "I don't want you! I like Hathaway best!" The Goon looked rather hurt at this, but he nevertheless set out across the museum yard with Awful's arms and legs whirling around him in all directions and Howard trotting after. Behind Howard came Ginger Hind, grinning all over his bruised face. "I want *Hathaway* to carry me!" screamed Awful.

"Go on," said the Goon. "You like me, too."

"No, I don't! I want Hathawa-ay!" Awful wailed.

"Shut up, Awful," Howard said, trotting alongside. "You *know* Hathaway lives in the past. You're hurting the Goon's feelings."

Awful at once became hugely contrite. She flung her arms

162

around the Goon's neck and burst into tears. "I like you, too!" she blubbered at the top of her voice. "I do, I do. You're a lovely Goon. You're my favorite Goon in all the world!"

The Goon's face, under the next streetlight, was an unusual brick color. Howard was horribly aware of Ginger Hind trotting a few yards in the rear, listening and grinning for all he was worth. He was resigned to Shine's knowing they had seen Hathaway, but this was a bit much. "*Do* shut up, Awful!" he said.

But Awful continued to shout endearments at the Goon, all the way past the Poly and halfway along Zed Alley, where she passed quite suddenly into a loglike sleep and snored, with her wet face pressed against the Goon's neck and the rest of her dangling. The Goon was afraid to disturb her and carried her like that in giant tiptoe strides all the way home. Howard followed the Goon, and Ginger Hind followed Howard, until the Goon made the final giant stride across Hathaway's moat and went into the side passage of number 10.

Howard stopped there and waited for Ginger Hind. Ginger Hind stopped by a red cone six yards away. "Come on," said Howard. "What are you waiting for?" Ginger Hind said nothing and did not move. He may have been afraid that the Goon was waiting in ambush down the passage, but Howard did not care. He walked toward him. They both were about the same height, and Ginger was older, but he was wiry where Howard was solid. There was still enough light to see to hit him by, and Howard knew he would win. But Ginger Hind shuffled away backward. "Like that, is it?" Howard said nastily. "Doesn't it look so much fun without the rest of your gang?"

Ginger Hind said defensively, "Shine said follow you but not hurt you."

"You couldn't hurt me," said Howard. "Not on your own." He took another step forward. Ginger Hind backed again.

"I've got my orders," he said.

There was a scared, undecided note to his voice which made

163

Howard thoroughly disgusted. "Orders!" he said. "Shine put a hex on your mind. And you let her!"

"Yeah?" said Ginger. "How do you think you know that?"

Howard turned away. "Because," he said over his shoulder, "she tried it on me, too. That's how." He left Ginger Hind standing by the red cone and jumped across the moat. He was, for some reason, so annoyed, disgusted, and agitated that he almost missed the side passage and jumped into the wall. He had to save himself with a sideways sort of scramble. Just as well he'd managed to, he thought as he strode rather unsteadily down the passage. Ginger Hind would have laughed like a drain if he'd fallen in the ditch. Funny the way Ginger Hind had gone from being a great threat to just seeming pathetic. Forgetting the wine, Howard thought that it was probably because he found out that Ginger Hind descended from Hathaway, too, and was only a relative like Auntie Mildred.

Then, just outside the kitchen door, it hit Howard. Ginger Hind was no relative of his. Nobody was, as far as he knew. He did not know *who* he was. But surely, he thought as he opened the door, Mum and Dad would know.

Catriona and Quentin were sitting facing each other across the purple heart on the kitchen table. Catriona did not have her earplugs in, although the television was blaring Viennese waltzes and the drums were distantly thumping below in the cellar. Quentin had his arms folded and his mouth set. The air was thick with the row they had been having.

Too bad, Howard thought. "Mum . . ." he began.

But just then the Goon came stooping in under the door to the hall. "Put her to bed," he announced.

Catriona murmured, "Oh, thank you," rather absently, and Howard somehow changed what he had been going to say.

"Mum," he said, "Dad. I went and saw Hathaway. He didn't send that letter about the taxes, but he says he'll help find the money. And he's going to stop digging up the road."

164

They all were looking at him, even the Goon, as if they were amazed. "Howard," said Catriona, "what's the matter?"

"Nothing's the matter," said Howard. "Hathaway's OK. He really does live in the past, you know. About four hundred years ago. You descend from him, Mum. Dad may descend from him, too. He says we've got to get hold of Erskine. Erskine and Venturus may be covering up for Archer."

"Yes, but—" said Catriona.

And Quentin said, "Now look, Howard—"

Howard said, "Now I'm going to do my violin practice." He pushed past the Goon and went away upstairs. There he disconnected his mind and scribbled tunes on the violin and thankfully went on an imaginary flight in his best spaceship, out beyond Sirius, toward the center of the Milky Way. The noise he made did not seem to disturb Awful at all. When, after about half an hour, the radiation from the packed stars got too intense, Howard came back from the center of the galaxy and went to have a look at Awful. She was fast asleep. He went downstairs to find that the Goon had borrowed them an armful of fish and chips from somewhere. Howard went upstairs again and asked Awful if she wanted any, but she just bit him and went to sleep again.

Howard was helping the Goon eat Awful's share of chips when Fifi put her head around the back door.

"Want some?" the Goon said, hopefully holding his plateful out toward Fifi's face.

Fifi shook her head. She looked very happy and businesslike. "I've only looked in," she said. "Archer's outside in the car. We're going to have supper at the Bishop's Arms. I came to say I'm leaving." The Goon stared at her, stunned. "I've decided to move in with Archer," Fifi explained. "We're getting married. Mrs. Sykes, is it all right if I come back and collect my things tomorrow morning?"

"I . . . suppose so," Catriona said, looking a little stunned, too.

165

Fifi beamed. "Thanks," she said happily. "'Bye, everyone."

Her head vanished. The back door shut. The Goon uttered a great howl and dashed out into the hall. He gave another howl there, and they heard him dash somewhere else. As Howard was picking up the chair the Goon had knocked over, there came a mighty bursting crash. Silence followed. The drums still boomed from the cellar, but the rest of Torquil's music seemed to have stopped.

Quentin said to Catriona, "That creature of yours seems to have destroyed our television."

"That creature of *yours*," Catriona corrected him. "It was useless anyway."

"There is no way," said Quentin, "we can possibly afford another."

"That," said Catriona, "is entirely your fault."

This icy exchange was interrupted by the Goon, who came sliding in around the door, drooping guiltily. "Telly just got broken," he said. "Came to pieces in my hands."

"Oh, really?" said Quentin. "It sounded more as if you'd thrown it."

"Flew across the room," admitted the Goon. "Can't think how." He grinned placatingly. "Find you another one?" he suggested. "New one might get better programs."

"I'd prefer to go without," Catriona said firmly.

"Pay you back somehow?" pleaded the Goon.

"Yes," said Quentin. "You can. You can take us to see Erskine."

The Goon looked at Quentin, and Quentin looked back. The Goon seemed to be struggling with feelings rather too large for his brain. "Won't like it," he said at last.

"I'll be the judge of that," said Quentin, imposing his will on the Goon, the way he did with students. "Take us."

There was a long, grudging pause. Then the Goon sighed gustily. "Take you tomorrow."

"Why not now?" said Quentin.

"Got reasons," said the Goon. "Can't say."

166

And there, it seemed, the Goon stuck. He would not explain, and he would not argue; but he would not take anyone to Erskine that night. He went and cleared up the broken television instead. "Well, I suppose it makes no difference when we go," Quentin said.

On Saturday morning Hathaway was as good as his word. His men woke them at dawn again, noisily filling in the moat and all the other holes in Upper Park Street. Awful howled with agony. She had a headache that morning and could not understand why. Catriona howled at the noise also, but more softly. She put her earplugs in and stayed in bed. But Awful got up and tried to make everyone else miserable, too.

"I hate Mum, I hate Dad, I hate Howard. And the Goon," she chanted. "Mum is cross, Dad is fat, Howard is stupid, the Goon is ugly. The only one I like is Hathaway."

"You used to like Fifi," Howard said.

"Fifi's gone boring," said Awful. "There's something wrong with my tea. It tastes of drains."

"Nothing wrong with it," said the Goon. He had made the tea. "You look wrong. Pale yellow. Hangover."

"You have hangover hair then," said Awful. "Hangover butter. Hangover toast. Hangover sun. I think the world's ill."

At this, Quentin said Awful must go back to bed. Awful refused. She had heard by then that the Goon was taking Quentin and Howard to see Erskine, and she wanted to go, too. Catriona was the one who stayed at home.

Howard went up to see Catriona with a cup of the Goon's tea. He was afraid she was staying in bed because she was so angry with Dad. But when he saw her, lying with her earplugs in, looking thin and white, with the noise of the road mending filling the room, he saw she really was sick. Catriona raised herself on an elbow to take the tea with a grateful smile. And she began to talk without remembering to take her earplugs out.

"Oh, Howard, bless you! I don't know what I'd do without you! Don't look so worried. I'm just tired out. This has been the

167

most dreadful week I've ever lived through. You'll have to forgive my not coming to see Erskine. He's probably just like Torquil, and I can't face another! Besides, somebody ought to be here when Fifi moves her things out. And I suppose Awful's going to insist on going, and your father's going to give in to her as he always does! Howard, you're to look after Awful. I trust you."

"You're always telling me that. I *do* look after her," Howard said, forgetting Catriona could not hear with the earplugs in.

"Yes, I know you will," Catriona said, smiling affectionately. "You're very good with Awful. Just look after her. Don't leave her on her own, there's a dear. If I know you're keeping her safe, I won't worry."

"Yes, all right," Howard said, sighing. He wanted to ask Catriona about how she came to adopt him, but it was no good if she could not hear him.

The Goon looked rather put out when Howard came downstairs without Catriona. "She not coming?" When Howard had explained how tired Mum was, the Goon considered deeply. "No car," he said. "Need money. Need to go by bus. Need boots, too. Need to go in the sewers."

At this news Quentin swiftly put on his red and black checked coat before the Goon could borrow it and turned out Catriona's purse. By some miracle, there was a five-pound note tucked in the back of it. Howard and Awful hunted for boots in the hall cupboard.

"My brain's loose," Awful grumbled. "It keeps rolling about when I bend."

"Shut up," said Howard. "Put those boots on." His own Wellingtons were on Quentin by then. Howard had to make do with the old pair that had a hole in the left foot. After that, to his surprise, they were ready to go. He had supposed the Goon would hang about in order to see Fifi again before she left. But Fifi had still not come to collect her things when they left the house.

Ginger Hind, on the other hand, was already on duty. He

168

slouched after them on the other side of the road, keeping his black eye warily on the Goon, and stood watching in a shop doorway while they waited for a bus in Park Street. Howard tried to ignore him. Even if Shine knew they were going to see Erskine, there was not much she could do about it with the Goon there. They waited for twenty minutes.

"This day's got a hangover," Awful grumbled. Howard knew what she meant. It was a cold gray day, and the sun was only a yellow smear among the chimney pots. It depressed him. He wondered if he had a hangover, too. He refused to believe he might be having forebodings.

After the second twenty minutes Quentin said, "I deplore the way Hathaway runs these buses. He's quick enough to dig our road up, but otherwise, he simply doesn't try."

"It must be quite hard to run things from hundreds of years in the past," Howard protested.

The Goon suggested, "Learn to drive?"

"Never," said Quentin. "My mission in life is to be a passenger."

Awful began chanting, "Hathaway, send a bus. Hathaway, send a bus." After a while it was almost as if the chanting had worked. Two buses came along together. There was room for them all in the one behind, but not, to Howard's pleasure, any room for Ginger Hind. He came sprinting up just as the bus started to move, only to be turned away when he got there.

Lost him! Howard thought gleefully, and he enjoyed the slow bus ride much more than he would have done with Ginger among the passengers. He found he was quite excited at the thought of meeting Erskine at last.

The bus took them right to the other end of town—the part on the map at school that had been marked "Industry"—and dropped them at the end of a row of little red houses that were all joined together. Beyond that the town just petered out into big khaki-colored sheds that looked like factories, although they did not seem to be working, or wide fields mostly made of weeds and half bricks.

169

"Who farms industry?" Howard asked, thinking he or she did not seem to be doing a very good job.

"Shine," the Goon said after some thought. "Not interested."

"I can see that," Quentin said impatiently. "Where to now?"

The Goon bent down to a manhole cover in the road at their feet. He hooked his large fingers in it somehow, and somehow he tore it up, leaving a square dark hole with an iron ladder leading down into it. "Down here," he said. "As good as any."

"Or as bad," Quentin agreed. "Lead on then."

The Goon swung himself into the hole and went swarming down the ladder as easily as a baboon down a tree. Quentin followed slowly. "I think," Quentin said to Howard with only his face sticking out of the ground, "that our friend has at last found his true home." Then his face disappeared. Awful climbed into the hole, too. Her headache was going. Howard could hear her saying excitedly that she liked this place as he climbed into it after her. The ladder was screwed into slimy brick wall. The hole grew rapidly darker as Howard climbed down. There was a sound like a river rushing below and a growing putrid smell.

"Isn't it *smelly*!" Awful said cheerfully when Howard arrived beside her on a grayly seen brick platform. The rushing sound was very near and loud there, and Awful was right about the smell.

The Goon picked up a large electric lantern from a niche in the brick wall. As he did so, there was a hollow clanging thump from above. Thick darkness fell.

"The lid seems to have shut," Quentin remarked, sounding a little nervous, out of the nearby thick dark.

"Bound to," said the Goon. He switched on the lantern. By its light they could see an arched brick passage, running to left and right, and black liquid decorated with yellow foamy blobs, also running from left to right. Howard quickly decided not to look too closely at that liquid. Things were being carried past in it that he would rather not know about.

170

Luckily there was not much time for looking. The Goon set off quickly to the right, carrying the lantern, and they had to hurry after him in order to be able to see. The arched brick ceiling was rather low. The Goon had to walk doubled over, and his black figure ahead looked like a vast crab. Shadows and light slid off the damp bricks, and the rushing of the liquid was soon mixed with the sloshing of their four sets of feet. The smell was worse. They were stirring things up. Howard glumly felt cold nastiness seep in through the hole in his left boot. He was going to have to throw those boots away after this. Before long he and Quentin were having to bend over like the Goon because the roof became lower still. Uneasiness grew in Howard. He kept longing to straighten up, and the more he knew it was impossible, the more he longed.

"Do you still like it?" he asked Awful, sloshing ahead of him.

"Sort of," she said.

Quentin must have felt like Howard because he began to talk, almost nonstop, in a very hearty way. Bits and pieces of his talk came back down the tunnel to Howard, mixed with sloshing, light glinting, and the smell. "Sort of sameness to a sewer . . . seen one yard of it, you've seen it all . . . does Erskine stand this? . . . See Erskine as rather a small man, possibly a dwarf about the size of Awful. . . . Private, of course . . . way to solve family problems . . . problem family . . . only met Archer so far . . . Fifi and Archer. Fifi's a nice girl, but . . . help seeing Fifi as the worst possible wife for Archer . . . Fifi clasping her hands and adoring . . . bound to make a man like Archer . . . even larger opinion of himself . . . Fifi in the ego-boosting line—"

Howard was not wholly surprised when the Goon suddenly swung around, glaring light into their faces. "Shut up!" he said to Quentin. "Shut *up* about Fifi!" It was possibly just the light shining upward on his face that made it look so savage.

Quentin shielded his eyes. "Don't you like Fifi? Of course, I'll shut up if you prefer. Please go on. I want to get out of here." And when the Goon had turned around and gone slosh-

171

ing on, Howard heard Quentin whispering to Awful to find out what had annoyed the Goon so.

Howard sighed incredulously as he sploshed after them. It seemed impossible that his father had failed to notice the Goon's huge devotion to Fifi. But he supposed that Dad had, after all, had rather a lot of other things to take up his attention.

They sloshed for what seemed hours. Howard's left boot was full and heavy when he suddenly found that the rushing liquid was parting company with the walkway. It went pouring thunderously away into the dark. The Goon's light picked up a small metal ladder leading to a stout metal door. The Goon reached up and tore the metal door open, causing them all to blink in the wan gray daylight that came flooding in. In the greatest relief they all scrambled up the ladder and out the door. Beyond was a concrete platform looking over a vast pit full of earth, ashes, tumbled tin cans, and motor tires.

"Here," announced the Goon as the metal door thumped shut.

They looked slowly around. To one side of the pit there were mounds and humps, some square and regular, some old and odd-shaped. On the other side there were new metal sheds with rows of yellow rubbish vans lined up outside them. Ahead was a vast modern-looking building, all gleaming pipes and faintly drifting smokes.

"Rubbish incinerator," the Goon said, pointing to the building. The sight seemed to please him.

They looked behind them. There they saw the fields of weeds and bricks, the khaki sheds, and, at the edge of the view but still not very far off, the row of small red houses where they had got off the bus.

"We could have walked here over those fields," Quentin pointed out. "Why ever didn't we?"

"Only two ways I can cross the town boundary," said the Goon. "Sewer or rubbish van."

Quentin, Howard, and Awful turned slowly back to stare up

172

at him. They had to tip their heads to look at his face properly. It was looking down at them with a sarcastic grin, and it did not seem stupid at all.

"Something tells me," Quentin said faintly, "that you may be Erskine."

CHAPTER THIRTEEN

The Goon nodded. He looked as savage as he had looked glaring in the sewer. They saw he was very angry indeed.

"Wh—what's wrong?" Awful said.

"Ask Venturus," said Erskine. He said it with utter contempt. And while they were still wondering why, he looked over their heads and said, "Got the place ready?"

Someone said, "Yes." They found they were surrounded by cheerful men and women in yellow coveralls and hats who all seemed to be wearing large white gloves. And cheerful though these people were, the way they grinned put Howard in mind of Hind's gang.

"Put them in it," said Erskine, and turned away.

Large white gloves seized them from every side. Someone said, "Better come along quietly," and they found themselves being pulled across the concrete platform. Nasty liquid squirted out of the top of Howard's left boot with every step he was pulled.

"But I don't understand!" Quentin protested. "What is this about?"

There was a fierce Goon shout from behind them. "Stop!" Everyone stopped and turned around. Erskine stretched out a long arm with that knife of his at the end of it. The knife beckoned. Howard was brought back, sploshing nasty liquid as he came. "Your dad," said Erskine with his hands on his hips, leaning down to glare at Howard, "said Archer hadn't a clue. Tell him *he* hasn't. Him and his talk! But someone has. Haven't they? Stay locked up till someone comes clean." This was a joke. A wave of hearty laughter went around the crowd in yellow coveralls.

"Yes, but why are you so angry?" Howard said.

For a moment he thought Erskine was going to throw his knife at him. But he said angrily instead, "How would *you* like to spend thirty years in a sewer? Know it's been that long. Rest of them think it's thirteen years. *Know* it's been done twice now! Flaming muddle or flaming fraud. Don't care which. You lot stay here till I find out how. Send a van to get your mum later." He clicked his fingers, and Howard was bundled away again. Scared as he was, Howard was interested to hear that Erskine still spoke in the same way. Evidently he had not had to do much pretending to be the Goon. A great Goon roar followed him, above the sploshing of his boot. "Write *me* some words! Or stay and rot!"

They were bundled on, to a hole in one of the odd-shaped mounds. They were pushed up an earthy passage inside, where the way was half-blocked by a new-looking metal door. Here they were each given a sharp shove, so that they stumbled on into the space beyond. And the metal door was shut behind them with an easy, oiled, grating sound followed by a booming click. The door had no handle on the inside.

Howard sat down on the nearest pile of rubble and emptied out his boot. It was obsessing him by then. The space they

175

were in was bare except for piles of stone and earth which had been made by the walls of the place collapsing. One mound of rubble sloped nearly up to the roof. At the top of it was a small gray space of daylight. Howard twisted around to look up at it as he shook the last drops from his boot. It was blocked by a rusty iron grating. The ceiling above was made of old cobbles and slightly arched.

"Yucky!" said Awful. "That boot smells foul!" It did. It was the same smell that had come off the Goon in whiffs when he first arrived.

"I think this is part of the old castle," Quentin said, looking around. "Possibly even the dungeons. Do you think our friend means us to stay here forever? I suppose we shall find out." He and Awful sat on piles of rubble, too. Nobody said anything else for quite a time. Nothing happened. The damp earthiness seeped into them, and they all shivered.

"Howard," said Quentin at last, "have you any idea what's made him so angry? I thought we treated him quite well, considering."

Howard considered, as slowly and dismally as ever the Goon had. "Some of it has to be about Fifi, I think. And he thinks we know what your words do to keep them here. And he seems to have worked out that it's Venturus doing it. But I still don't see what's made him so mad."

"I did notice," Quentin said glumly, "that he always kept out of the way when Archer was around. I thought it was respect or something. But now I see that he didn't want Archer to know he was sitting in our house, making his own investigations all this time."

"Archer knew, stupid!" Awful said. "He watched through the light bulbs. The Goon didn't want Archer to come in and say, 'Hello, Erskine' and let *us* know. He's mean and sneaky! I hate him now!"

Howard knew exactly how Awful felt. He felt cheated and betrayed. It was worse than Dillian. The Goon had seemed to want them to like him, and he had ended up almost being a

176

friend. And all the time he had been so helpfully taking Howard and Awful and Quentin to see the other members of his family, he had been simply using them to find who was doing what. No wonder he did not want Shine to get hold of them. He wanted them himself. "He stinks!" Howard said angrily. That made Awful laugh. "Well, he does!" said Howard. "Let's see if we can shift this grating."

With a good deal of sliding and scrambling, he managed to get near enough to the top of the mound of rubble to get a hand on the grating. He shook it. As he had rather feared, it was set so solidly into the earthy wall that he could not even rattle it. Awful, of course, would not believe him. She came scrambling up the rubble to shake the grating for herself. Since she was lighter than Howard, she could get right up to the bars. But they would not budge for her either. As for Quentin, he did not even bother to look.

Dad's being a passenger again! Howard thought angrily, standing halfway up the mound, looking down on the bowed shoulders of the red and black checked coat. It really annoyed him sometimes, the way Quentin let life carry him along. Fancy running up a twenty-three-thousand-pound bill for taxes. Fancy writing those words all those years without bothering to find out why! At that moment Howard almost understood why Erskine was so angry. It didn't seem possible! Yet Howard knew that with Quentin it was both possible and true. Provided Quentin was comfortable, provided he could sit at his typewriter in peace, he did not let things bother him. He could even talk about himself as a taxpayer and not notice that he wasn't. Selfish, Howard thought. It almost made him glad that Quentin was not really his father.

That was a thought. Howard slithered down the mound to Quentin. "Why didn't you ever tell me I was adopted?" he said.

Quentin looked up, so obviously unaware of Howard's angry thoughts that Howard felt mean. "Stupid, wasn't it?" he

177

said. "Because we like to think of you as ours, I suppose. It was so extraordinary finding you."

Awful came back down the mound in a sliding rush of cobblestones. "There's a guard outside up there," she interrupted. "I can see his feet."

"Bound to be," said Quentin. "Erskine won't leave much to chance. Looking back over what I know about him, I can see he's a persistent sort of chap, probably as obstinate as I am." He sighed heavily and looked gloomily at the earthy floor between his Wellingtons. "It worries me that he intends to fetch Catriona here," he said. "She's in one of her ill spells."

"He's a bit afraid of her," said Howard. "He may put it off."

"Do you think that Goon is really afraid of anything?" asked Quentin.

"Yes," said Awful. "Archer and Shine and Mum."

"Tell me about how you found me," said Howard.

"Ah, yes," said Quentin. "It passes the time. It was snowing, you see. I remember this coat of mine was new then. I'd bought it with my first money from teaching at the Poly. I'd started teaching there to make ends meet because we were in a really bad patch, me with writer's block and unable to write and Catriona without a proper job. We both were miserable. Catriona wanted children, and we didn't seem to be able to have any. Anyway, I was crossing the Poly forecourt to get to Zed Alley, hurrying because of the snow, when I heard this feeble cawing noise off to one side. I always wonder what would have happened if I hadn't stopped to look. It was you. A baby. I'd never seen a baby so thin and blue and feeble. The doctor we rushed you to said you were barely a day old and must be really tough to have survived at all. I picked you up. You were frozen. I wrapped you in this coat and ran home with you to Catriona. She told me I was a fool not to have gone straight to the doctor, but I think she was glad to have a hand in it, too. She fell for you on the spot, you see. Something about your face, she said, and the shape of the back of your neck. You were in the hospital all the next month, and she

178

visited you every day. And she said all along that we'd adopt you if nobody came forward to claim you—which nobody did. So we adopted you."

Quentin looked up at Howard earnestly, even though he was smiling, too. "That's it really. Honestly, Howard, we've never regretted it. It wasn't just that everything started to go right after we found you—I met Mountjoy and started being able to write again, and Catriona got the ideal job—we *enjoyed* you. You seemed to teach us how to be happy. Do believe that. You found out last night, when you came in looking so upset, didn't you? Did Hathaway tell you?"

"He keeps records and archives," Howard said. "It's one of the things he farms." He was not sure that Quentin's telling him this had made him feel much better. Worse, maybe, because parents who leave you outside the Poly in the snow cannot be very nice people.

"Tell me about how you adopted *me* now," said Awful.

"I can't," said Quentin, "because we didn't. You were born in the usual way. I don't know what we did to deserve you."

Awful knew this, of course, but she had hoped all the same. "It's not fair!" she said. "I want to be adopted, too. Not boring and ordinary."

"I'll give you away willingly," said Quentin. "Particularly if you're going to sulk."

This did not amuse Awful at all. Even when Howard pointed out that this meant she really did descend from Hathaway, she was still annoyed. She went scrambling crossly up the pile of rubble to the grating again, where she relieved her feelings by calling the guard names. "Stinky-poo!" Howard heard her call. "Your feet smell like sewers! The rest of you is brown and sticky all over!"

The guard responded with natural annoyance. The earthy room went dark as he knelt down and put his face to the grating. "If you don't shut up," he said, "you know what I'll do? I'll take this grating out and get you!"

Awful said, "What are *you* doing here?"

Howard took off and was halfway up the mound before the guard had finished speaking. He scrambled up beside Awful as she turned around and called, "It's not a guard! It's Ginger Hind!"

"I know," said Howard. And he called through the grating to Ginger, "Did Shine tell you we were here?"

To his disappointment Ginger Hind said, "Don't be daft! How could she? Followed the bus on my own feet, didn't I?" So that meant there was no way of playing Shine off against Erskine that Howard could see. On the other hand, Ginger seemed ready to talk, as if he wanted to impress Howard after the disgust Howard had shown last night. He said, "Saw you go down that hole. It stood to reason it was a sewer and came out here, so I came over here and listened till I heard you. What are you doing down there?"

Howard took a risk and said, "Erskine locked us up."

Ginger Hind roared with laughter. Then he sat down comfortably with his back to the grating. "Good for Erskine!" he said. Then he said, "Who is this Erskine anyway? Shine talks as if Erskine scares her, and Shine doesn't scare easy."

"You've met him," said Howard. "The Goon. Huge, with a little head."

There was a flurry of light and dark as Ginger hastily threw himself flat outside, with his face close to the grating. "Thanks for the warning!" he said sarcastically, but he said it almost in a whisper. Then he said, "Hey, I thought he was a friend of yours! What's he doing locking you up?"

"He turns out to be Shine's brother," Howard explained. "They hate each other." He was getting somewhere with Ginger; he knew he was. "There are seven of them running this town—"

"And each one is more pernicious than the last!" Quentin called out. He had scrambled halfway up the mound, too, where he proceeded to undo all Howard's good work by making an impassioned speech to Ginger. "You listen to me, my boy. If these seven maniacs are allowed to go on, they'll take

180

over the world before long. They have to be stopped. I ask you, as a citizen of the world—"

"Do shut up, Dad," said Howard. But Quentin paid no attention. He went on and on. Ginger's nose and his black eye pressed against the grating, so that he could stare down at Quentin with sarcastic wonderment. Then he yawned. Howard knew he was going to go away out of sheer boredom any minute, and their only chance of getting out of here would be gone. *"Shut up, Dad!"* he bellowed.

Quentin noticed that Howard really meant it. He stopped. "Your old man likes the sound of his own voice, doesn't he?" Ginger said. "See here. What you said last night about Shine. It bothers me. I do what she says because I respect her—or I thought I did, till you went and said that! You didn't mean she tried to put a hex on your mind, did you?" He said it coaxingly. He wanted Howard to say it was just one of those things you said. It had obviously been worrying him a lot.

"Sorry," said Howard. He felt as mean to Ginger as he had just been to Dad. "She did. It was like arm wrestling, sort of." And he did his best to describe the almost indescribable way thoughts from Shine had come flooding through his head and beating down his resistance.

He was helped in describing it because Ginger evidently knew exactly what he was talking about. Before he had got very far, Ginger's head was nodding angrily and his face was turning bitter and disgusted. "The fat *cow!*" he said. It was hard to tell whether he despised himself or Shine more. "Yes, you're right. That was it. That's just it. Only with me there was a lot about how marvelous Shine was. Worship Shine. Fat cow! I hate being used! OK. Want me to get you out of there?"

"Please!" all three of them called up, and Howard at least felt meaner still, because they were using Ginger now.

"Hang on while I find something to heave on this grating with," Ginger said. His face moved out of sight, and the rest of him, very cautiously, slid away.

The next few minutes were nerve-racking. It could be that

181

Ginger did not intend to come back. It could be that Erskine would spot him. And where they had been convinced before that Erskine was not going to come near them for hours yet, they now expected him to come bursting through the metal door any second. Quentin labored his way to the top of the mound, and they all three stood under the grating, jittering.

"Do you think he's not going to come back?" Quentin whispered more than once.

Ginger came back with a long iron bar and a stout old can to pivot the bar on. "Make it a proper lever," he explained to Howard as he wedged the bar among the holes of the grating.

"Yeah. Good thinking." Howard agreed, because it was.

Ginger actually shot him a sort of bruised smile as he crawled away to the other end of the bar. Then, to judge by the grunt and the squawk of metal, Ginger threw his weight, stomach down, over the other end of the bar. The can crunched, slowly. Metal chippings, rust, and earth spit down on Howard, Awful, and Quentin. The grating juddered as Ginger jiggled it. The earthy walls around it heaved. Ginger swore and grunted again. And the grating came out, together with a lump of wall that would have brained Quentin if Howard had not pulled him out of the way.

Howard blinked stuff out of his eyes and heaved Awful out of the ragged hole left by the grating. He scrambled out. But it took him and Ginger, each kneeling and hauling on an arm, to get Quentin squeezed through the space.

"Keep down!" Ginger panted as they dragged.

Howard ducked in a hurry. He knew now why Ginger had been crawling or lying flat. The mound they had been in was low on this side. He could see the incinerator and the metal sheds with the lines of rubbish vans if he knelt upright. There were people in yellow coveralls wandering about near the vans. He kept his head down and pulled.

Quentin came out with a rubbly rending and without most of the back of his red and black checked coat.

"Come on. Run for it!" said Ginger.

182

They scrambled up, bending over, and ran, out across the weedy field of bricks, toward the nearest khaki shed. Howard's left boot was still wet. He could hear his feet go *splart*-thump, *splart*-thump, as he ran, with the occasional *splunch* when he jumped a pile of bricks or slid down a sloping place. He could hear his father gasping like a dying whale. And horribly soon, he could hear faint shouts behind, followed by the grumbling of heavy engines.

Their heads all turned at the sound. Two rubbish vans and a big yellow sewage tanker were on the move, drawing out of the lines and turning to come after them. Yellow-clad people were racing to jump on the backs of the vans. They put their heads down and pelted on across the field. Quentin's gasps filled the air.

By the time they reached the nearest shed the vans and the tanker were a third of the way across the field and Quentin was finished. There was no hiding place in the shed. Vandals had smashed enough doors and windows to show them it was bare inside. They hurried on around the shed, where Quentin simply stopped. He leaned one hand on the khaki wall and fought to breathe. His face was white and wet. Awful's face was scarlet, and she was clutching a stitch in her chest.

Ginger and Howard looked at each other. "What do we do?" said Ginger. "Your old man's had it for running."

Howard looked about. On the side nearest the road the sheds stood in a muddled cluster. On the other side they were spaced out, with weedy gaps in between. He pointed away from the road. "I'll go that way and draw them off. You take Dad and Awful and hide near the road until they've gone after me. I'll come find you when I've lost them. Where will you be?"

Ginger nodded, knowing Howard could run fast. "I might as well take them to my house. Twenty-six Spode Close. New Estate. OK?"

"OK," said Howard. And since the sound of heavy engines was now rather near, he set off running at once.

183

He was still perfectly fresh. The only thing that annoyed him was the *splart* of his wet boot every time he trod on it. *Splart, splart, splart*, it went because he was sprinting hard so that the people in the vans would see him first, before they got around the shed and saw Ginger and the others. And see him they did. Howard heard a hooter blaring and caught a sideways glimpse of the three huge yellow shapes swinging around to follow him before he flung himself into hiding behind the next shed.

He made off again before the vans had come into sight. It was almost fun. The sheds were spaced over a lot of ground, with tall weeds and derelict machines in between. Howard crouched behind a great rusty machine and looked back, beyond the three yellow vehicles lurching around and around the shed he had just been at, to the place where he had left Ginger. There was no one there. Ginger must have made it safely with Dad and Awful to the sheds near the road. Howard felt light of heart and set off to lead the rubbish vans a dance. *Splart*-thump, *splart*-thump, he went, not too fast, across the bushy space to the next shed, bending down as if he thought he was keeping hidden. Behind him the blare of hooters and the roaring of engines told him they had seen him and were coming after.

Howard laughed as he went off his very fastest, *splart, splart, splart*, intending to hide behind the next shed while they searched that one. But they did not stop to search it. They came on and spread out, grumbling in a line, to cover as much ground as possible. Howard was forced to go on running, never quite out of sight, through weeds, around rusty machines, and alongside old sheds. Help! he thought. I forgot Erskine's not stupid! And he *splart-splarted* for dear life now, right through the old industrial estate, with the three vans grinding close behind.

He burst out through a clump of tall weeds to find nothing but a bricky field ahead, with a road and distant houses beyond that. With nothing to do but keep on running, Howard ran, *splart*-thump, out across the field. Behind him he could tell by

184

the violent roaring that the tanker at least had stuck in the weeds. But the two rubbish vans were thumping their way through and lurching out into the field after him. Howard knew he would be caught soon unless there was a miracle.

"Hathaway, send me a bus!" he panted as he ran. "Hathaway, send a *bus*!" It was a stupid waste of breath, but it had seemed to work when Awful said it.

And there, to Howard's amazement, was the long red shape of a bus, coming from beyond one distant row of houses and making its way toward the lonely bus stop at the edge of the field. Howard set his teeth and pelted, *splart, splart, splart*, toward the bus stop. The people in the rubbish vans, seeing what he was doing, sounded their hooters again and put on speed. Luckily, because of all the bricks in the field, they were not able to drive flat-out. But Howard could tell from the clattering and rattling behind him that they were coming as fast as they dared. By this time Howard was gasping like Quentin. His chest hurt, and his eyes blurred; but he kept on running, feeling in his pockets for a bus fare he did not think was there.

"Archer!" he gasped. "Money! Quick!"

His fingers closed on a piece of paper that felt like a pound note. He dragged it out as he ran, and it was a pound note. Another miracle. The bus, meanwhile, drew to a stately halt at the bus stop and stood there. Howard waved the pound note at it feebly, almost too breathless to lift his arm. And the driver, instead of driving away, opened the bus doors to show he had seen. By this time the rubbish vans were only yards behind. One veered off sideways to cut Howard off from the bus. But it veered too sharply, or it must have hit a brick. It spun around sideways and stopped. Men in yellow jumped off the back and ran to catch Howard, but Howard had just time for a last desperate *splart, splart* to the bus door. He flung himself up the steps and flung the pound note to the driver. The driver shut the doors and drove off, rattling change down for Howard as he drove.

Howard flopped into a seat, wrestling for every breath he

185

took, and sat with his head turned backward to watch the rubbish van that was still moving lurch up onto the road to follow the bus. The men were running back to the one that had stopped, and it was turning to follow the first van. Behind that the sewage tanker was lumbering across the field to join in the chase, too. But here the bus went in among the houses, and Howard lost sight of them all.

The bus driver must have wanted his lunch. He roared through the outskirts of the town so fast that Howard began to hope he had escaped. But it was Saturday. As they got farther into town, there were lines at the bus stops and traffic in the roads. The bus stopped for each line, and in between it went much more slowly. At the fifth stop Howard saw the rubbish vans in the distance behind. At the sixth stop they were nearer. And by the seventh stop, not so far from the Town Hall, they were nearer still. Howard could see now why they were coming so fast. The two vans were driving side by side, nearly filling the road, with the tanker racing along behind. The traffic going the other way was in chaos. Cars were having to go on the sidewalks to get out of their way.

Well, Howard thought, there have been two miracles now. It's worth a try. "Dillian!" he said. "Dillian, send the police to stop those rubbish vans. Please!"

A lady who had just sat down beside Howard stared at this boy talking to himself, but Howard barely noticed. He was too busy craning back to watch the big yellow vans gaining on the bus. They passed the Town Hall, and nothing happened. Beyond, in High Street, there was full Saturday traffic, and the bus crawled. I'd better get off and run! Howard thought. But the bus doors were shut because the next stop was around the corner in Corn Street. The rubbish vans were plowing through the traffic like a solid yellow wall, and they were now only fifty yards away.

Then, to Howard's huge relief, he heard the nee-nawing of sirens. Low blue lights flashed past the bus windows. Howard was not the only person who stood up to watch a line of police

186

cars go howling down on the rubbish vans. "I should think so, too!" someone said. "I don't know what those drivers think they're doing!" The bus started to move fast again as the person spoke. It was swinging around the corner as the police cars drew up across the road in front of the great yellow vans. One van had trouble stopping. Howard glimpsed it mounting the sidewalk. The door of its cab came open, on the side away from the police cars. Just as the bus went right around the corner, Howard saw a huge long-armed shape with a tiny head swing itself out of the cab and leap down on the sidewalk.

Only one person Howard knew was that shape. The moment the bus stopped in Corn Street, Howard dived for the door. He was out and running down the nearest side road before he had time to think. But fast as he was, his eye caught a sight of a vast, small-headed figure whirling around the corner into Corn Street. And the chances were that Erskine had also seen him. He was awfully close.

Howard tore down the small winding street. His boot had dried a bit on the bus, so that it now went *spuff, spuff, spuff*; but he was tired, and his legs ached. He knew he was not going nearly fast enough to get away. On the other hand, he was running right into Shine Town, with the disco quite near and the cathedral towering above. He forced himself on around the corner, *spuff*-thump, *spuff*-thump, and thought that, yes, well, it was worth another try. The first three miracles had probably happened quite naturally, but Howard could not think of anything else to do.

"Shine!" he panted out. "Torquil! Stop Erskine for me! Hold him up somehow at least!"

He ran around another corner, uphill into Palace Lane, going slowly now, *spuff*-thump, *spuff*-thump, and aching all over. The thing that had said "MITER CLUB, GAMBLING" that night was indeed the bishop's palace, he saw. That must have been Shine's idea of a—

A terrific noise broke out behind him. Howard jumped and ran looking over his shoulder. But whatever was happening

187

was around the corner, out of sight. Some of it sounded like a brass band, some of it seemed to be disco music, and some again was plain shouting and yelling. People ran downhill past Howard, either to join in or to see what was going on. The noise got louder still. Now Howard distinctly heard several sharp cracking bangs. Gunshots? Oh, no! Howard thought. Fireworks. But when the next bang came, he knew it was a gun.

"Dillian!" he gasped, pounding uphill. "Police! Shine's overdone it!"

Sure enough, almost at once, the noise was increased by the nee-nawing of police cars. And Erskine had still not come around the corner into Palace Lane. There was no one in the lane except Howard by now.

That proves it! Howard thought. It really does! And he tried not to think of Erskine and particularly not to think of Erskine as the Goon. He went on at a reasonable jog trot, *spuff*-thump, *spuff*-thump, past the cathedral and into the park. And he thought as he jogged: The one he had to find was Venturus. The only possible thing to do was to find Venturus; he was the one responsible for all this. But he had no idea how you found someone who lived in the future. Apart from a few inklings, that was. Come to think of it, he had a whole cluster of inklings: If even Shine joined in to help him against Erskine, then—But for some reason, he did not want to think about that. He found himself running home instead.

Hathaway's men had done a marvelous job in Upper Park Street. It was now smooth and black and level, with not a cone or a drill in sight. There were one or two places where the painted word "ARCHER" still stared at him from a wall; but people had been cleaning that off, and there was hardly any other sign of the trouble of the past two weeks. Howard spuffed swiftly along and dived into the passage of number 10. He burst open the kitchen door.

Catriona sprang up from the Goon's usual chair. She still looked ill. "Howard! What's the matter? Where's Awful?"

"Where's the car?" panted Howard.

"By the Poly," said Catriona. "Why?"

"Blast!" said Howard. "We'll have to hope he's followed me through the park if Shine didn't get him. Come on, quick! You have to get out of here before Erskine gets here!"

"Erskine?" said Catriona. But she was efficiently seizing her coat and her bag as she asked.

Howard took hold of her elbow and hurried her to the front door. He did not want Erskine to trap them in the side passage. "The Goon," he explained. "He was Erskine all along. And he's howling mad for some reason, and he may still be following me. He locked us up, and when we got out, he chased me right across town." The road was empty. Howard dragged Catriona out of doors and down toward Park Street.

Catriona dragged in return and hung back. "Locked you up? Chased you? Just you?" She was horrified. "Howard Sykes, *what* have you done with Awful? I told you not to leave her alone!"

"She's all right. She's with Dad," Howard said, pulling Catriona frantically toward Zed Alley.

"I don't count Quentin!" Catriona said. "He's far too absent-minded. *You're* the one I trust, and I told you to look after Awful."

"I *am* looking after her!" Howard shouted, exasperated. "She's with a friend in his house, and so's Dad. We'll go in the car and get them."

"Oh, I see." Catriona began at last to hurry as fast as Howard wanted her to. Howard paused to listen at the entrance to Zed Alley. It would be a nightmare to meet Erskine coming up it. But he could not hear footsteps, so he took the risk and hurried Catriona into it. "What a day!" Catriona gasped. "And Fifi still hasn't turned up. I didn't know whether to worry about Fifi or not. I suppose she's with Archer. What do we do when we've got Quentin and Awful? Drive somewhere where Erskine can't come? Oh, Howard, I used to *like* the Goon!"

"He was just pretending," said Howard. "I think we'll have

189

to find Venturus. He's the one. He's probably worse than Shine even. The trouble is, he lives in the future."

"I don't believe it!" Catriona said as they came out into the Poly forecourt. Howard thought she meant Erskine was there and jumped back into the alley. But although there were a number of people about, none of them was huge and small-headed. "No. I *can* believe anything of that family," Catriona said, hastening toward the car.

Howard understood what she meant and hurried after her. "Mum," he said, while she was unlocking the car, "where would you live if you lived in the future?"

"Goodness knows," said Catriona. She got in behind the wheel. Howard heard her say, above the noise of the starter, "In some house that hasn't been built yet, I suppose."

Light dawned on Howard. Venturus farmed education. He turned slowly to look across the forecourt to where the line of big yellow diggers stood in front of a building made mostly of steel girders and scaffolding. There was now a noticeable door-way in the middle, made of concrete blocks. It all fitted. It fitted with the way Shine, Torquil, Hathaway, and Archer all lived so close together. It fitted with the inklings in Howard's head.

"The door's unlocked," said Catriona. "Get in."

Howard bent down to the open window. "Dad and Awful are at Twenty-six Spode Close," he said. "It's in the New Estate. When you've got them, drive over and see Auntie Mildred or something—somewhere right away from here anyway—and don't come back till you hear it's safe."

"Aren't you coming then?" said Catriona.

"No. I'd better find Venturus before Erskine arrives," Howard said. He stood back. "Thank you for having me—adopting me, I mean."

"Oh, Howard!" said Catriona. "Listen—" Howard was already running, *spuff*-thump, toward the diggers, and did not hear her shouting.

CHAPTER FOURTEEN

Howard slipped among the parked diggers and stood looking through the half-made concrete door. It seemed unlikely, now that he looked, that anyone could live here. Inside, among the big girders, there was an empty space with a floor of yellow mud. There was nothing in the mud but puddles and trenches for drains. Well, Howard thought, if it didn't work, he would simply have to try walking into every half-built building in town.

He squared his shoulders and walked through the unfinished door.

Instantly all sorts of very queer things happened. Halfway through his first step, the doorway was complete around Howard—high and grand-looking. Before his left foot came down beyond it—*spuff*—he seemed to be pushing his way through a heavy swing door made of glass. It took an effort.

Howard pushed it open enough to slide around and put his right foot down beyond. To his surprise, that foot was not in a boot but in an old brown training shoe with yellow laces. Ahead of that foot in its trainer, he could see, rather mistily, a flight of four shallow marble steps leading up among the scaffolding.

He went up the first step. His left boot did not go *spuff* there because it was no longer a boot, but a neat shoe at least two sizes larger than the boot. It took quite a push to get himself and his right foot onto the second step. The training shoe on that foot was now black, and so were the jeans on the leg above it. The scaffolding around him had gone misty by then, and the earth floor had vanished. In a milky, transparent way he could see something like a marble temple stretching ahead. The third step took an even bigger shove, and the foot that came down on that step was larger still, in an old tennis shoe, with ragged blue jeans above it. At the fourth step, which took a real heave to get up onto, the marble temple looked almost real and Howard could hardly see the girders. His right foot came down on that step in a spongy, bootlike shoe and a tight white trouser leg. And it was the same kind of shoe and white trouser on the other leg when he forced himself forward on to the marble floor.

The temple was solid around him, vast and high and empty, with a humming somewhere in the distance. Venturus, it seemed, lived somewhere even larger than Dillian or Archer. Howard took a very much easier step forward and nearly fell over. He had simply not realized how big he had grown. He spread long arms for balance and looked dizzily down long white-trousered legs. He was, he saw, wearing a loose quilted coat, like a futuristic version of Hathaway's robe. And he must have been more than seven feet tall.

"I suppose I have to grow up to get to the future," he said out loud. His voice rang deeply around the marble spaces and made him jump. He decided that the best way to walk was by looking straight ahead. So he began balancing in careful strides down the long marble hall, silent in his spongy shoes.

There was a big mirror between the second set of marble pillars. Howard saw it out of the corner of his eye and thought the person there must be Venturus. But when the figure in the mirror whirled around to face him, he understood and tried to laugh.

Someone had painted a message on the mirror in large white letters: "THIS IS THE SECOND TIME!"

"I know it is," Howard murmured in his deep bass voice. "Hathaway, Archer, and Erskine all know, too."

He looked at himself with interest in the mirror behind the letters. "I wouldn't have known this was me!" he heard himself saying. Fully grown-up, he seemed to be built on the same huge lines as Erskine, except that—mercifully!—his head was the right size for the rest of him. His eyes were the same, but his face was so much thinner that it looked quite different. And the fringe he had been so pleased with was gone. He wore his hair longish and swept back in a way he did not care for at all.

"Looks horrible," he muttered, rumpling his hair about with a large hand, and turned away. "I wonder how big this place is." He found he wanted to keep speaking. Even his unfamiliar voice was better than the humming silence of this vast, empty hall. Howard walked on down it, unsteadily learning to balance his height, and thought he did not care for the place at all. If you judged by his house, Venturus must be as cold, proud, and unfeeling as the rest of the family put together. "He probably is, if he's stuck the rest of them here while he conquers the world," Howard said to himself.

He came upon proof of this at the end of the hall. Here there was a round antechamber with two vast arched doorways leading off it. On the floor of this round space was a heap of typewritten paper, some of it old and yellow, some of it white and new—a surprisingly small heap. Thirteen times eight thousand words did not make much more than two hundred pages. Venturus must have been using some other way for the first thirteen years, Howard thought, as he stooped unsteadily the long way down and picked up a page at random. He read: "Today all the rabbits started eating meat, a fact which was not noticed straight away. . . ." So this was where all Quentin's words ended up. It did not look as if Venturus were doing much with them.

Howard dropped the paper back on the heap and stepped around it to look through the left-hand archway. There was a huge domed marble room beyond, completely empty. Wondering what possible use such a room was to anyone, Howard scuffed past the papers to look through the right-hand arch. The humming seemed to be coming from there. He stopped in the doorway with a gasp of admiration.

It was another domed marble room, but this one had a spaceship in the middle of it. The spaceship was the most elegant thing Howard had ever seen. It had a sheeny surface of some substance Howard did not know. It was like a slender blue bolt, raised on a gantry to point at the domed roof. Howard could see the dome was designed to open and let the ship out, and he could see the ship was designed to take off under its own power, without a rocket to lift it into orbit. So there really must be some form of antigravity, he thought. It made him realize for the first time that he was truly in the future.

The ship was obviously not quite finished. Robots were working on it—not man-shaped robots, but things like elegant little diggers or metal giraffes. They were working as busily as people at all sorts of tasks. Perhaps they were being controlled from some of the banks of installations around the walls of the room. Howard looked around at the readouts, small lights, and ranks of little square buttons. Like the queer robots, they all were strange and compact and most beautifully designed. Venturus had technology here that made Archer's look like flint axes.

Since none of the robots seemed to notice him, Howard tip-

194

toed wonderingly in to have a closer look at the ship. It made him feel odd to be the only human being in the place.

The nearest robot trundled up to him. Howard froze. But the machine only spoke to him, in a voice like a mouth organ. "Advise not to enter ship," it said. "Final tests entail vacuum in interior."

"Is it nearly finished then?" Howard said, almost whispering with wonder.

"Takeoff planned for twenty-one hours tonight," the machine mouth organed. After that it ducked a metal scoop politely and trundled back to its work.

Then where is Venturus? Howard wondered. He went to look at the nearest control console. Since the robots took no further notice of him, he daringly put out one of his new large hands and pressed a square button that was third in a row of six. A piece of the wall above lit up and formed into a picture of Dillian. She was sitting by an arrangement of flowers near the fountain in her home, and she had her blankest, angriest look. There were earphones over her golden hair with a microphone attached. "Darling," said her voice, from a grille below the buttons, "must you always contradict me? I tell you that at least two of my family are about to take our organization over, and you just have to move without me. I want *this* country at least in our hands by tomorrow night."

Rather shaken, Howard pressed another button and found himself looking at Shine instead. She had a smoking gun in her hands and a black eye as bad as Ginger Hind's. She turned to look over her shoulder and shouted, "Where's that boy Hind? I'll murder him! Why has he got to disappear *now*, when we're all ready to go!"

Howard pressed the first button then, sure that he would get Archer. He did. Archer's face glared out of the screen at him, its eyes like blue holes. He was furiously angry. "Get off my screen!" he shouted. And the screen went blank as if Archer had cut a connection.

195

Did Archer know me then? Howard wondered, pressing button number 4. Hathaway. The image on the wall this time was misty and remote, as if even Venturus's technology had found it hard to go back six hundred years or so. Hathaway seemed to be up a tree. Anne and William were balanced on a ladder just below him, and the faces and arms of all the other people in the house were bobbing in and out of view lower down. Everyone was in such fits of laughter that it took Howard a moment to gather that they all were trying to rescue Bess's kitten from the top of the tree.

I was right about Hathaway, Howard thought. But it gave him an uncomfortable feeling of spying. He hesitated before pressing the fifth button, for Torquil, but he still went ahead and pressed it. Torquil seemed to be in the cathedral. He was dressed as a priest this time, in black robes and a white surplice, and he seemed utterly dejected. He was sitting all alone on the steps of an altar, with his hands clasped around his robed knees, just staring. He clearly thought he was private. Even more uncomfortable, Howard hurriedly pressed the last button, telling himself it really was important to know what Erskine was doing.

The picture showed the rubbish pit, with the incinerator in the distance, but there was no sign of Erskine anywhere in it. Then Shine did shoot him, Howard thought, and he was surprised how upset and guilty this made him feel. He was leaning close to the picture, searching the background, in case Erskine was somewhere in the distance, when he heard, quite unmistakably, the distant sound of the glass door thumping open. Venturus was coming.

Howard stabbed the button to turn off the picture and sped in great strides on his new long legs, out of the doorway, and in a long leap across the antechamber over Quentin's words, to where he could lean around a pillar and look down the marble hall.

It was Erskine. Erskine was coming up the four steps, lunging up each one, fighting the difficulty, but there was no

196

change in him at all as he came. He was just the same when he reached the top, except that his leather jacket perhaps looked older still. Howard dodged back around the pillar and listened to Erskine striding down the hall toward him, quite unable to think of what to do. If he hid, Erskine would simply stride through the place, the way he had stridden through the Town Hall, until he found Howard. The only comfort Howard could see was that he and Erskine were now more or less the same size.

Erskine came to the anteroom. When he saw the papers, he nodded. They seemed to be what he expected to see. He seemed to expect to see Howard, too. He simply leaned his back against the pillar opposite Howard's, folded his arms, and looked at Howard.

"Set Shine on me, didn't you?" he said. "And Torquil."

"Shine didn't shoot you?" said Howard.

"Missed," said Erskine. He added with satisfaction, "Blacked her eye."

Howard folded his arms and leaned against his pillar, too. "How did you know I was here?"

"Obvious," said Erskine. "Nobody can get here when you're not. You finished now? Or do we go around another thirteen years?"

If Erskine had landed out with a great Goon fist and hit Howard in the stomach, he could scarcely have given Howard more of a shock. He clutched the pillar with both hands and stared at Erskine.

"Ah," said Erskine. "Thought you didn't know. Tried to find out. Then tried to make you see. Almost worked. You came here."

"Thought I didn't know what? What do you mean?" said Howard. He did not want to believe what Erskine seemed to be saying.

"Didn't know much at first," Erskine went on remorselessly. "Just knew it had happened before. Outside town in sewage plant. Remembered. Went to see Archer. Archer played all his

197

phone tappings for 1970. Venturus always good at not being bugged. All Archer had was Quentin Sykes saying, 'Two thousand every quarter day then.' Came around. Didn't even know it was words then. Knew *you*, though, straight off."

"The others didn't," Howard said. "Are you sure?"

"Am sure. Others all grown-up when you were a kid." Erskine grinned and corrected himself. "When you were a kid *first*. Except me and Torquil. Surprised Torquil didn't remember. I did. Only five years older. Worse kid than Awful, Venturus."

I'm Venturus! Howard thought. Oh, no. I can't be! But he knew Erskine was right. There seemed to be a roaring in his mind, bringing with it knowledge and memory that told him that much as he hated the idea, much as he disliked the little he knew of Venturus, Erskine was right. He was Venturus. He hung his head, so that his new longish hair hid his face, and looked down at his spongy shoes, still struggling not to admit it. Almost the only thing he seemed to have in common with Venturus was a passion for spaceships. Yet memory kept coming in, clustering around that spaceship, telling him that the spaceship was the thing that had caused all the trouble. He had wanted a spaceship. He had wanted to go several times better than Archer. For that, he had used his brothers and sisters as a secret weapon, just as Awful used Howard. He had kept them in one spot for twenty-six years. And though that was probably a blessing for the world, Howard—Venturus, that is—knew that he had also made Quentin and Catriona adopt him, not once, but twice, and brought endless difficulties down on them. The reason he did not want to admit it was that it made him so ashamed.

He found himself making a sound that seemed to be a groan.

"Want to explain?" asked Erskine.

Howard—Venturus—looked up to see the Goon face wearing an expession of round-eyed sympathy. That made him ashamed, too. He had not expected sympathy. He deserved that Erskine should go on being angry. He was almost too

198

ashamed to explain, but he admitted wretchedly, "It was my spaceship. I could only get the technology to build it in the future. So I went there. But it was like Hathaway in reverse, and I found out the hard way, like Hathaway did. I stayed a year and a half, setting up the machines and programming them to build it. When I walked out of the door, I must have turned into a baby on the spot—only I didn't know I had, of course. That was the first time. I didn't realize what had happened until I was thirteen and my powers had started to come back. I seemed to remember things rather better that time because I walked in here at once and understood straightaway. That was what kept the six of you pinned down, of course."

Erskine frowned. "Don't understand."

The explanation lay a hundred and thirty-odd years back, behind a smear of blinding anger, long before their parents had turned them out. Howard-Venturus sighed. Erskine would not like remembering this. They all had been so angry with their parents. All the same, when you looked at the seven of them, you could hardly blame their parents. And when Venturus, the precious seventh child, who was supposed to have twice the gifts of the others, had grown up to be as bad a lot as the other six, they had had enough and turned them all out.

"Our parents," he said. "Don't forget you were all much older than I was and I was their precious seventh child. You all had come into your full powers and could do anything you liked, while I was still just an unprotected child. So they laid it on you: 'Look after Venturus. Don't let Venturus go off on his own.' It was just the same as me and Awful really. Catriona said this afternoon, 'Don't go away and leave Awful,' and I almost understood then, but not quite. But being our parents, they laid it on you really strong. As long as I was a child, without my powers, you couldn't go away and leave me. I think it was strong enough to come down through Hathaway to Catriona and Quentin. They did adopt me both times."

Erskine nodded. "Did it for me, too. Forgot."

199

"That's why they all had to help me against you just now," said Howard-Venturus. "But I really didn't know."

Erskine simply nodded again. He did not seem angry about it. And they both went thoughtful for a minute. Howard-Venturus was remembering the way he had indeed been worse than Awful, quite unscrupulously playing on the fact that the others had to look after him, running after them, making them take him anywhere he wanted to go. Erskine and Hathaway had always been surprisingly patient. The others had not.

Presently Erskine reached out a huge boot and stirred the little heap of papers. "What's all this then? Why the second time around? Any point to it?"

Howard-Venturus felt an Archer-like redness sweeping into his face. "You won't believe this," he said. "You probably don't remember. You and Shine got on to me the last time. It wasn't as bad as this time, but it scared me stiff. That's how I started remembering and came back in here. The spaceship should have been ready then. But it wasn't. It was an utter mess. I'd made a mistake in programming the robots. I had to do it all over again." He could have cried, even now, when he remembered the twisted heap of metal he had found instead of the beautiful ship he had been expecting. Thirteen years' work wasted! And his terror when he realized how his brothers and sisters would feel.

"The only thing I could think of was to do the same thing all over again," he explained. "But this time I planned it. I spent a day reprogramming the robots and arranging to pay Quentin and Catriona back for adopting me the first time." It had been a frantic day. He remembered how he had bullied Mountjoy and arranged for Quentin not to pay taxes and set things up so that Mountjoy would from time to time hear his voice over the phone. It had seemed a very generous idea.

"Just to pay them back?" Erskine asked unbelievingly.

"Well, I thought it might put the rest of you off the scent," Howard-Venturus admitted, "if you thought the words were doing it. But I didn't know they'd adopt me twice. I didn't

200

know! I really didn't know that when I went outside and turned into a baby, I was going to take everything back thirteen years with me. I'd no idea! I'd no idea it would be snowing then either. It didn't work out the way I expected at all."

The grin on Erskine's face seemed to say that it served his brother right. Then the grin faded. "Sykes won't like it," he said. "Won't like to think his words don't do anything. Be mad. Thought he knew. Think he did know last time. Think I told him about you." He puzzled a little. "Funny," he said. "Past not the same twice. Remember a bit. Fifi wasn't there last time. Or Awful." He sighed. "Pity I sent that letter about taxes. Mad with you. Mad about Fifi."

"Oh, was that *you*?" Howard-Venturus almost howled. *"Now* what shall we do?"

It was Erskine's turn to look uncomfortable. "Knew it was you keeping us," he said defensively. "Got mad. Didn't seem to be able to tear you to bits. Sent the letter, then took you through a sewer to see how *you* liked it. Didn't like it, did you?"

"No," said Howard-Venturus. He stared the long way down to his spongy boots, wondering despairingly what to do about it all. He hated being Venturus again, really hated it! He could always go out and be a baby again, he supposed. On the other hand, there was his spaceship.

"Two things," said Erskine, "you don't do. Won't stand for either. Don't go off in spaceship. Don't be a baby again." Venturus stared at him, wondering if Erskine read minds. "Stick to you. Make sure you don't," Erskine assured him rather grimly. "Followed you for that."

"I see," said Venturus. "So I just stand here."

"Got yourself in a mess," said Erskine. "Want me to get you out of it. As usual."

This was so like the things Howard said himself to Awful that it made Venturus laugh. "I ought to get out of it myself," he said. "If only I knew how."

"Should . . ." began Erskine. But they were interrupted by

201

an urgent ringing sound, coming from the room where the spaceship was. "What's that?"

"Someone wants me," said Venturus.

Three giant strides took him back to the domed room. Three strides took Erskine there, too. Erskine plainly did not mean to let Venturus out of his sight. Erskine's round eyes went rounder at the sight of the spaceship. While Venturus was searching for the right button—his memory was still hazy—he heard Erskine whistling with amazement at it. Oh, yes. The third red button was flashing. Venturus pressed it, and Dillian's lovely face looked out the wall at him.

"Oh, thank goodness!" she said. "You and Erskine! Venturus, dear, if you could just be a teeny bit easier to find, we'd all be much happier. And Erskine seems to have caught it lately, too. Now listen. Could you both be sweeties and do something about Archer? He's in the most frightful rage and threatening to blow up the town. He's already blown one gas main."

"Can't you deal with him?" said Venturus.

"Darling, I never *could* deal with Archer," said Dillian. "Besides, I'm awfully busy just now, and you two are the only ones Archer ever listens to. Do go. It's his worst rage ever."

Erskine said, "What bit him this time?"

Dillian shrugged. "Oh, Shine's been naughty and kidnapped Archer's young woman."

Venturus and Erskine looked at each other. "Fifi," said Erskine. "All right. We'll go."

"Angels!" Dillian smiled at them and vanished.

Erskine's great fist thudded into the wall where she had been. "Shine!" he shouted. "Get me Shine! Black her other eye!" Venturus had to reach around Erskine to press the right button. Erskine said, "What's Dillian doing? Too busy to see Shine."

"Taking over the country," Venturus answered. Then, as Shine appeared on the wall, he stood back and thought about

202

what he had just so casually told Erskine. This was how his family was. He did not like it.

"Oh, it's you again," Shine said to Erskine. She did not see Venturus. "I've had a bellyful of you today. Have you been getting at that boy Hind? I need him."

"Where's Fifi?" said Erskine.

"You mean Archer's girl?" said Shine. "Torquil's got her. We're trying to keep Archer quiet while we take over the things we want. Take a tip, Erskine. Grab this chance. It's Venturus who's doing this to us. He's posing as a boy. I should have realized the other night, when I tried to take him over and couldn't. But it's just come to me. He's going to be coming into his powers in a week or so. Be ready to move as soon as he does. I am."

"Where's Torquil put Fifi?" Erskine asked doggedly.

"Ask Torquil. Don't bother me now," said Shine, and vanished.

"Get me Torquil!" shouted Erskine.

"Better tell Archer first," Venturus suggested, and reached around him to press the top button. This proved to be a mistake. The wall lit up, but it lit in a storm of blue sparks, which came raining and spitting out of the wall into Erskine' face. Erskine backed away, with his leather jacket smoking. Venturus had forgotten what Archer's rages were like. He put his arm over his face and tried to turn Archer off. His hair sizzled and his skin stung, and the control button, when he reached it, was too hot to touch. He was wrapping his sleeve over his hand to try again when there was a run of blue sparks along the entire communications console, followed by a tremendous bang. The whole thing went dead, in a thick smell of burning.

"Bad rage," Erskine remarked. "Have to see Archer." He set off in great strides, out of the domed room, through the antechamber, and down the hall. He was halfway along it before Venturus caught up.

"Erskine! I can't go! I'll be a baby the moment I go outside!"

203

"Carry you," said Erskine, striding on.

"*Erskine!*" shouted Venturus, setting the echoes ringing. "Honestly, you really are a Goon sometimes! Do you want to spend another thirteen years in the sewers?"

This made Erskine stop. He pondered. "Go with me. Be Howard. Thirteen."

"I only wish I *could!*" said Venturus.

"Seventh child," said Erskine. "Might—"

The glass door thumped. Someone else began fighting his way up the four marble steps. They could not see who it was at first because the lower two steps were so misty. Erskine's round eyes turned to Venturus to know who it might be. Venturus shook his head. All he could see was that the person was quite small to start with. Then, as the figure put a foot onto the third step and heaved up to it, he saw it was Awful—Awful in the act of growing. What she was doing here, he had no idea, except that she was surely looking for Howard. And with that instinct that makes younger ones unerringly follow elder ones, particularly where they are not wanted, Awful had come into the unfinished building, too.

Awful grew as he watched. By the time she was on the third step she was a large, fat schoolgirl in a maroon uniform, with a sudden strong look of Shine. In fact, she was completely a fair-haired version of Shine. She heaved up onto the fourth step. There she was suddenly skinny and Awful again, but nearly six feet tall, with a scornful grown-up look. Then she came up on to the marble floor and became a student about Fifi's age, but much better-looking.

Venturus gaped. He had no idea that Awful would grow up that pretty. Beside him, Erskine's eyes popped, and a great admiring grin spread over his little face.

Awful looked at them both accusingly. "What's happened?" she said. "What have you done to Howard?" Then she looked down at herself. She looked horrified. She gave the well-known earsplitting Awful scream and ran away down the steps again, lunging from one to the other with her arms out and dwindling as she went. Her small, misty shape crashed out of the door and vanished, mistily sobbing.

"Marvelous!" said Erskine. "Chip off the old block!"

"Oh, shut up!" Venturus snarled over his shoulder. He was already racing after Awful. Awful had not recognized him. That made him feel worse even than discovering he was Venturus. He came to the marble steps and tried to bound down them as if they were ordinary steps. But it was even harder going down than it had been coming up. He had to lunge with his hands out, like Awful. And because he was thinking of nothing but getting to Awful at once and proving to her that Erskine had not eaten him—or whatever it was she thought— he made the right strange adjustment in his mind, not even noticing that he did it. He threw himself out through the half-built doorway as Howard again, and his left boot went *spuff* on the mud as he went.

"Howard!" Awful shrieked joyfully. She was sheltering between two of the diggers with Ginger Hind. Howard saw why. He had to put one arm up again. It was raining slightly, and Archer was using the wet air to express his rage most spectacularly. It was like coming out into a fireworks display. The lights in the Poly were flashing on and off. Sparks were pouring from all the outside lights, spitting blue and orange. And all the overhead wires were streams of running fire.

"Keep clear of the metal!" Howard called anxiously.

"What do you take me for?" Ginger called back. He slapped the big black tire he and Awful were leaning against.

Howard ducked and dodged. A seeming bolt of lightning lashed from the girders and sizzled in a puddle beside him. Archer was not supposed to hurt him, but Howard ran to shelter beside Ginger and Awful all the same. He remembered Archer and his rages now. "What are you doing here?" he said. "You said you'd take them to your house."

"I did. But they worried about you," said Ginger. "We all came back to look for you."

Erskine came out through the unfinished door. He must

205

have made the strange adjustment, too. His leather jacket looked slightly newer, and it was not singed anymore. Ginger backed away. Awful screamed all the rudest words she could think of. Erskine simply stood, surveying Archer's fireworks. "Better get to Archer," he said to Howard. "Remember still?"

"Yes," said Howard. "Be quiet, Awful. It's OK, Ginger. But how can we? The banks are shut."

"Show you," said Erskine. "Borrow this digger? Come under you really."

"Of course," said Howard. He looked up at the monster yellow machine towering over them and felt rather strange about it.

Erskine swung into the cab of the digger in one ape stride. As Howard swung up after him, Awful clung to the big tire and called up righteously, "Ginger and me have to come, too! Mum told you not to leave me." Erskine grinned.

Well, Howard thought, since Archer was not allowed to hurt him, the digger was probably the safest place in town at the moment. "All right," he called. And without thinking, he leaned around Erskine and started the digger. Its engine coughed and began trembling with mighty chugging.

"Ahem!" Erskine shouted through the noise. "Powers coming on?"

They were, too, Howard realized. As Awful and Ginger crammed into the cab beside him, and Erskine cocked up the scoop of the digger and sent it grumbling at top speed to the main gate of the Poly, Howard sat investigating the strange feelings unfolding inside him. It was not just the memory of the things he could do as Venturus. These feelings were new and growing, a little blurred and crumpled still, as if they were not quite sure of their final form, but they were strong. Howard was surprised how strong. No wonder the whole family just stretched out and took things if they wanted them. Beside those feelings, ordinary people just seemed feeble.

The metal of the gate flashed sparks as the digger chugged through. Erskine turned into the street, which was drenched in

206

raining blue sparks, and then, with an expert twist of the wheel, swerved into the park. They chugged straight across the park, in Erskine's usual way, through hedges and across beds of orderly tulips. There were a lot of people in the park, who all hurried out of the digger's way. They were surprisingly cheerful about it, and some of then even cheered. Howard understood why when Erskine deftly wove them out into the streets near the cathedral, under spitting, worming sparks from wires and lights again, and they could see out over the town. The whole town was a fireworks display, covered in a loom of bluish light, jetting and jerking spurts of white and yellow fire from every aerial. There were balls of yellow flame running down the cathedral spire. People had come to the park to be safe. And since the digger belonged to the Council, everyone thought it was on its way to mend the electrical fault. Well, in a way it was.

As they went downhill beyond the cathedral, there was a big explosion somewhere. They heard it even above the chugging of the digger. Erskine jerked. "Gas main," he said. "Blew a water main with it. Now I *am* annoyed."

So was Howard. People could be getting hurt or killed while Archer expressed his feelings. He was glad when he heard, faintly through the digger's noise, the sirens of fire engines. "Who farms the fire brigade?" he asked.

"Share it with Dillian," said Erskine, twitching the wheel to send the digger swerving through somebody's private parking lot. "Dillian does a careful job."

Though Erskine said this grudgingly, Howard knew he was right. Dillian was very conscientious. That was the trouble with her. Any country Dillian got to rule would have no chance to do anything Dillian did not want. She would think of everything. Now his powers were coming on, she might be doing just that by next week. By next week Shine, Archer, and Torquil would be trying to grab their shares. I shall have to be a baby again, Howard thought. And what's Erskine going to be doing?

207

The parking lot was almost empty. As Erskine rumbled the digger among the few cars there, Howard noticed that one of them was Archer's Rolls. Ahead was a huge blank-ended building, and that was surely the back end of Archer's workshop. Erskine lined the digger up with the blank wall. He lowered the scoop halfway. "Emergency entrance," he said. "Keep down." He put the digger into lowest gear and crept at the wall, roaring and shaking like an earthquake on wheels. There was an almighty crunching, cracking, and shrieking of metal. Erskine spread his great hands across his head and leaned sideways, squashing Howard, Awful, and Ginger down on the seat. None of them saw what happened. Everything for a few seconds went judder, judder, roar, roar. The digger stood still and shook.

Erskine sat up again. "That fetched him," he said with satisfaction. He ducked in a hurry. Fire and sparks exploded around the digger in clouds.

CHAPTER FIFTEEN

The fire cleared just as they all were quite sure they were going to be roasted. They sat up, sweating, and looked through rolls of smoke to find the yellow paint of the digger was brown and blistered. Its scoop was shoved some of the way through the wall of the building. But the wall was no longer blank. There was now a door where there had been no door before. Archer came out through it.

"How dare you knock down my house!" he shouted. He jumped onto the scoop of the digger and came running up the metal to the cab. He was so angry that his face did not look like a face. It was more like a white mask with blue eyeholes. "Oh, it's you!" he said to Erskine. His voice grated through the cab. "I thought you were Venturus. What do you think you're doing in this thing?"

"Use them, too," said Erskine. "Dig drains. Talk to you."

"Go away!" Archer shouted, putting his face to the glass opposite Erskine's. "I'm not talking to anyone!"

"Have to," said Erskine. "Blew a water main. Want satisfaction. People hurt."

"Who cares!" shouted Archer.

"Me," said Erskine. They glared at each other through the glass.

Howard put a hand to his head, as if he had just had an idea, and swept his fringe back. "Archer!" he called out. "We could get Fifi back for you." Archer turned to Howard. He looked at him, but he did not recognize him. He was too absorbed in his rage. "We'll get her back," Howard called. "But you have to stop all your fireworks first."

"What for?" shouted Archer.

"Won't get her without," said Erskine. "Distracting."

Archer folded his arms and balanced where he was, scowling. "If I stop"—his voice grated—"how do I know you'll get Fifi?"

"We promise," Howard called. "Keep your screen open. We'll get back to you as soon as we've found her."

Archer considered. He seemed to think Howard was honest. He nodded. "All right," he said, as if it were a big favor. It did not seem to occur to him that Howard was speaking like someone with inside knowledge, but it could have been that Erskine did not give him time to consider anymore. The moment Archer nodded, Erskine began swinging the digger around. Its scoop wrenched out of the wall. It turned so quickly that Archer barely had time to jump down. In fact, Howard had a feeling that Erskine actually tipped Archer off.

"Where are we going now?" Awful shouted as the digger rattled back across the parking lot.

"Torquil," said Erskine. "Before Shine gets to know."

As Erskine turned out into the road again, there were signs that Archer was already trying to control his rage. There was not quite such a shower of sparks spraying from the street-

210

lights, and the fires worming along the overhead wires were traveling more slowly. "Won't Shine notice?" Howard called.

"I'll go take her mind off it," Ginger shouted. "On conditions."

They all turned and looked at him. He seemed very determined about something, and he had gone very white. Several hundred freckles, which Howard had not noticed before, showed up bright yellow-brown all over Ginger's face, even mixed up with the purple of his black eye. Erskine glanced up at the wires. The fires there were now traveling in bursts, like fiery beads on a string. He stopped the digger by the curb. It gave giant rattling sobs, like Awful in a temper, and they still had to shout rather.

"What conditions?" said Howard.

"That Archer," said Ginger. "He scares me. Awful here says he wants to run the world. Right?"

"Do it better than Hitler," said Erskine. "Only like this in a temper. Have to keep him happy."

"He flies off like this when he's happy sometimes," Howard said. "You know he does, Erskine."

"Bound to," said Ginger. "He's that type, like my old man. And Shine's another. She's after the world, to. How many more of them are there?"

"Dillian," said Howard. "Torquil."

"And him," Ginger said, nodding his freckled chin at Erskine. "He's one of them, too, isn't he?"

"Only want to stop living in sewers," Erskine said earnestly. "Swear it. Want to travel. Might write a book. Want your dad to teach me how." While Howard was trying not to smile at this idea, Erskine said to Ginger, "Howard's one, too. Knew that, did you?"

"Erskine!" Howard shouted. "I don't want to farm anything!"

Ginger nodded. "I wondered if you were. Now here's the conditions." He swung himself half out of the cab and hung

211

there invitingly. "You stop Archer and the rest, and I'll keep Shine busy. If you don't, I'll set her on you instead."

Howard wanted to protest that no one could stop Archer, let alone the others. But he knew there was a way. He took a deep regretful breath, thinking of twenty-six years of work, elegant technology, superb engineering, stars in the viewscreens, planets circling the stars—all gone. "All right, we'd better get them on my spaceship somehow and send them packing into space."

"Spaceship!" said Ginger. He hung onto the side of the digger and stared at Howard. There was a gleam in the wide good eye and the half-closed bad one that told Howard he was looking at a fellow spaceship addict.

"I'll show it to you," he said.

"I think I believe you," said Ginger. "Many wouldn't. Make that a bargain, and I'll be off to Shine now. See you." He dropped to the ground and went racing off downhill, under the dying showers of sparks.

Erskine started the digger again and drove top speed toward the cathedral. Howard stared sadly ahead. Two days ago Ginger Hind had been out to get him. And now Ginger had, even though he had not meant to. Howard could have cried at losing his spaceship a second time. He barely noticed that the scoop of the digger had come loose after the attack on Archer's workshop. It gave out a loud clanking and made the digger weave from side to side. Howard was irritated to hear great Goon guffaws coming through the noise. Erskine was laughing and pounding the steering wheel with a great fist.

"Made it!" Erskine shouted. "Made you say it! Been working you around to it all along!" He glanced around at Howard. "Now going to make you do it."

Howard lost his temper. He unwisely called Erskine a gorilla and tried to hit him. Erskine stuck out the elbow nearest Howard and held him off with no trouble at all. He swung his other arm around, causing the digger to waltz about in the road, and brought that hand up against Howard's ear. Erskine

212

probably thought of it as a light pat. Howard saw stars. His head rang. Dizzily he saw the stone gateway to the cathedral court coming up at them. Howard would have said that there was barely room for a digger to get through that arch if it was traveling in the normal way, let alone with a loose scoop that was wagging from side to side. But somehow Erskine scraped them through it. There were clangs, and sparks flew that were neither Archer's doing nor in Howard's head. Awful laughed. She was loving this.

As they bounced and clanged across the cobbles in front of the cathedral, there were more sparks, spraying out of the floodlights and hissing in the puddles, but the balls of fire traveling down the spire had stopped. Erskine stopped the digger with a croak outside the west door. He hopped down. Howard slid down after Awful, holding his hot right ear. It was all very well, he thought, but Erskine had not had to be a child three times over, in order to get that spaceship.

"You were Venturus when we both were grown-up, weren't you?" Awful whispered to him as they climbed the steps. "You'll have to do what I say now, or I'll tell Mum and Dad."

Oddly enough, this made Howard feel better, because Awful had recognized him after all. "You try," he said. "Venturus can do things to you."

The cathedral door was locked because of vandals. But this did not bother Erskine. His knife came out, and there was a loud click. The door came open, and he strode in. A small verger in a black robe hurried up to them.

"Emergency," Erskine said to the verger. "Electric. Shorting all over town." And he strode on. The verger looked as if he might have protested if Erskine had been a size or so smaller. Howard felt the heat from his ear spread over his face. It was the Town Hall all over again. He followed Erskine up beween rows of chairs, past some ladies arranging flowers below the pulpit. The ladies looked as if they had wanted to stop Erskine, too. But when they saw the size of him, they suddenly became

213

very busy admiring a lily one of them was holding. Erskine strode on.

Torquil was in a side chapel. Knowing what Torquil was like, Howard thought the chapel ought to be dedicated to Saint Torquil—if there was such a saint—but it was called Dedicated to Private Prayer. Erskine stopped outside the chapel and edged himself, in a guilty, apologetic way, into a handy empty niche in the wall. "You speak to him," he whispered to Howard. Knowing what Erskine was like by now, Howard looked at him suspiciously. Erskine put on his most placating grin. "Torquil hates me," he explained, and he took hold of Awful's arm to stop her from going with Howard.

This made Howard quite sure that Erskine was pushing him into something else, but he could not see what it might be. He unlatched the wrought-iron gate to the chapel and slipped inside. Torquil did not seem to see him. He just sat on the altar steps, clasping his knees, under banners saying "British Legion" and "Mother's Union," staring unhappily at nothing. Howard was surprised. On a Saturday night there ought to be enough music and dancing coming up to keep Torquil happy for a week. And he was ashamed to be there. He could see Torquil wanted to be alone.

That took him back to the views he had had of all six, just now in the future. Torquil was not the only one who had been alone. Archer had been. So had Dillian. So, too, had he, as Venturus, been alone in his great marble temple. Shine had people with her, but they were minions. And Erskine's people in yellow coveralls were minions, too. The only one of them who had proper company was Hathaway, and he had to live in the past to have it. What a strange family they were, all sitting alone, all spying on one another, as if that were the only kind of company most of them knew. Thinking this, Howard began to wonder if his real reason for being a baby twice had much to do with the spaceship at all. It could well be simple loneliness. And he began to suspect what might be wrong with Torquil.

He went up to Torquil and coughed. Torquil looked up.

214

Howard saw him hoist a look of joking superiority onto his face. "If it isn't limpet boy Sykes again!" he said. "Or is bad penny or yesterday's chewing gum a better name? Go away. I want to be alone."

"I've come about Fifi," said Howard.

Torquil put his elbows on the knees of his priestly robes. He sighed. "Archer wants her back, I suppose. Tell him I haven't let Shine at her, but he can't have her."

"Why? Are you using her to help you take over the world?" said Howard.

"I don't *want* to take over the world!" Torquil said irritably, much to Howard's surprise. "I don't see why Archer should either." He stared dolefully into distance and said, as if he had forgotten Howard was there, "I wish I knew what I did want. Nothing seems fun anymore."

"But you told Mum you wanted America," Howard said suspiciously.

Torquil noticed him again. "Of course I did," he said. "I wasn't going to let the others know I was looking for a way to stop them. What was I supposed to do? Go on bended knees to your parents and say, 'Pretty please help me play a dirty trick on the rest of my family'? I've got *some* loyalty."

Howard chuckled. "It might have done more good with Dad. Have you ever thought why you called me limpet boy?"

"I did a good job keeping him obstinate," Torquil said. "And I've got Fifi. But I can't for the life of me think where to go from there. What did you say? I called you that for grabbing sleeves in grubby hands, of course."

"No, you didn't," said Howard. He pushed his fringe out of the way.

"Headache?" inquired Torquil, not at all sympathetically. He stared. His eyes widened, then narrowed, and he shot to his feet, towering over Howard in his black and white robes. Howard found it hard not to back away. Torquil was the most unpredictable one in the family. "Great Scott!" said Torquil.

215

"You're Venturus! And you're a foul little beast! It's *you* keeping us here, isn't it?"

He seemed to be hovering between rage and laughter in a way that was even more unpredictable than usual. Howard did not quite know what to say next. He was quite glad when Awful suddenly appeared at his elbow, having escaped from Erskine somehow. "You helped rescue us from Shine, didn't you?" Awful said to Torquil. "I saw you wink."

"Paint got in my eye," Torquil said haughtily. "I see you've got a limpet of your own now," he said to Howard.

"I'm not a limpet. I'm Awful," said Awful.

"I shouldn't admit it if I were you," said Torquil.

Awful laughed. "He's funny," she said to Howard. "And he's nice underneath. Erskine told me to tell you if I thought he was."

Torquil put his hands on his hips. "Erskine?" he said. There was a moment when Howard thought he was going to tower into a rage as bad as Archer's. Then Torquil laughed and relaxed. "All right, Erskine!" he called. "You can come out now!" He watched in a resigned way as the metal gate clicked and Erskine, at his most sheepish and Goonlike, came sliding around it into the chapel. Torquil began to laugh helplessly. "Erskine! You should just see yourself! What a look!" He pointed at Howard, still laughing. "And look at this! Limpet! I must have known deep down, Erskine. Wherever we went, it always used to come trotting along. Clung like a limpet! But he took care to have his face bashed up the first time I saw him and appear in the half dark the second time." Before Howard could protest that both those things had been accidents, Torquil had sobered up. He folded his arms and looked at Erskine. "What's it all about?"

"Where's Fifi?" said Erskine

"In the crypt," said Torquil. "And Archer's not having her."

"Need her," Erskine explained. "Help to get rid of Archer." Torquil stared. "Shine and Dillian, too," he added placatingly.

Torquil looked around all three of them. "But my dear chil-

216

dren!" he exclaimed. "Those three are fixtures! I've been trying to get rid of them for years, and it's like trying to move the sun and the moon and a rather fat star!"

"Thought you had been," Erskine said, satisfied. He did not quite look at Howard, but Howard knew he wanted him to know that he had been misjudging Torquil for many, many years.

"We're going to try to send them off in my spaceship tonight," Howard said. "Do you want to help?"

"Want to help!" Torquil was so delighted that he hitched up his robe and danced around the chapel. Then he let go of his robes, still dancing, and flung up his arms. The cathedral organ burst into sound and thundered out "Here Comes the Bride," louder even than the television at home. Torquil picked up Awful and swung her around as he danced. "Get rid of Shine! Get rid of Archer! Get rid of Dillian, and everything is fine!" he sang to the tune. Awful was laughing when Torquil finally dumped her on the ground, with another of his quick changes of mood. The organ stopped. "This is going to take careful planning," Torquil said. "Come to the vestry. It's more comfortable there."

He led them across the cathedral in great strides, with his robes rippling. Erskine followed, also in great strides. Howard and Awful followed, in a rapid procession, which the ladies doing the flowers watched disapprovingly, even though the procession looked more official now, with Torquil at the head of it. Torquil ushered them into the vestry, which was a great deal warmer and lighter than the chapel, a plain whitewashed room with cupboards at one end, and hung with black robes and white surplices for choirboys. Here Torquil sat on a damaged chair, Erskine doubled himself on to a worm-eaten pew, while Howard and Awful perched on leaking hassocks, and they discussed what to do.

It took longer than Howard hoped. He found he was thinking anxiously about Ginger before long. He hoped Ginger would be careful. No one had laid it on Shine not to hurt

217

Ginger. This was during the first of their two long arguments, after Awful had pointed out that Fifi would probably turn into an old woman when she went into the marble temple. Erskine, who was evidently feeling vicious about the whole thing, said, "Serve Archer right!" Howard said that was not fair on Fifi. Torquil said he did not think it was fair on Archer either. So that took planning for. And it all ended on a dubious note because no one knew if Howard's powers were far enough advanced to do anything about it.

The second argument was over who was to tell the right lies to Shine and Dillian. Erskine insisted that the only person to do it was Hathaway. "Only one they won't suspect," he said. "Nothing in it for him." Torquil refused to have anything to do with Hathaway. He went proud. He towered on his wobbly chair and said Hathaway had insulted him years ago and they had not been on speaking terms since. Erskine, in reply, went obstinate. There seemed to be a deadlock. Then Torquil haughtily consented to let them ask Hathaway, provided Torquil was not there when they did. Howard thought that would do, but Erskine went more obstinate still. Torquil, even more haughty, said very well, he would be in the room while they asked Hathaway, but he was not going to speak to him. Erskine stuck even at that. Torquil was to ask Hathaway himself, or nobody would. Torquil drew himself even taller and refused. Utterly.

This was hopeless! Howard sighed. "Oh, well, if you're too proud—"

"I am *not* too proud!" Torquil cried, springing up indignantly. "I'll show you!" He strode to the cupboard that filled one wall and flung it open. Inside, there were rows of priestly robes, but hanging among them were a great number of silken garments that did not look priestly at all. Howard recognized one as the Aladdin outfit, and then the Egyptian one, as Torquil rattled them along to leave bare wall. Luckily Torquil was too busy doing that to see the way Erskine turned and winked at Howard.

Awful went over and examined the garments admiringly.

218

"You are vain, aren't you?" she said. "You're far too wicked to live in a church!"

This pleased Torquil. Though his face still had a proud, tense look, there was also a slight smile on it as he seized a bishop's crozier from the corner of the room and pointed it at the wall. "Hathaway," he said.

A square of the whitewashed wall cleared mistily, until it looked like a window. Beyond it Hathaway looked up from reading a book in his study. "Torquil!" he exclaimed. He was so delighted that he fairly shouted it. He threw his book down and jumped up, laughing. "Torquil, this is marvelous!"

The proud look on Torquil's face wavered and broke up into a proper smile. "Hathaway," he said, "I'm sorry." He sounded as if he might be crying.

"Don't be stupid. I was to blame," said Hathaway. "Is something wrong? What's the matter?"

"No, no." Torquil wiped a hand hastily under his nose. "We're getting rid of the three elder ones. We want your help."

Hathaway picked his book up again in order to throw it in the air as he cheered. He was as delighted as Torquil had been, although, Howard soon gathered, it was the thought of getting rid of Dillian and Shine that pleased him most. His face took on a grin as evil as Awful's as Torquil explained what they wanted him to say. "I'll do it!" he said. "How shall I tell you the outcome? To you here?"

Erskine stepped up beside Torquil. "Make you free of drains," he said. "Get me through a drain anywhere I am."

"Ah! Here is the mastermind," Hathaway said laughing. "Erskine, how long have you worked for this?"

Awful began shouting that it was her turn to talk to Hathaway, so that Howard did not quite hear what Erskine answered. But he rather thought Erskine said, "Last thirteen years." After that Awful got right into the cupboard and pressed her face against the windowlike piece of wall, where she talked eagerly until Hathaway stopped her. She came sulkily out and said to Howard, "He says it's your turn now."

219

"Did you know me?" Howard asked, crowding in beside Torquil. This had been puzzling him.

Hathaway nodded. "Not straightaway," he said. "But when I learned you were adopted. Forgive me that I couldn't say. I had given you one shock by telling you that, and it seemed laid on me not to give you another."

"That was our parents," Torquil said, "of honored memory."

"Oh, forget that, Torquil!" said Hathaway. "Come visit me in the past when this is done!"

"I'd love to," said Torquil, and wiped his hand under his nose again.

After that they all went down into the crypt to look at Fifi. The crypt was low and dark and vaulted in all directions. It was so cold there that as they went down the stone stairs, their breaths came out as steam.

"She's quite warm," Torquil said defensively. "I wrapped her in all the bishop's robes."

Fifi was peacefully sleeping on top of a flat stone tomb, tucked in cloth of gold and hand embroidery, with white and purple gowns heaped on top of that. She was perfectly warm. Howard and Awful felt her to make sure.

Erskine looked somberly down at her. "Won't wake her after all," he decided. "Don't trust her not to tell Archer. Big bubble hanging over her with Archer in it." He sighed, but he did not seem nearly as unhappy about it as Howard had expected.

"We could lay it on her to go to the ship," Torquil suggested. "If we both do it, it should take."

Erskine agreed. They stood beside Fifi, Torquil stretching out his crozier, Erskine with his hands on his hips. Their breaths rolled out in clouds, from the effort they were putting in. Nothing seemed to happen—or perhaps a faint silveriness seemed to grow out of the embroidered coverings and gather round Fifi's head. Howard was not sure.

At length Erskine nodded. Torquil lowered his crozier and

220

mopped his face with his priestly sleeve. "If that doesn't take, it never will," he said.

"Archer now," said Erskine.

Back they went in procession to the vestry. The ladies had nearly finished doing the flowers by then. They had grown so used to the procession headed by Torquil passing them that they scarcely looked up this time. Inside the vestry Erskine heaved the worm-eaten pew over in front of the cupboard so that Archer would not see that they were with Torquil in the cathedral. He folded himself into it, and Awful and Howard sat beside him, Howard hastily plastering his fringe to his forehead with both hands, while Torquil stretched his crozier into the cupboard from one side. He snatched it out of sight again as soon as Archer appeared.

Archer was in his scoop, moodily eating a hamburger. Awful's stomach gave a sharp rumble at the sight. "You took your time!" he said angrily. "Where is she?"

They need not to have bothered to be careful, Howard thought. Archer was too wrapped up in himself to notice where they were. "Sorry," Howard said. "It took awhile because it turned out not to be Shine after all. Torquil and Venturus have got Fifi. We don't know where she is at—"

"What!" Archer yelled. "Call me up to say you don't know!" Sparks came spitting out of the wall at them.

"Stop! We know where she's going to be!" Howard shouted. The Aladdin outfit was smoldering. The sparks stopped. Awful leaned forward and rubbed at burning places until they went out. "Venturus," Howard said, "is going to carry Fifi off somewhere in his spaceship, but in order to do that, he's got to bring it into the present. He'll do that at nine o'clock tonight. If you go where he lives then—"

"I'll go there now!" Archer said, angrily.

"No. He's not there. You won't be able to get in," Howard said. It astonished him the way Archer did not recognize him.

221

"And if Venturus sees you, he'll do something else with Fifi. So go there just before nine—"

"You mean I've got to wait!" Archer hurled his hamburger at what was evidently his own screen. For a second they could see nothing but flames. But these flames were inside the wall somehow and did not seem to be hot.

Erskine pushed Howard aside and shouted, "Archer!"

The flames cleared away, showing Archer glowering at Erskine.

"Nine o'clock," said Erskine. "Hide in the ship."

Archer nodded. He even smiled a little. "All right. While I'm at it, I think I'll take the ship myself. I fancy owning a spaceship. Is that all?"

They had not needed any of the explanations they had carefully thought up. "All but one thing," said Erskine. "Sykes family found Fifi for you. Need rewarding. Thirty thousand pounds. Quentin Sykes hard up."

Howard was ashamed of this part of the plan, and he hoped Archer would refuse. But Archer said cheerfully, "Fair enough. Let's make that thirty-five." He swung casually around in his seat and pressed buttons. Howard tried to console himself with the thought that Archer was after all a millionaire, and he would not need money in space. At this a dim memory came to him. Venturus had ordered gold bullion stored aboard the spaceship. He would in a way be paying Archer back. He was feeling better about it as Archer swung his chair back, saying in his pleasantest way, "There. Thirty-five thousand pounds. It'll go through on Monday. Is that all now?"

"Yes," said Erskine.

"Then get out of sight," said Archer. "None of you are beauties."

Torquil rapped his crozier on the back of the pew, and the wall became blank whitewashed stones again. "I think he might have thanked you," he said. "He wasn't to know you weren't doing him a favor."

222

"Never does thank people," Erskine said as he heaved the pew away.

Yes, Howard thought, Quentin was right about Archer. He threw money about, and he never thanked people because he thought everything was his anyway.

"I'm starving!" Awful moaned. "Ginger's mum only had cookies, and there isn't even any borrowed food at home now."

"We shall see about that at once," said Torquil. "Just wait while I get out of my robes." He pulled his cassock over his head and ducked out of it. Underneath he was wearing black priestly knee breeches and a black priestly shirt. "I might as well stay like this," he said. He unhooked a black jacket with silk lapels from the cupboard and put that on.

"You need a top hat," said Howard.

"I know, but they don't suit me," said Torquil. "Shall we go?"

The cathedral was dusky and empty. The ladies and the verger had gone. Torquil tapped the west door with his crozier, and it swung open to show the floodlights on, shining steadily and without sparks, and the blistered and battered digger standing at the bottom of the steps. "I refuse utterly to ride in that thing," Torquil said.

"Refuse to ride in your hearse," said Erskine. "Hate funerals."

"Let's walk," Howard said hurriedly. "It's no distance."

They walked, through the blue dusk, until they came to the supermarket in Church Row that stayed open late on Saturdays. Torquil said to Howard and Awful, "Wait here for us." The two of them stood and watched through the windows while Torquil and Erskine went into the shop. At the door Torquil raised his crozier. Instantly every soul in the supermarket froze, in whatever position he happened to be at that moment. Some of the positions looked rather uncomfortable. Torquil nodded at Erskine, and the two of them went around,

223

gathering things off the shelves. Torquil did the gathering. Erskine held the things—a mighty armful by the end.

"You could do that," Awful said thoughtfully. "Will you do it for me in a toyshop before Christmas?"

"No," said Howard.

"Why?" said Awful.

"Shops are Torquil's," said Howard. But that was not the real reason. It was that glimpse of Awful coming up the steps into the future, when she had suddenly looked so like Shine. Erskine was right to say Awful was a chip off the old block. She was. And Howard was determined not to let her grow up a bad lot like the rest of them.

Inside the supermarket Torquil was coming sailing toward the door. Erskine, loaded as he was, put out a long leg and contrived to hook his boot around Torquil's black silk ankle. Torquil looked back in surprise. Erskine nodded to the cash desk, where the check-out girl was frozen with one hand in the air. Torquil shrugged. He stretched out his crozier and tapped the girl's outstretched palm with it. A large pink check appeared there. Erskine bent to look at it and nodded, and the two of them came on out of the shop. Behind them everyone came to life again. The check-out girl looked at the pink check in her hand, rather puzzled, and then put it away in her cash drawer.

"Honestly, Erskine," Torquil was saying as they came out. "I don't *always* forget to pay. I remember quite often. Howard, take some of this load off him. It's making him grumpy."

They all were carrying things before long. By the time they turned off the beautiful new surface of Upper Park Street down the passage of number 10 even Torquil was delicately carrying a frozen chicken which had slithered out of Erskine's arms as he turned the corner. Howard had to balance his load on his knee, like Anne Moneypenny, to open the kitchen door.

Catriona and Quentin sprang up with cries of relief, and Catriona ran to hug Howard, load and all. Ginger Hind stood up, too, painfully, and took the cotton wool from his second

224

black eye in order to grin at Howard. Behind the shouting and confusion, Howard heard Torquil say guiltily, "Woops!" and thump his crozier on the doorstep. The drums in the cellar stopped beating at last.

"Not you again!" Quentin said to Erskine. Then as Torquil, too, stooped under the door and came in, he said, "Good God!"

Torquil bowed to Quentin. He swept up to Catriona. "I apologize," he said, and kissed her on both cheeks. Since Catriona was not the kind of lady this happened to much, she was flabbergasted and could not think what to say.

Erskine dumped his load of food on the table. "Come to say sorry," he said. "Business meeting." Then, in his usual way, he marched on through the house to Quentin's study. Howard followed him there, and together they took a look at what Archer had done to the new red typewriter. "Seems good," Erskine said. "Should work."

Howard knew it was better than good. Archer, in his way, was a genius. Even as Venturus, Howard knew he would not have been able to fix that typewriter half as well.

"Everyone, as always, is welcome to help himself to all I own," Quentin said, following them in, "but I'm still not clear this applies to Goons. Just what is going on now?"

Howard grinned at him fondly. Quentin might have his faults, but he had been right about Archer. He was right about the right things. "I need some more words from you, Dad," he said. "And this time they have to be good."

CHAPTER SIXTEEN

Howard changed his boots at last. He had to throw his socks away, too. The left one had stuck to his foot, and he was even thinking of washing his feet when Awful shouted that the feast Torquil had provided was ready. Howard hurried downstairs then because he wanted to be the one who explained everything to Quentin and Catriona. He wanted to do it without telling Quentin that his words had been useless all this time.

He was halfway through this tricky task when Torquil said, "Oh, but surely—" and stopped with a yelp. Erskine had kicked his shin. Howard thought he was probably the only one who noticed. Torquil went white with agony, but he had the sense not to say anything else.

Ginger was being equally tight-lipped. He kept protesting that Shine had not hurt him at all. "That's not true, Howard!"

Catriona said. "You should have seen him when he came in!" She was so concerned about Ginger that Awful got jealous and threatened loudly to be bad.

And bad she would have been had not a voice spoken suddenly out of the plughole of the sink. "Erskine!" it said hollowly. "Are you there?"

Awful's face shone. "That's Hathaway!" She scrambled from her chair and rushed to the sink. "Hallo, Hathaway!" she called. "Can you hear me?"

"Very piercingly," said the hollow voice. "Erskine?"

"Here," said Erskine, leaning his elbows on the sink. "Done it?"

"I have indeed!" The plughole gave a windy laugh. "I spoke to Shine first. She was beating some wretched lad, who ran away when I spoke—for which she was disposed to blame me until I gave my news. Venturus, I told her, had formed a plot with Archer and Dillian to imprison the rest of us and take a third each of the world. I told her that their means to do this was a ship belonging to Venturus, where they would meet at nine tonight. For that purpose Venturus would bring the ship into the present day for a short while then. And I besought her to go there for me since I was fixed in the past."

Erskine laughed. "Shine react?"

"She certainly did!" said Hathaway's hollow voice. "That Archer should plot with Dillian was too much for her to bear. She will be there. Then I spoke with Dillian. This is why I have been so long. I gave her the story that Shine plotted with Archer and Venturus, ditto, ditto, and she would not at first believe me. I was forced to invent many circumstances—I have not lied so much since I moved here—but it came to seem to me that Dillian would also go, not because of Shine or Archer, but because she has always feared and dreaded Venturus. Erskine, tell Howard to keep out of her way."

"Will do," said Erskine. "Want to watch tonight?"

"Torquil can tell me," Hathaway said windily, "when he comes to visit."

227

Torquil leaned over the sink, too. "I'll come straight on to you," he said. "But I warn you—if it goes wrong, I shall be running, and I shall have to bring all the others." Awful, at this, looked as if she were hoping things would go wrong.

"All will be welcome," said Hathaway. "But, Torquil, I did warn you, did I? Stay with me more than an hour, and you will be old in your own time."

Torquil laughed. "You mean, I have to stay for good then? Well, I shan't mind that if you won't."

Hathaway's voice laughed, too, like someone blowing across the top of milk bottle. "I'll see you," he said, and ended with a plop, as if a plug had been put in the plughole.

After that they all began to look at watches, and Quentin paced nervously about, reading the notes he had made about what he was to write, over and over. Howard began to feel so nervous, too, that in order to take his mind off it, he hunted in the back of the cupboard until he found the mug which Erskine had chipped with his knife when he first came. As he had expected, the deep glazed gouges on one side were not a G, but a crookedly carved E. For Erskine. The marks on the other side were meant to form a V, for Venturus.

Erskine saw Howard turning the mug in his hands. "Knife slipped," he explained. "Thought you knew then. Trying to tell you I knew, too. Day after. Realized you didn't. Kept trying to hint." He seized Howard's wrist and turned it around so that he could see Howard's watch. It was twenty to nine. Erskine surged to his feet and strode to Quentin's study. He came back carrying Archer's red typewriter and a hunk of paper. "Time," he said.

"Gentlemen, please!" murmured Torquil. "Thank goodness! I was beginning to think the clocks had stopped!"

They made another strange procession as they went down Hathaway's smooth new road and along Zed Alley. Erskine strode ahead with the typewriter. Quentin followed, in the backless red and black checked coat, making a striking contrast with Torquil and his black knee breeches and swallow-tailed

228

black coat. Torquil and Quentin were getting on surprisingly well together, chatting and laughing. Torquil had to bend over Quentin most of the time because he was almost a foot taller. Catriona followed with Awful. Awful was tired and dragging rather. Last in line, Ginger limped along beside Howard. Ginger was still taking a very gruff and unnoble line. "I'm not coming to help, see?" Ginger kept explaining. "I want to take a look at that spaceship."

Howard suspected that Catriona's sympathy had embarrassed Ginger. "I haven't seen inside it yet," he said, "but it looked like a real beauty."

The Poly forecourt was darker than usual because the Poly was shut for the weekend. Most of the light came from a big white moon, scudding through wet clouds behind the empty girders of the new building. Erskine stopped there and parked the typewriter on a digger.

"Come on, young Venturus," Quentin said. "Do your stuff."

This was the part Howard was dreading. He went to stand with Erskine and Torquil opposite the gray outline of the unfinished doorway, feeling small, uncertain, and powerless. How could he fetch a whole marble temple with a spaceship inside all the way out of the future? He couldn't. It was a mistake. He was just an ordinary person.

"Get on with it," said Torquil. "We'll help, but the main pull has to be yours. You made the thing. You must have got enough of your powers back by now to do that."

"Must remember how," said Erskine.

It was true. Howard could remember. But it was rather the way you remember being able to suck your own toes as a baby—not something you did now. "I'll try," he said.

They tried. Howard looked up at the scudding moon and thought earnestly of the temple and of himself fetching it. He thought of himself beckoning it. He tried to imagine himself as Venturus and remember the way he had felt then. He tried every way he could think of. On either side of him he could feel

229

Erskine and Torquil trying, too. But nothing happened among the dark girders—nothing at all. Howard tried again. Nothing again. Oh, it was hopeless!

"No good," Erskine said dismally. "Gone wrong."

Torquil lost his temper. *"Howard!"* he shrieked. He stamped his buckled shoe. "You are simply not trying, you stupid little squirt! Fifi will be here in five minutes. Then Archer and Shine. Try!"

"I can't," Howard said hopelessly.

"Oh, yes, you *can!*" screamed Torquil. "Do it, or I'll twist your ears!" He held his crozier aloft.

Howard clapped his hands to his ears. The pain in the ear Erskine had boxed was excruciating. "Stop it!" he gasped.

"Then *try!*" Torquil yelled at him. "Try, or I'll—" He raised the crozier higher.

Howard tried. He was terrified in case his ear came off. He tried urgently. And like the time he had resisted Shine, he quite suddenly found his way into a new layer of his own mind. Then it was obvious. It was almost easy. He reached into the future and fixed a white moonlit strand of his mind to the marble temple and began to pull it back to him. It was like pulling a kite out of the sky. The temple was more difficult to control than a kite. Howard was not sure he could have got it in alone, but with Erskine and Torquil pulling strongly and steadily behind him, they began to tow it into the present. White moony mist appeared among the empty girders. The mist hardened and hardened, and the lines of the temple started to appear.

As soon as they did, Howard almost let go and let it spring back into the future again. Ginger made a scornful noise. Ginger was right, Howard thought. The temple was plain ridiculous. If he had not known he had made it himself, he would have called the person who built it a lunatic. Four towering statues of Venturus held up a roof which was a head of Venturus, giant-size, looking heroic and noble and, to Howard's shamed eyes, utterly stupid.

"Howard!" said Torquil threateningly. There was another tweak at his ear.

Howard gave up looking at the temple and simply concentrated on getting it there. He guided it down the last twenty years, brought it gently to a stop, and anchored it firmly a year ahead from now. They had agreed on a year ahead because that would give Howard full use of his powers when he went inside.

"Nicely done," said Torquil. "Get on into it."

Howard sprinted for the dark square of what was now a glass door, calling to Ginger to come, too. As he pushed the door open, the marble hall inside lit up, as long as a football pitch. He saw his foot come down in the brown training shoe with yellow laces, but this time his other foot came down in the pair to it. It was much easier to get up the steps. Howard arrived at the top only an inch or so taller. Ginger arrived several inches taller, but without his two black eyes and not limping at all. He kept up with Howard easily as Howard raced down the hall and through the antechamber with the papers and into the domed room where the spaceship was. The robots were all motionless now, frozen into strange attitudes, like the people in the supermarket.

The first thing Howard did was to direct one to go and take away the papers from the antechamber. Archer must not find those. "Is the ship finished?" he asked it.

"Work completed five minutes ago," it mouth organed. It had to trundle around Ginger on its way to the door. Ginger was rooted to the spot, staring at the spaceship.

Howard hurried forward and ordered its air lock open. The lock did not slide. It opened, just as he had hoped, like the pupil of an eye, widening in layers of rings. He could hardly wait for it to finish, there was so little time. He jumped inside. Lights came on here, too, showing a cabin like the inside of a luxury yacht, with thick red carpet from wall to wall. There were silver goblets on the table and pictures on the walls—real paintings in big gilt frames. The marvel was that though the ship was pointing upward, the salon seemed to be level. It was the domed room outside that appeared to be tipped downhill. Ginger gave a squawk of amazement at this as Howard raced for the controls.

He looked at the console and shook his head sadly. The red foam pilots' couches were about all right, but Venturus had gone mad over the controls. There were banks and banks of unnecessary buttons, levers, and dials. He had been trying to go one better than Archer. And he had. "This looks pretty complex," Ginger said over his shoulder.

Howard was glad he had brought Ginger. He was going to need four hands. "I was afraid of this," he said. "You hold down those two blue levers over there and those three red switches over your head. Don't let go."

Ginger did so; it meant he was spread-eagled across the console. "This is ridiculous!" he said.

"I know," said Howard. He had to leave Ginger like that while he himself leaped from side to side, programming the ship to take off in twenty minutes. He locked it on course for Alpha Centauri and instructed the computer not to permit manual override for any reason until after that. Then he shifted Ginger to some more controls and set about making it impossible for the ship ever to return to Earth. Then he shifted Ginger again.

"I could design better controls than this in my sleep!" Ginger said, obediently spreading himself out in a new direction. "What's this ship called?"

"Venturus!" Howard said disgustedly. The last piece of programming was tricky. The ship had to allow everyone who arrived to come in, but it was to let no one get off. Howard was not sure he could do it. He did the best he could, but that part was really going to be up to Quentin. "Right," he said. "Let's go." He ran through the salon and leaped down into the domed room. As the room miraculously came right and level about him, he realized he had remarkably few regrets.

Ginger lagged a little, but he caught up with Howard in the

232

now empty antechamber. "You know," he said as they ran side by side down the hall, "you and me could design a better ship than that if we put our heads together."

"Yes," said Howard. "Let's."

"Make it *Venturus Mark Two!*" Ginger called out, leaping down the steps. "And I tell you what—" But at that point he became a year younger. "*Ow!*" he yelled, hobbling. Both his black eyes were back. Howard had to help him through the diggers and across the forecourt.

The others were waiting at the small side door to which Quentin had the key. Quentin unlocked the door and took them inside the Poly building, walking almost too fast for Ginger, and turning on lights as he went. In the foyer the caretaker met them accusingly.

"Mr. Sykes, isn't it? 'Fraid you'll have to leave. Poly's closed for the weekend, sir."

"So sorry, Mr. Forbes," Quentin said. "I have to give these people an urgent seminar, and all my books are in my room upstairs. It's very important. They all have a big exam tomorrow." He carried on walking while he spoke and arrived at the stairs.

"All of them!" exclaimed the caretaker, his eye running from Torquil to Ginger and then on to Awful.

"All of them," Quentin's voice came back from halfway upstairs. "They give me all the oddballs to teach—everyone from giant morons to eight-year-old geniuses. Hurry up, all of you!"

The caretaker stood back helplessly and let their procession go past. Howard tried not to laugh. Dad, in his way, was as bad as Erskine.

In the room upstairs Quentin was rapidly arranged with a low angle lamp, the typewriter, and plenty of paper. Torquil opened the windows so that they could see and hear what went on in the forecourt. Catriona prudently locked the door. Everyone else found a tubular metal chair and sat down.

"When do I start?" Quentin asked expectantly, winding paper onto the red typewriter.

"Up to you," said Erskine.

Quentin looked at his notes, sat back with his eyes closed for a moment, and then leaned forward. Instead of starting to type, he said, "One thing puzzles me about this arrangement with Mountjoy." Howard looked at him in alarm. He was surely going to ask what use the words had been. But Quentin said, "That time just after Awful was born, when I was too tired to do the words. Somebody stopped all our services and machines. Who was it? It couldn't have been Venturus— Howard—because he was only five at the time."

"Was him," said Erskine. "Angry about Awful. Did it from memory. Did it mostly from memory just now."

Erskine was right, Howard knew. The feelings and knowledge he had been using without thinking inside the temple were strong and clear and piercing, compared with the fuzzy way he felt his growing powers now. So Torquil had made him fetch the temple from memory! He found himself looking accusingly at Torquil, who bit his lip guiltily and laughed back. And Howard realized another thing. He needed Torquil. Torquil was the only one in the family who could ever make him do things he did not want to do. "Don't go and stay in the past," he said to Torquil. "You can come back the same if you think the right way. I did it just now when I came back from the future."

The laughter faded off Torquil's face a little. "Ah, but," he said, "you forget. You're the seventh child. You can do things none of us can do."

Quentin announced solemnly, "I now begin." Everyone was quiet while he tapped away at the keys. Howard watched the words coming over Quentin's shoulder. "The first to appear was Archer . . ."

"Archer's coming!" Awful called from the window.

Howard sped over there to look. Archer's Rolls was nosing its way through the main gates, silvery in the moonlight. Its headlights blazed across the light streaming from the door of the temple.

234

"'in his Rolls,'" Quentin murmured as he typed, "'headlights . . . light from temple . . .'"

Below, the car stopped. Archer sprang out and stood looking at the temple for a moment. Howard squirmed rather. Then Archer leaned into his car and brought out a number of things.

"What's he carrying?" whispered Ginger.

"'laden with a number of strange objects . . .'" murmured Quentin, tapping away.

"Yes, but say what they are, Dad," Awful whispered at him.

"In due course," said Quentin. "I only have ten fingers."

"You only type with two!" Awful said scornfully.

"But I go damn fast," Quentin retorted. "Besides, I don't know what the things are." And he typed, "probably designed to secure the spaceship as his own."

By this time nobody knew whether to look at what Quentin was typing or to watch Archer out the window. Howard, Catriona, and Torquil all were hurrying back and forth, laughing incredulously. It really seemed to work.

When Howard next looked, Archer was walking in through the lighted glass door of the temple. They saw him jerk himself up the first step. Then he was out of sight.

"'out of sight,'" Quentin murmured. "Quick, someone. Tell me where he hides in the spaceship."

"In the toilet, of course," said Ginger.

"Thanks," said Quentin. He was rattling away merrily now. "'in the toilet, where he was at first far too busy arranging his equipment to realize that he was unable to leave the ship. When he did notice—'"

"Oh, no, Dad!" said Howard. "You'll get him mad and he'll short something out."

"Hush," said Quentin. "Allow for inspiration." And he typed, "it was only as a pleasant languor and a sense of wellbeing. He sat down and poured himself a drink, waiting for Fifi. She was not long in appearing."

"Fifi coming now," Erskine said, looming over Catriona at the window.

Howard pushed in between them to see. Fifi was running. Howard had expected her to move like a sleepwalker. But she was obviously wide-awake and so sure she was going to see Archer that the silvery haze Torquil and Erskine had created around her had actually formed itself into a cloud above her head. In the cloud was a silvery shape that seemed to be Archer wearing shining armor.

"'seeing Archer as a knight in shining armor,'" Quentin murmured behind him, clattering away. "'On she sped . . .'"

In the courtyard, Fifi raced between the diggers and plunged through the temple door.

"'and there at last was Archer, her own dear Archer,'" murmured Quentin. "Will somebody tell me just how slushy they want the next bit to be?"

"My dear Quentin," said Torquil, "I'm sure you don't need us to tell you that."

"How about a row of stars?" Catriona suggested, going to look over Quentin's shoulder.

"Stars might give the game away, don't you think?" Quentin said, clattering feverishly.

"Yes, but you've got to make sure they can't leave the ship," Howard called anxiously.

"What do you think I'm doing?" Quentin demanded. "Very well, too! It ought to be censored. 'We will now leave the lovers'—somebody feed me some chocolate—'and turn to the next comer.'"

Torquil produced a bar of chocolate. Howard and Awful broke it up and were feeding it into Quentin's mouth as he typed when Ginger said in a loud whisper, "Hey! This looks like Shine!"

They ran to look. Shine had come with minions. Her big bulletproof car was drawn up in the center of the yard. Men with guns were piling out of it, and one was ceremoniously opening the door for Shine. They could hear her leather creaking, even through the noise of the typewriter, as she climbed mountainously out. She was also carrying a gun.

236

Everyone turned accusingly to Quentin. "She's brought a load of people!" said Ginger.

"Of course," said Quentin. "I put them in because it's obvious she never goes anywhere without them. How many are there? I put six. I don't know how they all got in the car."

There were indeed six guards, all stalking closely about Shine as she strode to the temple.

"*Do* something about them!" said Howard. "The ship won't take that number!"

"Coming to it," said Quentin, typing hard. He typed, "Torquil raised his crozier."

Beside the window Torquil's eyes widened as his hand went up, holding the crozier aloft. Everyone began tiptoeing back and forth again, between the window and the words, to see Quentin type that Shine abruptly ordered four of her men to stand guard outside the temple and then to see Shine actually do it. Quentin typed, "The four outside stood like statues, obedient to the power of Torquil's crozier." And the four men outside did. Shine and the other two guards pushed their way through the glass door into the temple.

"You let two in," Erskine said reproachfully.

Quentin, as he typed, grinned just a little fiendishly. "I hadn't the heart not to. The way you planned it, you had the women on that ship outnumber the men by three to one. All I've done is make the numbers even."

It seemed to everyone that Quentin was getting an undue sense of power. He was rapping away at a furious pace now, grinning as fiendishly as Awful. Erskine plunged toward the window and plunged back again. He seized Howard's wrist and looked at Howard's watch. "Dillian's due," he said. "Bring her in. Move those men. Smell a rat. Won't go in."

"One moment," said Quentin. "I'm extending myself on the conversation aboard the ship. Shine's language is spectacular. And they've just realized they can't get out. Shine thinks it's Archer's doing. Isn't that what you wanted?"

237

Erskine punched his own hand in his exasperation. "Move those men!"

"Ready now," said Quentin. He typed, "Shine's remaining men—Erskine, by the way, found himself quite unable to hit Quentin—climbed into the car and drove away."

Erskine's face, as he read this, made Howard snort with laughter. Outside, the four guards jumped a little, looked at one another, and went back to Shine's car. "Bring Dillian!" Erskine more or less shouted as the car drove away.

"In a second now," said Quentin. There was an interval of intense typing.

"Here's a police car," someone at the window whispered.

Howard and Erskine dived to look. There was indeed a police car. It drove to the center of the forecourt and stopped. The headlights went off. The light inside came on, showing them the fair hair of Dillian. Nothing else happened. Dillian seemed to be just sitting with her window down. Quentin continued to type, in a long rattle.

At last, Dillian opened the far door of the car and got out. She was wearing a mink coat and, to everyone's dismay, carrying a rifle.

"Don't worry," Quentin murmured. "Archer won't let her shoot holes in the ship."

Dillian rested the rifle on the roof of the car, so that it was roughly aimed at the window. "Venturus!" she shouted. "Venturus! Is that you typing up there?"

There was a frantic scramble as everyone, by common consent, got away from the window. "Dad!" whispered Howard.

"Sorry," said Quentin, typing hard. "Haven't you ever heard of a character running away with a writer? I fancy Dillian. She sounds to be just my old-fashioned type."

Dillian's voice came up from below. "I can hear you, Venturus! Stop that typing!"

"Just finish this sentence," said Quentin.

Dillian lost patience and fired at the window. The shot screamed above Quentin's head and crashed into the wall near

238

the ceiling. Plaster came down like a landslide. "Reloading," said Erskine, pressed against the wall beside the window.

Howard was on his hands and knees underneath the window. "Dad!" he said. "Stop her!"

Torquil, pressed against the wall on the other side of the window, said, "That caretaker fellow has just come out into the yard now. Send him in before she shoots him!"

"I can't! I didn't do him! He came out by himself!" Quentin gasped. He was sweating. "This is going all wrong!"

"Oh, really!" Catriona said angrily. Howard, to his horror, felt her shove him aside with her knee. He looked up to see Catriona leaning out of the window.

"Mum!" he said. "You'll get shot!"

Catriona took no notice. "You down there!" she shouted. It was her angriest and most booming voice. "Yes—you, woman! You with the dyed hair and the gun! I'm talking to you! Just you stop that, do you hear? I've got my two children up here, and I'm not having it. You should be ashamed of yourself, loosing off like that!"

While Catriona was shouting, Torquil tiptoed hastily to Quentin. "Come on!" he whispered. "Type! While she's distracted. 'Dillian turned without another word and walked into the temple.' Quickly!"

Quentin nodded and typed madly.

"Keep yelling, Mum!" Howard whispered. Whether she heard him or not, Catriona was fairly launched, and she continued to thunder at Dillian. Howard looked at his watch. Erskine grabbed his wrist and looked at it, too. "Barely two minutes now," Howard whispered.

"And I shall have you arrested!" Catriona thundered out of the window. She turned away from the window. She said, in her normal pleasant voice, "Well, she seems to have gone. Aren't you finished yet, Quentin?"

"Just getting her into the spaceship," Quentin said. "Does it take off without my help, Howard?"

"Yes, any second now," said Howard. "Come and look."

239

Quentin typed a loud full stop and stood up. They all crowded to the window and looked into the yard, where the caretaker still stood, looking suspiciously at the strange moon-lit building inside the scaffolding. A wide smile of light appeared in the domed roof, to the right of the great head of Venturus. The smile widened like a moon, to half, then three-quarters, and then to a blaze that struck upward into the blue clouds of the night. There was a gigantic mutter of power, so enormous that the window rattled and everything in the room shook. The girders, and the temple with its opened dome, blurred with it. Their ears went dead. Then, slowly rising from the opened dome, came the spaceship, silvery and stately, up and up, straight as a pencil, into the light of the dome, up out of that light, into the light of the moon, faster and faster and faster. Their eyes followed it up, then up, until its tail spurted white light. A blunt cough of energy came to their dead ears. Against the moon they saw the ship slant sideways and become a shooting star for a second, up and out.

"Cor!" said Ginger.

Howard looked back at the temple in time to see it collapsing and fading into the future as it collapsed. Venturus had built it too weak. How stupid, he thought. He did not mind. He never intended to go there again.

The thunder from the spaceship came, delayed, and shook Howard into noticing Quentin tiptoeing to the typewriter again. Howard got there first and disconnected the thing Archer had done to it. "I was only going to write, 'They lived happily ever after,'" Quentin said, injured. "But I suppose it *is* unlikely."

Behind them Erskine luxuriously stretched long Goon arms. "Go and travel now. See the world," he said. His eyes slid to Catriona pleadingly. "Come and see you every year?" he asked.

"Of course, if you want, Erskine," Catriona said warmly.

Howard looked at Erskine warily. He rather thought Erskine's eyes had flicked on to Awful after that. She was lean-

240

ing against Torquil, yawning her head off. Awful saw Howard look and beckoned him over. "If you do things to me," she murmured sleepily, "I shall tell Dad about the words. I saw Erskine kick Torquil."

Hm, thought Howard. He had been thinking it was his duty to stay and help Quentin and Catriona bring Awful up, to make up for all the trouble he had caused them. They would not want her to be like Shine. Now he saw he would have to bring himself up not to be Venturus, too. Because it was quite possible that Erskine would come back one year, saying he had taken a look at the world and decided he would like to farm it. When he did, he would offer Awful a share. Howard saw that he and Awful both would have to be ready for that day. He thought that since this was his third time around, he might just manage to get it right for a change.

Stories
✠ of ✠
Swords and Sorcery

⚜⚜⚜⚜⚜⚜⚜⚜⚜⚜⚜⚜⚜⚜⚜⚜

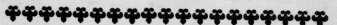